Acclaim For Aaron Patterson's
Dream On

"New authors come and go every day. Very few come on the scene with the ability to weave a tale that will make you sad to reach the end, longing for more. At a time when the world needs a real hero, Patterson delivers big with the WJA's Mark Appleton—an unlikely hero for the 21st century."
—*The Joe Show*

"Aaron Patterson spins a good tale and does it well."
—*W. Parrish*

"Aaron Patterson has such a unique ability of keeping the reader on edge with an undeniable urge to never put the book down. The characters are captivating and mysterious in their own ways, creating a storyline that's difficult to find in most other books."
—*Samantha S.*

"Patterson shows great potential!"
—*Donna Conrad*

Aaron Patterson

Dream On

Book Two In The WJA Series

StoneHouse Ink 2011
StoneHouse Ink Boise ID 83713
www.StoneHouseInk.net

First Hardcover Edition: July 2009
First Paperback Edition: July 2009
First eBook Edition 2009
Second Paperback Edition 2011
Second eBook Edition 2011

The characters and events portrayed in this book are fictitious. Any similarity to a real person, living or dead, is coincidental and not intended by the author.

Patterson, Aaron, 1979
Dream On: a novel/ by Aaron Patterson. 1st. ed. p.cm.

ISBN 9780982607824 (Paperback)
Library of Congress Control Number: 2010902251

Cover design by Paul Higdon

Stonehouse Ink

A thanks to my wife for putting up with me and my two natures, and to Joey, Donna, and Samantha.

Dream On

Rise of the Red Dog

Two natures beat within my breast,
One is evil one is blessed,
The one I love the one I hate,
The one I feed will dominate.

CHAPTER ONE

I WATCHED IN VAIN as my life slipped away and there was nothing I could do about it. Time is a heartless father, and in its never-ending *ticks and tocks*, time smiles at me as if to say, "I have you, I control your life, and you will do as I bid—or else!" I can feel my own heartbeat, and that, too, is ruled by time, beating in perfect rhythm as if my own heart conspires against me.

You can never take your future and bend it to your own will. If you try, then time, or maybe even your own heart, will throw a banana peel on the ground and you'll tumble and end up in the same place I am. I was a careful man and tried to keep my eyes on the ground in order not to step on something or into something that would take me. I was ready for anything. However, nothing could have prepared me for this…this place, and this feeling of finality and judgment!

Mind-numbing darkness crept all around me with a stench that hit my senses like a freight train. At first, I thought I'd been buried alive in someone else's grave, and the smell was the decomposing body I shared a box with. Then, after a few days, or weeks, I can't say which for sure, I figured out that the stench was me. I was the terrible taste in the stale air that I tried to breathe! I was trapped in a wooden box that gave me about a foot below my feet and six inches above my head. I felt around and touched the lid, only to find that there was a mere foot of space in front of my nose. *I am dying!* The thought made me want to scream and struggle, kicking and smacking with everything in me to free myself and drink in the sweet morning air that used to swim through my lungs. I did, in fact, do just that for so long that I passed out with exhaustion and woke up in the same dark place, but this time my head ached with a pounding that not just one aspirin would cure. I would have believed I was already dead; however, the pain shooting through my body told me otherwise. I understand that you don't know me and that I'll never see you or know your name, but I need to tell someone what happened, and how I was to end up dead, or almost dead!

My name is Mark Appleton. I know, not too flashy or "in your face" hero kind of a name. I'm no different than you, the stock broker working his sixty plus hours a week, or the guy standing on a highway holding a stop sign in a construction zone. I am your everyday, ordinary, run of the mill American guy, and I'm in a casket—my casket. I was buried alive and from what I can tell, I'll not be escaping any time soon. So, why would someone do that to me, you might ask?

Well, I have a job that involves a little different approach than your average mail carrier. You might say my job is to deliver messages to those in this world who think they can commit any evil they dream up without repercussion. I encounter people every day who would love to see me dead… hung by my neck and swinging in the breeze.

That's where I come in, I am their repercussion! I'm an assassin, who is what some might call a vigilante or a mercenary of sorts. I know, I know, but lying here in a cramped box, talking to myself, I can't help but wonder how I got the job or how I ended up in a pine box underneath a ton of dirt.

The voice recorder in my watch is the only way you will ever know my story, so here goes…

* * *

THE DAY WAS EVERYTHING you could imagine a beautiful

spring day to be. Birds chased each other through the trees, and flowers opened up to drink in the sun's warmth as if awakening from a long slumber.

I was on my way downtown to meet my wife for lunch at our favorite diner on Sixteenth Street. It was a Mom-and-Pop kind of place, with the best homemade soup you could buy in New York City.

K was a teacher in a private preschool, and most of her classes were finished by noon, so it was easy for her to break free for lunch. We tried to meet at least twice a week when I was working in town. The diner was packed as usual, but I found a table in the back where we liked to sit.

K was running late, but I didn't mind, it gave me time to think and watch all the people standing in line waiting to order. A tall, older gentleman in a pinstriped suit looked at his watch for the twentieth time and sighed out loud, as if his time was more important than the rest of the people in the diner.

The city is no place for a dawdler or for people like me, who like to cruise rather than speed along like a freight train. I looked through the menu as if I'd never seen it before. Who knows why I even looked at it. The menu had been the same for the last twenty years, and I was going to get the same thing, as always. However, I looked anyway. You could never tell, there might be something new, and it might be wonderful.

K walked into the small diner and the place hushed as if a movie star had just walked into the room. She was a stunning woman with golden hair that curled naturally, and the sunlight always seemed to hit her just right. She had a presence that one couldn't explain. Everyone looked at her as she walked to the table and sat down in front of me, never noticing that all eyes were on her. Then again, no one was looking, but everyone was looking.

"Hi honey." She leaned over and kissed me on the lips. Her kiss was soft and one I would never tire of. "You order yet?"

"No, I was just looking to see what I wanted."

K laughed. "You always get orange chicken, what do you

mean you were 'looking'?" Her smile lit up her face and made my heart skip a beat.

"True, but you never can tell when they'll come up with a dish that draws me in. I was thinking about the French dip today, and a bowl of clam chowder." I looked at her with one stern eye as if I really were considering trying something new.

"I see, well I'm in the mood for chicken, maybe a salad." She played along. The waitress was an older woman who happened to be the owner's wife. She was average height and had a round face and white hair, pulled back in a neat bun. Her name was Deborah Palmer, but everyone called her Grandma P. James Palmer was a short, fat man with a small mouth. They'd started the diner twenty years ago in December with their life savings. Back then, it was possible to start a small business from nothing, and now it was their pride and joy.

"Hello you two, shall I bring out a Dr. Pepper and a Diet Pepsi?" Her voice wavered just a bit, but not enough to show her true age.

I nodded and smiled at her as she hurried off to get our drinks. "So, how was class?"

"Really good. We have the cutest little boy, David. He doesn't care about his colors or numbers, but he loves to draw. He's good for his age, too, very talented."

"He gives you his drawings, doesn't he?"

"And only me! He says I'm his 'favrite teachr' in all of his drawings!" K smiled, and her eyes sparkled like diamonds. K loved kids and her teaching was the one thing in our lives that gave us a sense of normalcy. I never said anything about my work, and she never asked, but there was always something in her eyes that told me that she was worried about something.

The drinks came back along with Grandma P. She looked at K and smiled, making more wrinkles on her face but taking years off all at the same time.

"So, what can I get for you, dear?"

"I think I'll have the chicken salad with ranch on the side." Grandma P. looked at me with old, gray eyes that at one time were full of life and spunk, but now just seemed calm and content.

"And I'll have the orange chicken with a bowl of your clam chowder."

K laughed and kicked me under the table. "Told you. You're so predictable!" Maybe I was, but it was so good, I could eat just that chicken forever.

"What do you want to do this weekend?" I asked.

K took a sip from her soda and half closed her eyes as she thought about the question. "I think we should take Sam to the park, and then go on a date in the evening and get a sitter for Sam."

"Oh, a date! Sounds like fun. You have anything in mind? Maybe dinner, a movie, and then find a quiet place to park?" I was aware of the stupid grin on my face, but I didn't care.

"What are we, teenagers? I was thinking of going miniature golfing, and then parking!" K giggled, and I rolled my eyes.

"And I'm the teenager? You know I'll beat you, and then you'll get mad and the night will be ruined."

"Ha, you will bow at my golfing-god feet. I'll wipe the floor with you and your little ball!"

"I think you're spending too much time with children. You think we all play like preschoolers."

"That's why I'll beat you. All men are just big kids, much the same as preschoolers."

I watched K as she ate and talked, noticing her little smiles and the way her nose scrunched up when she found something funny. K didn't seem to have a care in the world, and that was just the way I wanted it. By the time we were done, the place had all but cleared out. A few people still sat around finishing their meal; everyone else was headed back to the old grindstone.

Today, I was going to Atlanta for a meeting with a man who called himself *The Magician*. He had escaped from five different prisons and ten jails. He had the habit of disappearing, so the nickname stuck, and to most, it was not a name they ever wanted to hear. His ties to the mob ran deep, but even they had begun to fear him and would love to see him fall prey to a premature death. He was a loose cannon and had done enough to get noticed by my boss.

We knew of twenty-two murders that he had personally committed and countless rapes in and around the Atlanta area. The FBI and local authorities had a hands-off policy on him. They were just as scared of him as his own crime family was, and I had a feeling he was an informant for the FBI, in trade for a free pass as far as the law was concerned.

When he kidnapped a sixteen-year-old girl named Hanna Marcella, it was the last straw. She wasn't someone most people would care about, just an orphan who'd been in and out of foster care from the age of seven. However, Solomon, my boss and founder of the WJA, had a heart for kids, especially orphans. Hanna was found a week later in a junk yard. The Magician had gotten tired of her.

I couldn't read the file on him all the way through. Most of the time I wanted to know who I was to meet with, but in this case, it was too much.

I kissed K and left the diner. I had to be ready to go to Atlanta in an hour. My meeting was set to go down at seven p.m. and with any luck, The Magician would disappear for good tonight.

Abracadabra!

* * *

A TALL, BEARDED MAN sat in a lounge chair sipping a glass of vodka. The smell filled his lungs, causing him to smile to himself. It was the smell of victory. He looked out over the warm sand to the ocean. The water washed up onto the sand, making a soft sound as it hit the beach and rolled along the shore. Bali was warm and inviting. A slight south wind blew, and the smell of salt water and tanning oil made him hungry. He thought of what he planned to do with his day, but shoved the thoughts from his mind with haste as he sipped his drink. He was alone, and that was just the way he wanted it.

His villa was beyond modest, pushing the extreme. It overlooked the ocean to the east, and massive, rocky cliffs jutted from the ground behind his villa. The deck attached to the house could have been another bedroom by itself, and it stuck out high above the ground and clung to the cliff face like a bat. Marble and concrete made up the floors, and all the walls were old wood beams ripped from some long ago shipwreck and mixed with raw stone that gave a rugged look to his décor.

Taras Karjanski loved to flaunt his money, and he had plenty to show off. Much of his wealth was stolen or given to him in trade for a life. He loved money, almost more then he loved himself. Then again, who wouldn't love *The General?*

Placing his now empty glass down on the tiny wooden table next to him, he got up and walked through the white sand and inside on the ground floor where his office was located. Getting an internet connection around here had taken some doing, but it was worth it. His laptop hummed quietly as it booted up. He pulled a fresh bottle of vodka from the bar that stood in the rear of the office. After a few minutes, he was able to get online and onto his family's website. It was secured with a voice identification command, as well as a fingerprint scan, just to log on. The Russian Mafia was believed to be dead; however, Taras liked being the underdog. It made the surprise of the attack that much sweeter.

The red dog is in the woods

He typed his message and sent it off. Moments later, he got a response.

The woods have been harvested

A smirk spread across his face as he read the message. His brother did have a good sense of humor. It would be a shame to have to kill him.

* * *

KIRK WESTON LOOKED DOWN at his belly, which was on the rebound. He'd been in hiding and out of work for too long. His old boss back in Detroit would be angrier than a woman on a diet if he knew his *favorite* detective was still alive. But Kirk

Weston was not planning on going back to the force anytime soon. He rather liked being dead.

He thought about how he had been assumed dead after being kidnapped and left to die in Puerto Rico a year ago. He remember the pain of being tortured and shot in the chest. Luckily, when the building was laid waste by a few well-placed bombs, he just happened to be a few hundred yards away. The next day, when he went back to look the place over and see if he could make more sense of the situation, he came upon a dead man in the rubble. The guards had been blown to bits, with a few scattered around here and there, but one in particular caught Kirk's eye. *What was a man dressed in an Armani suit doing out here in the middle of nowhere?* The well-dressed man had a suitcase handcuffed to his wrist. This made the detective bells go off in his head. Kirk decided to look into this mystery further. The suitcase was filled with over one million dollars in cash.

Bali was just the vacation Kirk needed. He'd had a rough year. Who was he kidding, he'd had a rough life! Now as a dead man, he had suddenly become rich.

Kirk spit on the ground as he watched *The General*. He was not in Bali just for the ocean breeze and the margaritas. His instincts as a detective couldn't be turned off just because he was on vacation. He muttered and took a bite out of a glazed donut. He had bugged *The General's* villa, and set up surveillance when he first followed him to the island. He was amazed at what you could buy on the internet and at Radio Shack. The plane ticket to Bali he had found in the suitcase helped, but Kirk liked to think he had figured out this plan on his own.

Stupid Russian!

Kirk tried to keep himself focused as he watched his new friend chat away on a personal dating site. He'd seen his face in the small cell where he was beaten and almost killed. He knew he was supposed to be dead, and this man was responsible. This didn't have anything to do with justice or "doing the right thing." *This was revenge!*

The Russian was up to something. Kirk didn't know what exactly, but he had his suspicions. It looked like he was getting ready to leave Bali and make a trip to Russia. Kirk was packed and would follow him to see if he could uncover what this Mafia boss had cooked up.

A phone rang in Kirk's pocket.

"Hey kiddo, what's up?"

"I want to go surfing later with you, you come?" The island teen had taken a liking to Kirk. He was sixteen and had taught Kirk how to surf and navigate around the island. He was a tall, skinny kid and had the wildest black hair Kirk had ever seen. At first, Kirk hated the water, but after a few times out, he began to crave it. The smell, the sound, and the feel of its raw power under his feet as he rode a wave. It was a little piece of heaven and, in his life, that was a hard thing to find.

"I can't today, bud, I might have to go out of town for a few days, but I'll let you know."

The boy hung up after agreeing to have a dinner of pork and roots at his parent's house later. The family had taken him in on more than one occasion, and the pig was his favorite dish.

Kirk looked around his bedroom and back at the monitor. He had twelve cameras set up in Taras's house, but all at once, he was gone! Kirk switched from one camera to the next looking for the Russian.

Nothing.

Then he heard a knock at the door.

CHAPTER TWO

I SAT IN THE humid car outside a bar called Mugg's. I hated Atlanta, and this job didn't improve my disdain for the city. In fact, I think I hated it more now than I ever did in the past. It was muggy and had to be over a hundred in the shade, not to mention the dirty streets and buildings.

I looked at my watch. With the TAXI ride and the time change, I could see that I had an hour before I had to meet with The Magician. I used one of the company's cars and turned the air conditioner to high, hoping that it would help, but found that it only made it colder and still just as sticky. Picking up my .45, I screwed the silencer onto the end of the barrel. I would use another weapon in most cases, but I needed to frame the mob for the kill to get the families fighting with each other.

The two families were the Fontanas and the Massinos. Between the two, they kept the authorities busy and scared. Most of the mob or the Mafia had dissipated, but they never disappeared completely. They just went underground and were heavily involved in politics, gambling, and racketeering. Most of the time they could be found in the Senate or kissing some baby at a political rally.

The Magician was a Fontana. He'd worn out his welcome in his own family as well as in Atlanta, and all the way to the coast where he liked to do business. If he died, it would be a relief to everyone, but would still force the hand of the Fontanas in order to save face. If one of your own was killed, you had to repay the debt or it would be like blood in the water.

The sun would be down soon. Darkness suited my work, but even the nightfall gave no rest from the heat. I slid my hand over the silver .45 and traced a line on the cold metal. It was smooth and had a faint smell of oil and gunpowder. It was weighted just right and felt good to hold, just the way it should. Every weapon was custom fitted, and in most cases, made for the person who would be using it. I didn't need anything special. I could get the job done with just about any weapon.

I went over the plan of attack again in my mind. I knew there would be bodyguards and that they would be armed. That didn't worry me much; it was the initial frisk that had me worried. I had to get in with the weapon and get by the guards. The last thing I wanted was for one of the guards to find me with a gun, which would mean more blood and a bigger mess to contain.

I still had a few tricks left to play, and I suspected they would be showstoppers tonight. Taking a pair of black gloves from the glove box, I pulled them on. They looked like any ordinary pair of driving gloves but with one minor detail: they made metal virtually invisible! It was a long shot, but I was sure I could pull it off. Most of the time they frisk you but don't touch your hands. They plan on being able to see anything you might be holding, and I hoped that was the case tonight.

After stretching my fingers in the tight gloves, I picked up the .45. It touched the metal contacts in the palm and thumb of the glove. The silver metal shone for a moment, and then like water, it washed out of sight. You could still see it if you knew it was there. Everything you saw through the gun was a little distorted, but in a case like this, in a bar with bad lighting and guards who might even have a few drinks in them by this hour, I had a chance. A smile crossed my face as I looked, or tried to look, at the gun. It was amazing what the WJA scientists could do. Placing the gun on the seat, I grabbed my coffee mug and just about spilled it all over myself—I guess aluminum is metal, too.

* * *

TARAS KARJANSKI CLOSED HIS eyes and sank into his seat as the Boeing 747 took off. He smiled as he felt the pressure from the giant jet engines pushing him into the backrest. He wondered how anyone could sit in an airplane and be afraid. He loved the rush and the power of the engines as they fired and sent the plane into the air and over the ocean.

He peered at the flight attendant as she passed his seat to check on the lower class people in the back. He could smell her perfume and thought of how easily he could reach out and snap her thin, little neck. He tried to shake the thought from his mind. When he first had a thought of such violence, he was only a boy. Papa's farm was not much, but they still ran a few hundred sheep. Russia was struggling to survive after the war, and he could remember many nights going to bed with his siblings, hungry and angry.

Taras loved the sheep and loved tending to them on the plains, far away from anyone or anything. He used to lie outside with the sheep instead of in the tent where his father slept. He could never understand his father. He was a man of few words and a quick hand. Most of the time that hand landed across his face, which was better than when Papa found a stick or some other object to use for punishment.

Taras could still remember the night he began to change. It might have been the isolation, or maybe he was just a bad egg. He was fuming and cursing after a beating. He could feel his heartbeat calm as he imagined hurting his father. In his mind, he always won, but it was only in his imagination. He could feel the rage build up. He could kill his father! Sometimes he wanted to. He looked down at the lamb in his arms and thought how helpless it was and how powerful he was. He thought of how easy it would be to kill it. Just twist its neck, and end the lamb's life.

Then, he did it.

When it was over, he was covered with blood, and the remains of the sheep looked like a wild animal had attacked it. Taras fell to the ground and cried. He couldn't believe what he'd done. He tried to wipe the blood from his hands, but it wouldn't go away. It stuck to his fingers like strawberry jam. Standing over the murdered, innocent lamb, he looked over to the tent where he could see a flicker of light. *You made me do this!*

Wiping a tear from his cheek, he ran into the woods to get away from his shame. However, the more he ran, the closer he came to his fears. His father's voice filled his head. He screamed and cursed his father for making him kill.

Months went by, and little, twelve-year-old Taras found himself killing every night. It started to feel good, even normal. With each kill, his hunger grew deep inside like a starving beast. He would go all day waiting for nightfall, when he could kill under the blanket of darkness.

His father thought they had a wolf problem and hunted him every night with no luck. His killings got more and more brutal as the years went by. He tried to control it, so he resorted to killing off the neighbor's cows and goats, but the hunger wanted more than sheep and goats. He wanted something with a soul.

Someone claimed to have seen a red looking dog killing a sheep, and he became a legend in his village. No one knew that he was the Red Dog. He didn't even know if it was him that the villager saw, because he would sometimes pass out after a kill, not remembering what he had done. He liked the legend though, and took the name for himself with pride.

Taras snapped back to the present as the pretty, red-headed flight attendant touched his shoulder and smiled. "Can I get you anything to drink, sir?" She was even more beautiful up close then Taras could have imagined.

"Yes, my sweet." Taras could be charming if he wanted to. "I would love a glass of scotch, on the rocks."

He brushed her hand and lingered just a second too long. She blushed and smiled. "Right away, sir." She hurried off to get his drink.

During the rest of the flight he made small talk with the redhead, flirting with her every time she was within earshot. She didn't seem to mind and even responded by giving him her phone number before he got off the plane at LAX. He knew he was older than her by almost twenty years, but, without his beard, he was a striking man to behold. The scar above his eye only added to his mysterious appearance and seemed to draw the opposite sex, like bees to honey.

* * *

KIRK STOOD AT THE front door with his gun drawn as he looked through the peephole. He relaxed a little and opened the door when he saw that it was the FedEx man. "Package for you, sir." The long dreadlocks of the native shook as he spoke. He looked at Kirk with a big smile on his face, showing all of his white teeth.

"Hey, Frank, you going to the game tomorrow?" Kirk asked conversationally.

"Oh, Mon, I wouldn't miss it for anyting." Rugby was still alive and well in Bali. The local team was called the Bali Geckos. "You going, sir?"

"No, I wish I could, but I've got to go to the States for some business. Go Geckos, and death to anyone who stands in their way!" The dark man raised one hand, gave Kirk a high five, and laughed with a cackling, deep baritone that reminded Kirk of a giant in a movie he once saw.

Kirk took the package and waved to Frank as he walked away. It looked to be some sort of CD. He wondered if it was from his new silent partner. He'd been getting anonymous information on The General for the last six months. It always came in a package without a return address. Kirk tore it open, pulled out a CD, and read the letter.

The General is also known as Taras Karjanski. Here is

his file and accomplishments. He has been off the grid for the last year, but we believe he is alive. He is considered highly dangerous and hostile.
    P.S. You are still dead.

Included in the package was his old shield and a set of passports with the name, "Wes Kirkwood." It was a lot easier to get around when you were dead, and now with new credentials he would be unnoticed. He smirked and slipped the badge on his belt. It felt good to have it again. He missed being a cop on some level; however, living the life of ease wasn't bad, either.

After reviewing the contents of the CD, he zipped up his suitcase and waited for the cab to pick him up. He couldn't believe what he had seen on the disc. The General was one smart guy, and if he was still connected to his old buddies, he could be one dangerous man.

He wondered if the WJA was behind the notes and the information he was getting on The General. He had a feeling they knew far more than they were letting on.

A horn sounded as a cab pulled up in front of his villa. Kirk smiled when he saw the rainbow colored cab. Only in Bali!

* * *

THE FLIGHT TO LOS angeles was long and boring. Even the in-flight movie made Kirk want to jump from the plane without a parachute. *The Good Shepherd* was one of those movies where you wondered if the directors had even watched it themselves! Kirk could feel his old mood creeping over him as he got closer to the States and farther away from his comfortable hideaway. He was not one to look at things in a positive manner or to see much good in anything or anyone. In his little world on the beach, he was a different person, and it felt good. Now he was back to work and had a killer to catch.

The flight attendant smiled at him as she handed him a bag of peanuts and asked what he wanted to drink. She had a youthful face but wasn't very attractive. Her body was too large to be wearing the size she so desperately wanted to be, and her nose was flat, like it had been smacked with a frying pan.

Kirk gave her a nod and went back to the morning paper. Kirk had looked around the plane when he was searching for his seat and couldn't find one good-looking flight attendant. *Why couldn't I have gotten a pretty one, is that so much to ask? They should screen them better.* At least the woman sitting across from him was nice on the eyes. She read her book and tried to pretend not to have noticed him; however, he knew when he looked away that she stole a glance and liked what she saw.

After a chicken sandwich and a can of Pepsi, Kirk leaned back in his seat and closed his eyes. He could remember being in that cell and how the cold concrete floor made him shiver. He still had scars all over his back, and his feet felt like shoe leather. The scars would always be there. They were a constant reminder of his past and what he was out to do.

Kirk used to be the lead detective in the Detroit Police department until he snubbed his nose at authority one too many times. He had been one mistake from being put on traffic duty for the rest of his career.

The General was a Russian who ran what was left of the Russian Mafia from LA to New York. He had a few younger siblings. Their parents were assumed murdered when he was only thirteen years old, but no one ever found the bodies. The rumors were that a Red Dog had killed them. In Russia, they had no idea that their legend was a real person.

Kirk had tracked him to Bali after he escaped from the compound in Puerto Rico. The World Justice Agency had attacked and tried to rescue him but believed he was dead after the building had exploded. If the information he was getting in the mail was from the WJA, then they must have found out he was alive and well, but still didn't know The General's whereabouts.

Kirk Weston was a man of luck. Most of the time it

was bad, but when it was good, it was very good. After the explosion, he went back to see what he could dig up on The General.

After Kirk had arrived in Kasamba, using the tickets in the briefcase, he soon discovered that his enemy was the owner of a villa just up the beach.

To the rest of the world, Kirk Weston was dead. He had been kidnapped and killed, never to be heard from again. That was fine with Kirk, and he rather enjoyed it. No one to bother him or tell him what to do. His ex-wife had remarried, and he didn't have any other family to speak of...so, life was good.

The airplane jerked Kirk awake as it hit a rough patch. He looked around and saw that everyone was settling down for the long trip. He rubbed his hand over his smooth, bald head and sighed. It was hard to believe he was going back to the United States. He couldn't think of many good memories there, but then again, he never liked people, and America sure had a lot of them.

CHAPTER THREE

I LOOKED DOWN AT my watch. It was time TO make some magic. My stomach tightened, and I couldn't believe I was nervous. I had dreamed about this evening and how everything was going to go. Not that I looked forward to it, but I had this thing down…

A single bead of sweat dripped down my face. I wiped it away with the back of my hand and opened my car door. The car was a Dodge Neon so I would blend in, unlike most of the local law enforcement. They all drove big Fords or black SUVs—the masters of blending in. Just as I imagined, a black stretch limo pulled up in front of the bar and the driver waited for his boss to come out. He would be waiting a long time.

I held onto the gun a little too tightly. It was in my right hand as I walked toward the bar. The lights were on outside, but it still looked dark. This place represented everything that was wrong with this city. Old, broken down bricks and a window boarded up with plywood. The street lamp flickered on and off, making my shadow fade in and out, like a phantom. A train rumbled by behind me as I walked up three steps to the front door. The building had a bar on the main floor and apartments on the second, but I doubted anyone lived there. The rooms were used for other things. In one window, a small light made its way through the split plywood and spilled into the night.

Two mooks stood in the doorway with tailored suits and overbuilt bodies. They looked at me and opened the door without a word. I felt the cool air hit my face as I entered. The air conditioning felt good, but it didn't help my nerves.

I waited.

The bar was just about empty. An older man with a patch over one eye sat at the counter and sipped on a Budweiser. He didn't even look up when I came in. It made me wonder if he was even aware of my presence. I was dressed in a nice suit with a black tie. My blond hair was short and spiked just the way K liked it. I looked the part of a punk *wannabe* mobster, which was half the battle. The bar was long with beer signs hanging on the wall and a big mirror behind the counter. A short, fat man looked at me with deadpan eyes, and he wiped his mouth with the end of his dirty white apron. The place could hold fifty or so customers, but the rush was still an hour or so out. Everything was ready for their money, and then the drinks would flow. Wooden tables and chairs sat all around. A green felt-topped card table sat in the corner with a stack of well-used cards next to red, black, and white poker chips.

"This way." One of the mooks led me to a back room with a wooden door and a fogged over window, with lettering that read, "Office." Before I went in, he looked at me with the universal look that said, *you know what to do*, so I obliged, put my hands against the wall, and he patted me down. I'd left a knife in my pocket so he'd feel like he'd found something and would be satisfied.

It worked.

He smiled with a big dumb grin and opened the door to let me inside. He never even looked at my hands, and I tried to loosen my grip so it didn't seem like I was holding something. But it was too late for them anyway.

I was in!

The office was littered with newspapers and clippings pinned to the wall from about three feet up all the way to the ceiling.

Murder in Cape Town leaves police baffled.
Fifteen-year-old girl missing.
Banker found in his own vault, throat cut.

He was a collector of his own art, and he could care less who knew about it. The old wooden desk had a large stack of money sitting off to one side. The Magician sat looking over his accounting books, which were piled on the floor. One thick one sat open on his desk.

He pointed to a chair across from where he sat, without looking up.

I sat down and looked at his accomplice who glared back at me. He was all of six-feet-seven and had a head of thick, raven black hair. He wore a white dress shirt and a Glock in a Galco shoulder holster. He didn't seem overjoyed to see me, and I didn't send any love in his direction either. The two mooks who let me in left the room and shut the door behind them.

"So, you think you have something I want?" The Magician finally spoke, looking up at me with a set of dark brown eyes. He had thinning black hair and a splash of gray ran through it like spider webs. He was built like a linebacker with a fat neck and wide shoulders. I saw that he was not packing a weapon, but I knew that in or under his desk, he would have a shotgun, unless he was completely stupid.

I started to speak, but he jumped in. "You better have what I want, because not just anyone can get a meeting with me. And you, my friend, are on borrowed time!" He slurred his words and chewed on a dingy toothpick. His Italian accent made him hard to understand.

We had forwarded him ten million to meet with us, hoping to make a business arrangement. He responded with a meeting time and place. We had him hooked, and all that remained was my part. I thought again about my sweet daughter Sam and imagined this pig taking her. I remembered all the little girls he had kidnapped and killed. I did not need to think on it long. The reason I was here came to mind, giving me the strength to begin.

"Mr. Fontana, I am here to talk to you about your future." He started to butt in again, but I stood up as my instincts kicked in. I knew it would enrage him that I dared to stand without his permission, but I needed him mad. I needed him to be so mad that his judgment would be clouded.

"No, you listen to me! Your future is set in stone, Magician." I spat his nickname out as if it were poison, and his face turned red from the neck up. "You are here tonight to pay for your sins. I am here to speak for the families you have touched with your dirty hands!"

The bodyguard hit the floor with a thud before he even knew he'd been shot. The gun in my hand was just an extension of my arm. The magic of The Magician was about to run out, and as he stood up, I pulled the trigger, sending a bullet into his chest. His body shook as he tried to catch his breath. I moved over his desk and pushed him backward. The chair he was sitting in splintered and broke apart under his weight. He grunted and gurgled as his lungs filled with blood.

I landed like a tiger, crouched on his torso, and looked into his dark, empty eyes. He tried to push me off, but I shoved the barrel of my .45 into his neck so hard that he froze and glared up at me with hate flashing through his eyes, like lightning in a thunderstorm. Leaning down, I whispered in his ear just before I pulled the trigger.

"Sweet Dreams!"

* * *

A REDHEAD LAY ASLEEP in her bed, looking peaceful as an angel. Her delicate eyelids covered her blue eyes and the moonlight cast a glow over her face making her look more beautiful than a runway model.

She's so beautiful, so sweet.

Taras Karjanski looked down at her and touched her soft skin with his hand. He stood over her and let his fingers feel her cheek ever so gently as if she were made of glass and, if he pushed too hard, she might break. He considered himself lucky to have met her and hit it off so quickly. But he was a charmer, and he knew he could have any woman he wanted.

Mandy Buckingham told him about how she grew up in Venice Beach, California, and began working for the airlines when she turned twenty. After a year, she moved to Los Angeles to focus on her desire to be an actress. Her parents were both lawyers and hated the fact that their only daughter was off chasing a dream they believed she would never attain. Mandy worked out like a machine and had natural red hair and a smooth, creamy complexion.

It was a scary thing—to be sucked in to where the caged monster hid, and to tease him and let him out to play, even for a moment. Just one time, and it would change your life forever. Taras knew all about playing with the caged beast, he liked the thrill and fear that came with living on the edge.

The night was still young for the Red Dog. He left Mandy's apartment without a sound. She had a simple walkup: one bedroom, a small kitchen, and living room that was a dining room, as well. Looking down at his watch, he noticed that it was one in the morning…plenty of time to hit a few clubs, check out the night scene, and get into a little trouble.

He walked in the shadows as he made his way down to the corner drug store. LA was still alive and bustling with activity even at this hour. He loved to see all the people and think to himself how fragile their lives were. He was a killer walking among them, and they didn't even know it. *I am the highlander! No, I am more powerful than he. I hold life and death in the palm of my hand.* He liked to watch the Highlander movies. He felt like he could relate to someone who was immortal. He was immortal after all, just below a god. Maybe one day, he would kill God and take His place.

Most mobsters or mafia bosses would have bodyguards and private jets carry them wherever they went. Taras Karjanski liked to be alone. It reminded him of the plains of Russia, with fields full of sheep. His operation was strong in the LA area, so he figured before he made his rounds, he would finish off the night with a nightcap. He ruled with fear. His goons knew that at any moment he could show up to check up on them, and he would do anything to keep his subjects under control.

Before Taras knew it, he was in the middle of downtown. He could hear music from the dance clubs and looked around for one that he deemed promising. Across the street he spotted a club called "The Duce." It had a tall, glass, knife-shaped sculpture jutting from the street into the air, with neon lights intertwined throughout it. Inside, the carpet was red, and the black walls contrasted with white booths and tabletops. Oversized cone-shaped lights hung on cords, like icicles waiting to fall on some unsuspecting person below.

The music was pop rock with a little jazz mixed in. Not much was said to the big black bouncer who guarded the door after Taras slipped him a thousand-dollar bill. In fact, he was granted a private table in the back overlooking the dance floor. Music pounded out something that Taras didn't fully understand. *Pop it like it's hot, or drop it like it's hot?* It didn't make any sense, but everyone on the main dance floor moved with the beat in one, fluid movement. People talked, laughed, and danced in packs that, from where Taras sat, looked like a sea of moving arms and bodies.

The place was packed and filled with excitement. Taras was in the mood to be alone, contrary to the Red Dog's mood. Much of his hate was for the way the people all seemed so happy. It made him want to burn the place down with all their smiling faces trapped inside.

The waiter took his order and returned with vodka in a short, fat glass that had two ice cubes floating in the clear liquor. It was an old cliché, but he liked the taste of it and hoped he could just watch the ridiculous people in peace. However, that was not what the Red Dog wanted, or what he was going to get.

A tall blonde and her slightly shorter girlfriend came over

to his table and smiled at him, as if expecting something for their efforts. The tall one wore a red dress that hit her just above the knees, and she had a huge rose pendant around her neck. The smaller brunette had a choker around her neck with a tiny, white flower in the middle, and a black dress. The colors almost made Taras think they might work at the club, but then, they must have been to the club in the past and dressed to match the décor.

"You girls looking for something?" He wanted to scream at them to leave him alone in his misery.

"You seem lonely and so sad…we thought you might like some company." The tall one slid into the booth next to him and the shorter brunette sat on his other side. He could smell the perfume on them and, mixed with the smell of the vodka in his glass, it made an intoxicating scent. He forced a smile, and took another sip.

"Okay, if you lovely ladies insist, then I have a few rules before we continue." The girls laughed and rolled their eyes as he began to explain.

"First, no names. Second, you will leave just the way you came—alone. Do you understand the rules?"

They nodded and the shorter one asked. "What if we break your little rules…then what?" She spoke in a whisper and Taras had to lean toward her to hear what she said.

Taras looked at her and, with no expression on his face, said, "Then I'll have to kill you."

They both stared back at him and after a brief pause, they both burst out laughing. If they only knew. He wasn't joking.

* * *

KIRK WESTON GOT OFF the plane and looked at his watch. A red dot blinked with a map outline where the numbers would normally be. He had found a bunch of Geek Squad stuff online. When you had a million dollars in the bank, you could get just about anything you wanted. The red, blinking dot was the location of Taras Karjanski, or at least it was the location of his wallet. Kirk had put a small tracking device in his wallet when he bugged his villa six months earlier.

After picking up his brown duffle bag from baggage claim, he got a cab and headed downtown. The Russian was on the move and was out way too late to be up to any good. It was two a.m., and Kirk was exhausted from the flight. Now he had to go chasing the Russian around when all he wanted was to crawl into a warm bed and sleep.

Los Angeles could be a beautiful city at times, depending on where you were. However, tonight something didn't seem right. Something was off about this entire trip. He knew that Taras was going to meet his family in Russia. *So why the stop in LA?*

The cab pulled up to an apartment building that stood four stories tall and was made of red brick. Each window had a green awning above it and the complex looked to be over a hundred years old, though with recent renovation. He paid the cabbie, walked up the steps and looked at his watch again. The little red light was blinking a few blocks down and he knew this building was Taras's last known location.

The apartments looked dark, but one had a faint light coming from beneath a blind. It was the one with the closest staircase, so Kirk decided to try that one first. *Why not? Not like I've got anything better to do.* He didn't know why, but he had a strong hunch that he was on the right track. What was Taras doing at an apartment building in LA anyway?

He made his way up the front staircase and looked up and down the street. No one seemed to be milling around, and worst case scenario, he had his badge. Kirk breathed in the night air as he tried the doorknob.

It was open. *Not a good sign.* The kitchen light above the sink was on and the faint smell of burning wood filled the room. The fireplace still glowed with the last bit of embers as it smoldered in the living room hearth.

By now, he had his gun drawn and his heart quickened as he made his way toward the bedroom. Everything was quiet in the house, and between the fireplace and the light on in the kitchen, it gave the idea that someone else was in the house. *Maybe one of his goons, or maybe a girlfriend?* Kirk was alert and every nerve was on end as he stopped in the doorway to the master bedroom.

The form of a sleeping woman made a lovely shape in the king size bed. He flipped the light switch, but the woman didn't move when the room filled with light. Kirk stopped as he read the rough message written in black marker on the wall above her bed.

"YOU THINK THIS IS A GAME, DETECTIVE?"

CHAPTER FOUR

I COULD FEEL THE clock as it ticked on without anyone or anything able to stop it. Everything seemed to be in slow motion. Even the paper in The Magicians big, black book floated to the floor with an almost silent sound as it turned over and over in the air. I could feel my mind jumpstart as my instincts came alive. The Magician had seen his last magic trick…tonight, the trick was on him. He would not do anyone else any harm, at least not in this life. I waited for the guards to burst into the room to see what all the noise was about, but they never came. The silencer was effective. I moved as fast as I could and did not make much, if any, sound as I carried out my mission.

The tall beast of a bodyguard looked up at me with blank eyes and a hole in his forehead where the bullet made contact with his brain. He never knew what hit him. Perhaps the last thought that passed through his brain was nothing short of genius, but then again, maybe not. Usually the type who were employed by men like The Magician were not the highly intelligent sort.

I didn't kill for fun or sport, and I had to shut off my emotions when I was on the job. If I thought about it long enough, then the dark beast inside might even find it enjoyed killing, when in fact, I did not relish it. I did, however, get some sort of satisfaction in knowing that someone tonight would sleep better without this killer on the streets.

A great man once told me that you had to remember your *Why*. *The Why* is what keeps you going when things are at their darkest and will keep you focused on what needed to be done. I had a daughter waiting for me at home, and a loving wife, and I wanted to see a day where they could be safe. I was not naïve or stupid, I knew that my small part wouldn't make much difference, but it made a difference to the family who wouldn't lose a loved one to this monster. I would never be a hero, not in this lifetime. The thing is…

Time to go, Mark.

I awoke from my thoughts and slipped out the back door of the office. No guards came to stop me, and I was soon back in New York with my comfortable slippers on and a warm cup of cocoa in my hand. I couldn't explain it, but nothing beat a warm cup of cocoa after a long day at the office.

* * *

KIRK WESTON RUBBED HIS shaved head and muttered. He searched his mind trying to figure out where he'd slipped up. He was careful and, to his knowledge, he was unseen by his enemy. However, the message written on the wall proved otherwise.

He stumbled down the dark alley behind the apartment building and turned toward the street where he found a pay phone. He dialed 911 and waited for the operator to answer.

"911 what's your emergency?"

"I want to report a murder."

"What is your name sir? Where are you?"

"In apartment 1A, on the corner of Sixth and Spring Street." Kirk hung up before the operator could ask any more questions. Walking down two blocks, he looked up the street, heard the sirens and saw the flashing lights from an ambulance. They wouldn't be getting much sleep tonight, and Kirk didn't think he would either.

* * *

"MORNING, BABE. YOU SLEEP okay?" I grabbed k around the waist from behind as she tried to pour a glass of orange juice.

"Like a baby. When did you come in?"

"Late."

"I see. You up for some scrambled eggs?"

"Always." I loved K's eggs. She always put a little cheese in them that made your taste buds jump for joy. "You look like—well…uh."

"Hm? You better watch it, mister, I haven't even taken a shower yet, slaving away in the kitchen to make *your* breakfast."

"I was going to say a ravaging beauty. I mean it. You look stunning, my love!" K smacked my arm and laughed. She was beautiful, with a smile that could warm you right down to your soul. We'd been married for almost ten years now, and it seemed like it was just yesterday that we met.

Samantha was seven and thought everything was hers or would be hers if she just batted her big blue eyes. Then again, maybe she was right. I couldn't resist her, even if I tried. I was a lucky man to have my girls. Sam never took advantage of me, though. She somehow knew that it was a special thing to have that kind of love from her father.

"So, what are you up to today?" K asked as she cracked an egg.

"I'm off today, so I thought I would take you to…well you'll just have to wait and see!" K turned to look at me with her deep brown eyes. "What? Sam's in school until three and you're off, too."

"Mark I have to work today, I—"

"—I called and had you replaced for the day, so you're all mine!" K's eyes brightened as she jumped in my arms. "You dog."

"Yeah, I know."

* * *

THE LOS ANGELES TIMES had a headline that would end

up on every news channel in the country.

MURDER, MURDER, MURDER!

"Three women found dead. A flight attendant was found early this morning, strangled in her sleep, and a couple of teenagers found two bodies in a dumpster behind The Duce nightclub early this morning. They were strangled and beaten so badly, it looked like an animal had attacked them."

The story went on about how the LAPD believed the murders might be linked and there could be a new serial killer on the loose. Taras looked at the paper and shuddered. It was hard to believe that someone could do that to another human being, let alone such beautiful women. But then again, he had enjoyed it, even if it did bring him a small amount of guilt.

They broke the rules. They disobeyed me!

* * *

THE DAY WAS JUST what i needed to get back down to earth. It was nice to have K all to myself and just mill around with nothing in particular to do. We went downtown and hit a few clothing stores where K bought a spring handbag. I never could understand replacing a purse every time the season changed, but it made her happy. I found a baseball hat that fit better than my old one. They only last a year or so before they implode on themselves and look like you stole them from a bum on Fifth Avenue.

After lunch at our favorite diner, we went to Central Park to sit and watch all the people, getting a few laughs at what we saw. I made up voices, and we imagined conversations of people who walked by. Most of the time it was making fun of them in a 'you had to be there sort of way.' I would try just about anything to get K to laugh. It was worth any crazy thing to hear her laugh. She was the best thing that had ever happened to me.

* * *

A TALL RUSSIAN LOOKED around as he walked from the

terminal in the famous LAX airport. He had a black backpack slung over his shoulder and dark sunglasses on, even though he'd been inside.

Taras Karjanski waited to see if the man would recognize him. The dark-haired Russian looked at Taras then walked past him, still looking for his older brother. He stopped and turned to look again at the man with a small scar above his eye.

"Brother!" Taras said. "You like? The surgeons here can do wonders, yes?" Taras smiled and gave his brother a hug. "I had the scar added for effect. You like it? Makes me look tougher."

"It has been a long time. You look good, Taras."

"Thank you. You still look like my brother." Taras laughed at his brother's confused look. "Come, I have a car waiting."

The airport was packed with people, which was not unusual for LA. Like a melting pot for the world, people from every different race and walk of life could be found coming or going in LAX.

Taras looked at his little brother as they walked out to the waiting car. He was a strong man with a head of thick black hair. He could tell that his younger brother had kept himself in shape and looked much more impressive than he did. *Strength in body will fail you brother. The mind is the real weapon!*

The Red Dog began to emerge from his slumber as they drove to the hotel where Taras was staying. He felt like a caged animal trapped in the car. Nowhere to go. Nowhere to hide. He had to get some air. He rolled down the window and breathed in deeply. He needed to think. His family business was about to become more profitable. His brother was about to be murdered, and the business would go on without him. His sister was in Russia running that end, and he had his hands full running the operation in the States.

When you think about most of the downright evil things people do, it almost always comes back to money. He wanted a bigger cut and this was his chance. Natasha was in on the plot; it was partly her idea. Their brother had burned too many bridges and used more of their merchandise than was acceptable. The Red Dog also knew deep down in the pit of his soul that his brother had been the one who killed his parents. This did not anger him because he loved his parents, but because he felt that the honor of taking their lives was his! He wanted to spill their blood, but his brother had taken that chance from him.

The Radisson was close to the airport and proved to be somewhat up to Taras's standards. When they arrived, Taras pulled around to the back of the building and parked the car. His room key got them in, and they were soon in the suite on the fifth floor. Taras made sure no one had seen them come in. The plan was even more perfect than he could have imagined. *I'm more sinister than anyone will ever know. I am a mastermind, and no one can even begin to compare to my genius.*

The smug look on Taras's face turned to horror when he saw a .22 pointed at his forehead. He didn't have time to react or even have a conscious thought before the silent bullet ripped through his skull. He fell to the floor in a heap as blood gushed from a gaping hole in the back of his head.

The Red Dog looked down at his deceased older brother and a single tear ran down his cheek. He loved him more than anyone would know, but his hate was stronger.

After wiping down the gun and shoving it into the back of his pants, he opened his black backpack, pulled out the old plane ticket, and replaced it with his. Then he took out a knife and peeled the skin off of his fingertips. He winced in pain as they tore free and the fresh skin underneath hit the air. He threw the fingerprint implants in the toilet and flushed them away. Never to be seen again!

After trading wallets, rings, and anything else that would lead the police to believe Taras was alive, he granted himself permission to smile. The new Taras Karjanski looked one more time at his dead older brother. He loved him, but his need for killing and lust had taken control. The Red Dog was not only hiding deep within his subconscious, but somehow was a shared awareness between the two brothers. The new Taras didn't even remember his real name any more, and had felt, and known, everything between his older brother and himself for so long that it felt natural to be him for real now.

Taras recalled how his sister had come to him with Taras's plan to murder him, but it didn't matter because he already knew. She wanted to warn him and form a contract to take over the family business. She said that he was the stable one and she feared Taras. If she only knew what loomed inside of him was now worse than anything that ever lived in her older brother...

* * *

SERIAL KILLER FOUND DEAD IN HOTEL ROOM

THE LA TIMES SPLASHED the headline across the front page as eager readers devoured the horror story as it unfolded. "Fingerprints found at the murder scenes matched, and so did a video surveillance tape from The Duce, which showed a man with a scar above his right eye leaving with the two murdered women. The LAPD has not yet released his name, but we believe he was part of the underground Russian Mafia."

Taras gritted his teeth as the old Soviet surgeon removed the scar and added a small one over his left eyebrow. This time he looked like a young Taras Karjanski. The older Taras had made it easy for him, changing his face to look like his little brother so that when they found him, they would assume he was the younger brother from his looks down to his fingerprints. Taras was good, but the plan backfired. Now, the new Taras could pick up where his older brother left off, taking his place in the family. He would have to lay low for a few months before he attacked again—and this time he had the perfect person to frame.

Time to play with the big dogs, Detective Weston!

* * *

THE MORNING NEWS WOKE kirk weston from a deep sleep in the Hilton Garden Inn. He rubbed his eyes and sat up in bed. It was eight in the morning, and his head felt like it was about to explode. He must have left the TV on last night, and after a few drinks, passed out. The newswoman looked like she was made of plastic and always had the perfect little thing to say. Kirk watched as the woman who had been murdered in her apartment was taken out in a body bag. He could see the news media as they tried to climb over the police barricades to get a better shot of the madness.

"Stinkin' vultures!"

The one-cup coffee maker would be just enough to get him going, but he would have to hit the java shop in an hour or so to really get going on the right foot.

So, you know I'm here, do you? He sat down on the edge of the bed and held his head in his hands. *Think, man. Where is he going?*

The red light on his watch showing where Taras was located was gone. Kirk assumed that Taras had found and destroyed the bug. *What are you up to?* The coffee was done, and Kirk grabbed a mug from the counter and filled it to the brim. He sipped as a thought hit him. "Money. Follow the money." Only one person from Kirk's old life knew he was still alive. A kid he had let off with a slap on the wrist a few years back, who was a wiz with computers.

CHAPTER FIVE

MOOCH WAS IN HIS twenties but looked like HE was still in his teens. The messy hair mixed with patchy, unshaven peach fuzz on his chin would unnerve most people just by his looks alone. His screen name was **HotHat007**. Kirk didn't understand the underground world of hackers. There were "white hats" and "black hats," but he didn't know who was what or who was higher than who. All he knew was that his pocket hacker had helped him out of a jam on more than one occasion.

"What do you want this time? Wait, don't tell me. You're tracking a killer of some kind and you want me to do something illegal." Through the phone, Mooch's voice dripped with sarcasm.

"Well Mooch, you trafficked in the dark side of the law on your own. I didn't think you'd have any problem running some borderline computer hacking for an old friend."

"How's Mom?" Kirk asked. He could tell Mooch was still living in his Mom's basement from the sounds coming across the line.

"Funny, but my rent is free, and she still does my laundry. Are we going to talk about my living situation or are you going to get to the point?"

Kirk rolled his eyes and took another glance at the girl

behind the counter. She was in her early twenties and Kirk could have been her dad, but he still half-considered asking her out. He took a sip of the dark, bitter coffee and turned his attention back to Mooch. "Taras Karjanski, aka the General. I need his financial records and last known associates."

"Oh, is that all?" Mooch mocked.

"Yeah. Think you can handle it?"

"Fine, but I want another thousand for my trouble."

"Five hundred. You don't pay rent and your Mom washes your underwear." Kirk didn't even skip a beat.

"Well played for a dead guy. Fine, give me twenty-four hours."

Kirk hung up the phone and smiled. He would have paid any amount to get more information on Karjanski, but sometimes it paid to be mean. It had served him well so far, why stop now?

* * *

MY WEEKEND WAS OVER faster than I would have liked, but then, getting back to work for most people was a drag when Monday came. I liked what I did—well, most of it. At the end of the day, I could rest in the fact that I was making a difference.

A few years ago, I never would have believed I'd be involved in a secret agency. However, my life was destined to be a life of mystery and intrigue. It all started when I was a baby. My parents were killed in an airplane accident, leaving me orphaned. The whole story of how I survived is still a mystery, and I have not been able to find much of anything explaining the accident. I was in the hospital when Solomon found me. He adopted me shortly afterward because I had no extended family, and no one ever came forward to claim me.

Solomon created the World Justice Agency. He would adopt children, give them a safe place to grow up, and then teach them skills to survive.

The WJA was not a part of any government, nor affiliated with anyone. It was self-supporting with many big-time investors, who were always kept anonymous. The children were trained with subconscious therapy and taught everything from combat fighting to advanced reasoning. Every child had to be under the age of three and, after they completed the program, they were placed in a foster home and integrated back into society. They did not remember the WJA or any training they had received, since the programmed training was planted deep within the subconscious mind, making that knowledge part of their instinct.

I could remember most of my childhood now that I was back in the program and doing memory exercises. If a child wanted to work for the agency once they were an adult, it was up to them. Everyone was given the option to go on with their normal lives, or they could reenroll in the program and build on the foundation that had been laid years before.

It was weird to have all this information in my head and not know it was even there. I could do so many things, and I knew stuff I never remembered learning—it just came instinctively.

The agency was run like the FBI or CIA, but with a slight difference. The WJA carried out justice without any court or jury. Each case was decided by the facts in order to balance the corrupt government that America had become.

I had watched a rapist walk on a technicality, and a murderer confess and claim he was temporarily insane, spend a few years in a hospital, and walk out a free man. The days of this madness were over. I'd always wanted to make a difference, to live in a world where the criminals were afraid of the law, not the other way around. Now they were.

The FBI had put together a special task force to take us down before the public got wind of our activity. We knew taking the law into our own hands was risky and could cause confusion; however, we took great steps to ensure that we kept to the background. To the average person, if a mobster was killed or a bombing killed a terrorist cell in DC, it was just a random act. Just two thugs or groups killing each other, which was fine by most Americans.

The WJA headquarters were right in New York City, in the Merc building. They ran a paper called the Global Adviser that reported about global warming and environmental impact that the earth is experiencing. The paper was a cover, to be able to interview people and get into places that we would otherwise not be able to get into. The environmental movement was a popular subject these days, and the WJA took full advantage of it.

The other side to the agency was the Growth Fund Program. Countries with little-to-no education were given schools and hospitals, started by the WJA. This created a place for the WJA to operate from without drawing attention to themselves.

The media, as well as the FBI, couldn't say anything against the paper or its funding projects, or it would look like they were against saving the earth, as well as poor children. The news media was our biggest resource. They had no idea, and championed our cause with energy and fervor.

The FBI and task force looking into the WJA couldn't make the connection and never would, if Solomon had anything to say about it. It also helped that Solomon had been the director of the FBI for twenty-five years and was sort of a hero, due to the number of cases he'd solved when he was with the agency.

I could not see myself doing anything else, now that I was a part of the World Justice Agency. I was finally doing what I was born to do.

* * *

THE UNITED ARAB EMIRATES had their hand in just about everything in the Middle East. The Russian Mafia had set up trade alliances with them and had companies based in Sharjah and Ajman. Their reach even went all the way down into Africa.

Taras Karjanski had been no idiot. He'd had his grubby paws in just about every operation, including dealings with the Taliban. He founded "Air Cargo Incorporated," a drug and arms operation that had fed the Taliban and the African civil wars for the last ten years. He was untouchable as far as the world was concerned. In fact, no one really knew who he was or what he looked like. His sister was the only person left alive who could pin anything on him. However, she was involved almost as much as he was. Natasha Karjanski was the local beauty, and her beauty was matched by her self-confidence. But that was not the part that could kill you. She ran the family business throughout Russia and Africa. She was The Boss, if you will, just under Taras, and in her part of the world, she was one of the deadliest people alive.

Taras trusted his sister to keep everything as it needed to be. Her business savvy had been implanted in her from childhood. Taras had been the one who started it all, after his parents were murdered when he was in his early teens. He began to get mixed up in the Russian Mafia and, before he knew it, he had an inline road to the high seat as Boss.

But it was all too slow for Taras and his sister, who was at his side every step of the way. He planned a hit, which would be all but impossible from any sane human perspective, but Taras Karjanski was not quite right in the head. He eliminated the Old Russian Boss and took his seat. However, the loyal followers of the former boss didn't take it lying down. But they were soon found dead, with their heads sent to the rest of the unconvinced followers in a burlap sack.

Taras had never noticed his little brother; to him it was as if he did not even exist. Natasha, on the other hand, was molding him to take Taras' place when the time was right. She called him Taras and even made him call himself by his older brother's name to bond him to it. By the age of fifteen, he was Taras, and she and he did everything together. She saw in him a talent for business and an ability to do what had to be done, no matter the situation.

Taras knew that in the last few years his sister and he had grown apart. She was busy with her dealings in Russia and he traveled too much to come back home to visit her much. He liked it better alone, anyway. It freed him to do as he saw fit, no one looking over his shoulder and no bodyguards to draw attention to him. The plan was falling into place, but Taras still needed one more ace before he went all in.

The war in Iraq and Iran had looked like it would never end for the United States. The president lacked the guts to do what was necessary to win, and frankly, Taras knew that the American people were the ones who lacked the stones to see poor, innocent people die. The situation was just what he needed to ramp up his plan. The best part was that he and his organization were all but invisible. The Russian Mafia was thought to be a dead group and wasn't considered to be a threat. Fifty, maybe a hundred at the most, were believed to be still left in the mafia. Just in Taras Karjanski's little world, he had over five thousand members, and his Natasha had around the same number. He was the Red Dog, and one day soon, he would rise up. *Then who will stop me?*

The new Taras Karjanski was different from the other Mafia Bosses. They paled in comparison to him. He was on the streets. He was doing hits. He was down in the muck doing what he expected everyone else in his organization to do. He was special, he was different, and no one knew that he was worse than the original. He was overlooked as a boy, but, now that he was Taras, with his reputation, the people who feared him found that Taras had changed. He was not rash and impulsive, but took everything in stride as if he didn't know the meaning of defeat. Now, he was unstoppable.

CHAPTER SIX

THE LAPTOP WARMED UP as kirk took a sip OF his third cup of black coffee. He looked at his watch and grunted in anger. The small, hometown coffee shop was just the place in which Kirk liked to sit and think. No one to bother him. The coffee tasted like tar or burnt soot, and that didn't leave many people who liked that sort of thing, so the place was usually empty.

Mooch was too slow for him. It always made him mad when he didn't get his way, and he wanted that information now!

A woman with a short skirt and boots with fake fur on the top of them, whined at the barista that her latte was too hot. Kirk glared at her and muttered something about her clothing choice. She looked at him with a blank look on her face, which was just what he'd expected.

His cell phone buzzed in his pocket and Kirk answered with his usual charm. "About time."

Mooch didn't seem to care that he had made the detective wait. "You think I could get a little respect around here. This stuff isn't easy, you know!"

"Well you sure don't make it look that way." Kirk didn't hide his feelings very well. "What did you find out?"

"Are you sure you want to get mixed up with this guy?

He's dirtier than a hog in a mud slide."

"Listen, Mooch." The punk didn't know how to keep his trap shut. Kirk didn't care to have the Feds show up at his door again. One phone call, and it would all be over. "Just give me the information."

"Fine, man, you can be a real grump. Anyway, this *General* is what you would call—er, well, a Mafia boss."

"The Russian mafia? I didn't think they were even around anymore."

"He has a sister named Natasha. She is, like, his number two, if you will. She runs things in Russia, and he seems to be doing a lot in the States and in the Middle East."

"What kind of operation? Drugs? Guns?"

"Yup, and something else, but I can't get anything on it other than it's in the works. Something big, though. His net worth is in the billions."

"Billions? With a B?" Kirk whistled and took another sip of coffee.

"Yeah, the guy has some serious coin, and get this—he has never been photographed or identified by anyone who lived to tell about it, other than his sister, of course."

"I've seen him, but I'm already dead, so what's the difference."

"True that. He's got something on his encrypted website you gave me that I thought was interesting. A codename—Red Dog. So I ran it through my database and it goes back to about the time he was twelve, back in Russia."

"What was this guy up to at twelve years old that would give him a code name?"

"Well, the story goes that this Red Dog would roam the streets at night and attack livestock. This Dog thing would kill and rip to shreds anything it could, terrorizing the town for ten years. He considers himself to be like this legend or something."

"Hm, I wonder why he took that name? Could be some sort of fantasy of his, killing like an animal." Kirk opened up the email that Mooch sent him and looked through the information on this Red Dog.

"And, like you wanted, I checked all the flights in the up coming week for anyone Russian, and guess what I got?"

"Just tell me, I'm in no mood for games."

"A man has a flight to Tajikistan tomorrow, and his name is Taigan Tian Tshan."

"And that would be cool in what way?"

"That's the name of a Russian dog breed. Come on, keep up with me."

"Very good, Mooch, I guess you can live yet another day in freedom."

"Hah, funny. Next time my fee is going up."

Kirk hung up before Mooch could say anything else to get him going. Mooch was a good kid, just a little misguided and into computers a little too much, more than what was good for him.

A flight to Tajikistan was leaving at ten in the morning. Kirk planned to be on it.

* * *

JILLIAN PORTER SAT WITH her note pad out and a serious look on her face. Her glasses made her look like a school teacher. She was what I would affectionately call a shrink, or a head doctor. I didn't care for them much, and in most cases, I would say they were a waste of a good college degree, but Jillian, in her mid-thirties, had a comforting way about her. I guess that's why she was so good at what she did. I never thought I would be sitting and talking to a shrink, but here I am.

Jillian was a tall woman with light brown hair that she kept pulled in a tight bun. She was good looking, but somehow never put herself out there as someone to be attracted to. Everything about her was professional and regulated. She was definitely WJA, and I had a feeling she had, at one time, been doing exactly what I was doing for the Agency.

I had the usual problem that almost anyone would

experience if you killed people for a living. My emotions were so tied up with my mind, and everything seemed to get all mixed up inside my head. I knew the people I had killed deserved to die or they would go on killing and harming innocent people, *but why did I have to do it?*

"Mark, tell me about your last mission. Was it hard, simple, or just part of the job?" Jillian was the WJA "house head doctor" and had been doing it for the last three years now. Solomon made it mandatory to see her at least once a month.

I thought about her question and something bothered me that I couldn't put my finger on. "A few years ago, I killed three men who were planning on bombing a supermarket. Afterward, I was terrified and felt so much guilt, I wondered if I'd done the right thing. And now it seems like I am becoming a different person."

I refused to lie down on that stupid couch, so I leaned back in the chair she had for me on the other side of her desk. I looked up at the indirect lighting and the countless books on the shelves hanging behind where Jillian sat. She tapped a notepad with a pencil and gave me a look of concern. "It went just as planned. I keep trying to remember the reason why I am doing what I'm doing. I have this fear that one day I won't feel anything anymore."

"So, you want to feel? You want to have guilt?" Jillian had found the deep secret that I might not have even known myself. I wanted to feel guilty. I wanted it to make me feel more human or make me force myself to keep my soul in front of me. I *needed* to feel guilty.

"I don't want this to be about revenge, it's so much more than that. I go over each and every case before I accept a mission. Sometimes I put up pictures of the victims so I can feel their pain. I don't like killing, but when I do it—it just feels right."

I could hear my own voice, and it sounded like I was on a narrow road to being a murderer, or worse. I shouldn't like killing, or have it come naturally. I should be forcing myself to do it. "Am I crazy?"

"No, you're just going through a natural process. It is not natural to take a life and feel nothing. You have the spirit of the helpless and the ones that can't speak for themselves with you." Jillian took off her glasses and leaned over as she spoke. I liked her. She had a sweet smile and always seemed to care about what you were really going through.

"Mark, you need to really think about why you're here, find the 'Why' of your life. Out there, you don't have time to think or decide if or how you're going to react. You need to settle that now."

Her words hit me in the pit of my stomach. She was right, of course, and I had to do some thinking. Another thing I had to decide was what I was going to tell K. I hated having secrets between us, and even though she said she trusted me, I felt that I owed her the truth.

I thanked Jillian for her time and hunted down Big B. I wanted to see if he had heard anything on The Magician, and if the mission had had the effect we were all hoping for. I really wanted to take some time off to think, but it wasn't in the cards for me.

"Hi ya, Mark. You done good with The Magician. The fight has begun between the two families, just as we expected," Big B said.

"Good, then they'll be at each other rather than on the streets. You look good. Did you lose some weight?" I smiled as Big B laughed, his big chest rumbling like distant thunder.

"Well, maybe a few pounds." Big B was six-foot-four and well over three hundred pounds, and most of it was muscle. He was a giant of a man, but gentle as a teddy bear.

I found my way to my cozy office tucked away on the fifth floor of the Merc building. Every agent had a job in the news publication, our cover; it was needed to keep up appearances. I tried to put the whole case out of my mind. It was over, and now I could relax. Relax. That was something I had a hard time doing.

My office door was locked and the key slid into the doorknob with ease, but something made me stop mid-turn. My senses were going off like alarm bells in my head. I looked down the hall and back the other way, toward where I had just gotten off the elevator. I pulled out my pistol from my shoulder holster and walked in.

Empty.

I kept my office neat and everything had its place on the desk. I was learning to be perfect in everything. I took in every detail because anything out of place was never good in my line of work. I scanned the room. Then I saw it. A newspaper sat on the desk, opened to the second page.

The paper stared back at me, the story headline read:

WHO IS KILLING OFF THE MOB?

The story was only a few paragraphs long, starting with the details of a Russian Mafia member found dead in a hotel room. He had been linked to a series of killings in the LA area. It also mentioned the death of The Magician and a few others who were in hiding throughout the country.

I turned to the front page and saw it was the Global Adviser, our own publication, and was dated two days ago. My brain turned over a few theories, and then it hit me. *Someone has been in my office, in my building! How did they get in here?*

I grabbed the paper and ran down the hall. I was being singled out. They knew who I was.

* * *

THE PLANE LANDED WITH a bump, and the brakes pushed everyone forward in their seats as the 737 slowed. The flight was headed to Dushanbe, Tajikistan, with a half-hour layover in New York.

Taras Karjanski had picked the flight specially. He got up from his seat and slipped into the bathroom at the end of the aisle. He smiled at himself in the mirror. He had long hair and a scruffy beard, topped off with bushy eyebrows. He looked like a stoned punk rocker who had never grown up. His disguise was perfect.

Of course it was perfect. Would he accept any less? *Where are you going? What do you think you will accomplish this way?* His head was a mess of voices and arguments. He pulled off his beard and wig. His jet-black hair looked good, and his contacts made his eyes blue instead of brown. He flushed the disguise down the toilet, took off his coat, and stuffed it in the cabinet under the small sink. His shirt was reversible, and after he was finished, he looked like an executive on his way to an important meeting. His brown leather suitcase had his updated passport, and in seconds, he walked off the plane with the other passengers.

His baggage went on to Dushanbe, as well as his follower who would be on the next flight. Detective Weston was smarter than anyone he had ever met. He shook his head and warned himself that pride would blind him. Detective Weston was smart in his own way, but in a few days, that would be taken care of.

* * *

AZER GEORGIAN WAVED DOWN a cab and got into a beat up yellow Ford, after it came to a screeching stop at the curb. The driver had dreadlocks and spoke like he was from the South Pacific. He smiled at his new passenger and took the piece of paper from his hand with an address on it.

"Your wish is my command, mon. We goin' downtown."

Azer looked at his watch, he had plenty of time. He had a meeting with an influential business contact. If he played his cards right, he would soon be the richest man in the world. And no one would ever know!

CHAPTER SEVEN

A COLD STEEL-BLUE BMW pulled up to the curb in front
of the Lalo Café on West Eighty-Third Street and parked. The
famous café was a popular place, known for its European style,
décor, and cuisine. As usual, it was crowded for lunch. A dark-
skinned man opened the car door and stepped out onto the
sidewalk. He had thin, well-groomed hair and dark sunglasses.
His driver was a short, fat man, with a bulge under his suit
jacket.

The Red Dog watched from his cab as they entered the café
and found a table right in the middle of the restaurant. *Smart,
Mr. Dior. You think you are safe in there with all of your drones
eating their soup of the day.*

The name he was using on this trip, the one the buyer
knew him as, was Azar Georgian. It was the name of a reddish
Russian dog that suited him perfectly. He liked to use names
that only he knew the meaning of. It made him feel like he was
in on a joke that only he knew the punch line to. *Time to party.
Are you ready to meet The General? I don't think you are. I
think you're scared of me, as you should be. Let's just get this
over with and move on.* Shut up you coward! Do it or go home!

Azar entered the café with confidence pouring from his
body like sweet oil. He was an impressive man, with hard arms
and square jaw that clenched a fat cigar between his lips. He

smiled with all his charm as he shook the hand of Mohammed Dior. Dior was the president of OPEC and owned over half of the world's oil refineries. To the rest of the world, OPEC was just trying to help keep the prices consistent as an impartial party, but in the real world, he was lining his pockets with millions each year. "Hello, my friend. You look wonderful, as expected." The Red Dog was out and laying it on thick. "I hope your stay has been pleasant."

The oil lord was sitting without expression and still wore his dark sunglasses, even though he was inside. When he finally spoke, it was with a thick accent. "You have something I want, Mr. Georgian. I won't waste your time or mine with small talk."

Azar smiled and pounded the table with his fist. The bodyguard moved his right hand with a speed that only came from experience. "I like you. Going right for the jugular. I think we will be getting along great, you and I!"

The crowded café was loud, and half of the people kept looking over to the table where the strange people sat. The presence of a clean-cut businessman in a ten thousand-dollar suit was a little out of place in this casual café.

You picked this place special, didn't you, Mr. Dior? You think you're safe from me. I could kill you without even trying, if I wanted to. "I want all of your shares in your company, and then you can have all of my shares. It will be an even trade."

The dark man laughed then took off his sunglasses. His eyes were dark black with pure evil seeping out like dripping wax. "You will get my shares when I have the deed to your company."

"And you shall have it." The Red Dog pulled out a thick folder from his briefcase. The deeds to twelve nuclear power plants were inside. "You may sign your name on the bottom of each of these and you will own enough power to blow up the world, if you wish."

Mr. Dior's face broke into a smile as he flipped through the deeds. He was going into business, the Nuclear Bomb business.

Do it! The Red Dog screamed. He was like a passenger in the back of Taras's mind, and it seemed that he wanted to take over rather than stay in the shadows.

The fat driver opened a laptop and began typing. The funds and shares were transferred to five different accounts throughout Europe that Azar had given them. After confirming they had made the transfer, the Red Dog hung up his cell phone.

"It has been a pleasure doing business with you, my friend." Do it, you coward! *Don't push me. I'm the one in charge!* The café had more than fifty people sitting in different places and even had a line out the door of impatient people waiting to get a table.

Standing to his feet, the Red Dog pulled out a .9 millimeter and shot the fat driver in the head before he even had time to react. Blood sprayed out the back of his skull and showered a man who was sitting nearby. The man screamed out in shock and jumped to his feet, his white t-shirt with a Nike logo covered in blood. As he stumbled and fell over his overturned chair, his shirt clung to his body like a wet rag.

The bodyguard toppled backward, and, as he fell, Taras swung the gun toward Mohammed Dior and sent three rounds into his face. The recoil of the weapon shattered the room with sound, and people began to scream and run for the door.

Taras shot two more rounds into the air and commanded the panicked crowd in a voice that stopped everyone in their tracks, the voice of a lunatic that did not even seem human as he thundered. "Everyone sit down, or I will kill every one of you right here where you cower!"

The frightened crowd stopped cold and looked at the tall Russian. He turned to meet their gazes and his dark eyes flashed. "Good, now, everyone sit down, I will be on my way, and no one else has to die." A tall kid in his mid twenties jumped up and cursed as he made a beeline for the door. Taras squeezed the trigger, the boy's head made a popping sound, and he fell to the floor like a sack of potatoes. His backpack went flying, and his ball cap, which he had on backwards, tumbled through the air, landing in the blood that drained from what was left of the kid's head.

"Anyone else want to die?" Taras smiled and let out a little laugh. "I thought not. I have one thing more to say." He bent down, took his deeds from off the table, and stuffed them back into his briefcase. He snatched the set of car keys from the table, as well. "If any one of you talk to the police and say so much as a word of what you saw here today, I will find you and then kill you and all of your family. Don't test me, and don't think for one minute that I won't do it."

The place was silent as he spoke. A woman to his left had tears streaming down her cheeks, and the men in the room looked beaten and stared down at the floor. Everything happened so fast that no one had time to think. With that, Taras walked from the Lalo Café, squealed the tires of the blue BMW, and disappeared around the corner.

The café filled with screams and cries, as the horror of what just happened dawned on them. The three bodies lay silent, and people tripped and slipped in the blood of the twenty-something-year-old kid as they tried to run from the café. In broad daylight, in the middle of New York City, the Red Dog had just murdered one of the most powerful men in the world!

* * *

"MARK, IT'S TIME TO take detective weston in." Solomon stood more than six feet tall and had a white, well-trimmed beard and glasses. "He's on the tail of The General, and we need to team together if we plan on catching this monster."

I had seen the reports on the local news about the murder in the middle of a crowded café and knew it was The General. I still hadn't gotten over the newspaper I had found in my office, but at this point, it had to be put on the back burner.

"Where is he?"

"On his way to Dushanbe. We have a private jet waiting for you at the airport. Our TAXI is too far away, and we need to get this guy before he does what I think he's planning on doing."

I had a feeling Solomon was holding back some important information, but what could I do? I knew this much—if Solomon was in a hurry to get this General, then he must be a very bad guy.

I grabbed a cab just outside of my building and called K on the way to the airport. She didn't answer, so I left a message. I wouldn't be home for dinner tonight. I hated the fact that she didn't know what I really did. But wasn't it worth her safety to keep her in the dark? I thought about how she and my daughter had been kidnapped, and the pain of almost losing them again was just too much. But not knowing didn't keep them safe back then, so how was it keeping her any safer by not knowing now? I had to tell her, it was eating me up inside. She was my soul mate, my love. I needed to be able to talk to her, to confide in her.

The jet was running as I pulled onto the tarmac. The engines roared in the evening air as I climbed aboard. I looked over my shoulder and saw the New York City skyline. It was a beautiful city, and I couldn't help but feel sad at what it was becoming. The city of fear.

The city was going to be rocked with nuclear bombs in fewer than two weeks. How did I know? I saw it in my dreams...I see it every night in my dreams.

* * *

A MUSHROOM CLOUD ROSE from the new york city skyline like an earthquake, as yet another bomb detonated. I could see two mushroom clouds now. The city, in less than an hour, was all but destroyed. The schools had been the main target, with hospitals next. In all, twenty-seven nuclear bombs went off, killing everyone in their paths.

The projections of the number of people killed, including from the fallout, came to more than eight hundred thousand, and half of the New York City's land mass was left uninhabitable.

I opened my eyes and bolted out of bed. Sweat poured from

my back and arms. I opened my eyes and looked around the G5. I knew it was just a dream, but my dreams always came true.

* * *

THE FLIGHT FROM LA to dushanbe was long and miserable. Kirk Weston stretched his legs as he reached for his carry-on. He was only about three hours behind Taras Karjanski by his calculations, and his tracking device showed that Taras was still close enough to get a signal. The device came back on once the plane started to descend into Dushanbe. He figured Taras has found it, or maybe it just quit working, but now that it was back, it worried him a little.

Why is he still in the airport? Could he be waiting for me? Kirk was always careful, but he just had bad luck. "If it wasn't for bad luck, you wouldn't have any," his Mom used to say.

The airport was dingy and hot. He tried to wipe the sweat from his forehead, but it didn't help. He looked around and didn't see his friend, the Russian. *Come on, neighbor, come out and play!*

Kirk looked down at his watch and carefully followed it to the baggage claim. Kirk cursed out loud and kicked the ground when he saw a single suitcase going around and around the baggage claim track. *Where was Taras? Fine, I'll take your suitcase and see what you've got for me.*

The black suitcase was heavy as Kirk hauled it over to an empty counter to look through his new and only lead. "Stupid, stupid, *stupid!* I should have known." Kirk sighed and unzipped the suitcase. A pair of pants and a shirt lay on top. Kirk mumbled as he went through Taras's garments, feeling like a pervert.

Something hard was mixed in with the clothes. Kirk felt it, picked it up, and looked in horror as the timer on a chunk of C4 counted down from ten. *The dirty bugger put a bomb in a suitcase for me!*

"Bomb, bomb, *bomb!*" Kirk screamed as he dropped the device and ran for the door. Everyone within ear shot screamed and ran when they heard him. No matter what language you speak, everyone knows the word *bomb*.

The ten seconds seemed faster to Kirk then it should have been, and as he ran to the exit, he could hear his heart throbbing in his head. The blood was pounding in his ears, thud, thud, thud. He could see a woman running with a child in her arms. She was screaming. He was screaming, too, but he couldn't hear anything. Just—thud, thud, thud.

You never know what you will think of when you're about to die. Maybe your family, or what you should have done with your life. Kirk could only think about this woman and her child, running. *The run of their lives.*

The bomb ignited and a ball of molten hot fire erupted from the baggage claim. Kirk had his hand on the door when he felt the heat from the blast hit him in the back. *I am going to die.*

The force of the bomb sent Kirk flying into the air. Glass and metal splintered past his head with a sizzling sound. He could feel something on his back. Heat, or maybe pain. He didn't know until he saw the ground coming up fast.

Kirk looked up from his back at the blue sky. A single bird grabbed his attention as a rain of fire and debris came down on him. The bird flew on, unaware of the chaos all around him.

The entire west side of the airport was blown apart, from the east end all the way to the south side, making a crater full of concrete and wood. The fuel from the nearby tanker truck made its own bomb and was thrown fifty feet into the air, tumbling end over end and exploding like huge fireworks.

The last thing Kirk saw was that truck falling from the sky and coming right for him. He knew he was dead already. He had seen the poor woman engulfed in flames just before he blacked out. He had been beat, but even in the face of certain death, he tensed every muscle in his body and braced for what would come next. They had tried to kill him once, and he would not go out like this, not on his back like a wounded deer. Kirk clenched his fists and screamed at the flaming truck as it came down on him.

* * *

A KILLER LOOKED OUT from a window that faced Central Park. The hotel was the perfect temperature and even had a mini-bar stocked with the best drinks. The newspaper the killer had left on Mark's desk had made an impact, but it was time to show Mark Appleton what a crime spree really was. "You think you can save the world? Then let's see if you can stop me!"

The killer smiled and took a long drag from a Cuban cigar. It was the best, and accepting anything less was out of the question.

The game had begun. Though there was much to do, and much to see. It was time to bring the World Justice Agency to its knees. There is no justice in the world, and anyone who thought otherwise was just fooling themselves.

The five-foot-nine killer walked over to a mirror, looked into it, and smiled. "You can call me Chaos. Hm…yes, Chaos will do. You want justice? Come and get it!"

CHAPTER EIGHT

THE FLIGHT TO DUSHANBE took longer than i wanted. I was getting used being able to travel halfway across the world in hours in the TAXI.

I'd requested Isis Kanika, and she'd agreed to come along to give me a hand with the mission. Kirk Weston could be a difficult man to handle. Between his flowering personality and his stubborn nature, he could be dangerous and irrational.

Isis sat on the other side of the aisle on the black G5 as we flew through the air at forty thousand feet. Isis was from Egypt originally, and had dark smooth skin and black hair that looked like silk. She was five-foot-seven, I guessed, maybe a hundred pounds, and her body was trim, fit, and strong. The person who underestimated her would be mistaken, for she was deadly with a knife and a master of hand-to-hand combat.

The airplane made a soft, droning sound, and I could feel the speed of the craft as we crossed the ocean. I wondered what it must feel like to be a powerful bird, like an eagle or a hawk. I could imagine soaring through the clouds, feeling the wet mist on my face and the wind in my hair.

"I am glad you came along on this mission, I miss having you back me up," I told Isis. I leaned on my elbows and tried to shake the uneasy feeling that was starting to cast its shadow over me.

"Back you up? I thought it was the other way around." Isis smiled. I was about to protest, but she held up her hand and said, "No matter who backs who up, it is nice to work with you again. Out of all the people I've worked with over the years, you are by far the most fun, not to mention interesting." Isis smiled with a look that said more than words could. "So, you still having…you know, dreams?"

"Yeah, they still come, just not all the time. They are much shorter, and I can tell at once if it's a glimpse or just a dream."

Isis was going through a file the agency had on Kirk Weston, not because she didn't know all about him, but out of habit. Isis probably knew more about the detective than anyone else did. She was in charge of his original kidnapping and did all the research herself.

"Have you been able to call them up, you know, make yourself glimpse something just by thinking about it?"

"No, not that I haven't tried. I think it only works if it's something with a strong emotional connection to my life or to me personally. Like with K, that was easy because I love her. But every time I try to force it with a job, nothing happens." Isis handed me the file and I flipped through it. Kirk Weston had been married to Debbie Hiet for eight years, and, after an ugly divorce, Debbie had moved back to Alpena, Michigan, to be closer to her family. They kept in touch here and there, but nothing worth reporting.

As if reading my mind, Isis said. "He loved her. I mean Kirk, he loved Deb. You can tell when something that ugly goes down, there is a lot of emotion on both sides." Isis seemed sad and the thought crossed my mind that she was not just empathetic, but knew what it felt like from first hand experience.

"Yeah, on the surface he seems so hard and controlled, but losing everything in the divorce—house, dog. The dog was the worst, no guy wants to lose his dog." My attempt at humor did not register and I chided myself for even making a joke when it was clear Isis was not in a joking mood.

"He is a good cop, but his attitude gets in the way. He would have been captain a long time ago if he could've held his tongue every now and then."

"That's why I like him. You never have to guess what he thinks or how he feels. It's just out there for everyone to see, and he doesn't care whose feelings he hurts. Good thing to have in a cop."

A crackle broke the air and the copilot began his announcement that they were being rerouted to an alternate airport. "There was a bombing at the Dushanbe airport. We have to land fifty miles further south."

I jumped up and rushed to the front of the plane. Isis was right behind me, but, before I could storm into the cockpit, a flight attendant stepped in my way. "What's going on? A bomb, how big, are we talking pipe bomb or a truckload of fertilizer?"

The skinny woman held up her hand in a calming manner and looked into my eyes as if she'd experienced things like this a thousand times before. She acted like nothing strange was going on, or at least, nothing to get all worked up about.

"Mr. Appleton, Miss, there is nothing we can do about it now, we just got the report in from the tower, and if there is still a tower to report to us, well, then, the bomb couldn't have been that big." Her dark brown eyes looked like coffee beans in her pale face. They had a cool, relaxed look to them, and I calmed down enough to go back to my seat.

I could feel the G5 bank toward the south and begin to descend. "We have a friend we are meeting in Dushanbe. He flew in before us. Is there any news on where exactly the bomb went off?" Isis asked as she put her hand on the brown-eyed flight attendant's arm.

"I do not know, but I can ask the pilot for you. I know you must be worried, but after all, this is the Middle East and things like this happen more than you think. I have been with the Agency for five years now and this is my route. This is the seventh bombing we've had to detour around. We even had one go off just as we took off last year, not two hundred miles from here." She shook her head and patted Isis's hand like an old woman trying to comfort a child.

The speakers crackled again and the copilot came back on with a tinge of fear in his voice. "The alternate airport is full due to the bombing, so they've opened an abandoned runway in a field to the west of the airport. Just so you know, it's dirt, and it could get a little bumpy. The flight attendant will instruct you in the emergency landing procedures."

My heart sped along, and my mouth was so dry that when I licked my lips, it felt like sandpaper on rough wood. Isis seemed calm and collected as usual, and that made me feel better. No use worrying about something I couldn't control, and I didn't know how to fly a plane, so I listened to the skinny brunette as she showed us how to hug our legs and tuck our heads between our knees.

I could feel the engine begin to power down, and for an instant, I glanced out the window. The desert below had jets, small aircraft, and a few big jumbo jets lined up on the available runways. To my dismay, a 737 stood off to one side in the dirt, wingless and on fire. Must be the alternate runway. Then the flight attendant tapped me on the shoulder. "The bomb went off in baggage claim. That is all I know." She smiled with perfect teeth.

"Thank you."

"Remember, keep your head down." I nodded and did just that. The G5 belonged to the Agency. Isis, the pilot, the copilot, the flight attendant, and I were the only ones on board. I was glad our pilot was an agent. It made me feel better knowing that he knew what he was doing, or so I hoped.

The jet slowed, and when we touched down, the airplane jerked to the left and pulled me up hard. The breath rushed from my lungs, and I sucked in, trying to keep my head down as instructed. The sound of rocks and dirt hitting the underbelly of the jet made me think of gunshots. Bouncing and jerking, the plane finally came to a stop and I looked up. Everyone was alive, and the copilot came back on the overhead speakers.

"Okay then, we made it. We don't have to taxi because we're in a field. I had to land next to our runway due to a 737 that crash-landed on our runway."

Isis hugged me as soon as we were safe on solid ground. I held her and felt a shake in her core, and then it was gone. I wondered if it had just been my imagination. She pulled away and we headed for the main lobby of the small airport. "You sure know how to show a girl a good time," Isis joked as she pushed through the glass door that led into a small, concrete-lined entryway.

"I planned the whole thing. I thought, what better way to add excitement to the mission than to have an emergency landing in a field?" I chuckled. It felt good to hear Isis laugh, too, and the mood lightened considerably.

Over my shoulder, thick black smoke billowed from the broken wing of the 737. People ran from the airplane like ants, and a ragtag fire crew sprayed water on the flaming wing. I considered helping out, but it looked as if most of the passengers were out and not in any real danger. I walked toward the east end of the airport to see about a rental car.

After some bartering and a few hundred dollars, we climbed into a late-seventies Volkswagen Beetle. It was yellow, with rust crawling up the fenders like a virus, but overall, it ran and had a full tank of gas. I figured it would take us as far as the Dushanbe airport, but after that, I didn't expect anything more from the worn car.

The old Bug smoked and sputtered, but it did the job. We rumbled on a dirt road with ruts and potholes, some just as big as our car. I could tell that Isis was nervous. She had met detective Weston before. When she was under cover, he had showed her a picture of her standing in the Merc building. Kirk Weston would know exactly what we wanted with him as soon as he saw Isis.

"You okay? I asked.

"Yeah, just nerves. I just hope he's alive." She sighed and looked over at me. Her brown eyes were dark and beautiful.

She had a soft exterior to her, but a strong, powerful side as well. She checked her watch and gear to make sure we had everything. She was very good at her job and always professional.

"I think the detective has a few more lives in him. If he could survive one bombing, then I bet he can make it through a second one. He's unlucky, but very lucky at the same time." I still had my doubts, but you never knew. I sent a text to our handler to let him know we were okay and on our way to the airport.

Every agent had a handler, someone who tracked your movements and kept you up to date on anything you needed to know. Mine was an Australian named Euon. He was the funniest person I had ever met. If something was embarrassing or could be turned into a joke, he was all over it. When I checked in, he promptly asked if I wet my pants, because stains are hard to get out, and he would not wash my clothes no matter how much I begged.

Forty minutes later, we came up over a small rise in the landscape, and the smoking airport came into view. It looked like a big hand from the sky had ripped off the west side of the building . Black smoke poured from the center of the blast, and screaming lights from fire trucks and local law enforcement cars flashed in the distance.

We drove right up to the smoking building and mixed in with the wandering victims and emergency personnel. The scene looked like it was right out of a movie. People walked around crying and holding a wounded arm or searching for a loved one with a look of pure terror on their faces. It was horrible.

After an hour of searching for Weston, we had turned up nothing. Isis looked worn out and I called in to headquarters to report that we couldn't find Detective Weston anywhere. We were going to have to spend the night and check the hospitals in the morning.

Isis looked at me with dark soot smeared on her face. A

small cut marked her left arm. I knew what she wanted, and I shook my head, "I can't. If it comes on its own, maybe we will get lucky, but I can't force it."

"Try. We need him and you know it. All I ask is that you try. Please!" Her pleading eyes stared at me, and I knew I had to give it a shot. I nodded, smiled weakly, and took her arm.

"Let's go, I need some sleep."

* * *

YOU'VE DONE IT NOW. Everyone will be looking for you! What kind of game are you playing? Taras Karjanski sat in his hotel room watching the six o'clock news. He smiled at the news reporter and all her blather and babble. He hated America and everything about it. The only good thing was how dumb and gullible everyone was. He had transferred the oil tycoon's shares, took the fake deeds to his companies, and thrown them into the fireplace. He had shot that pompous know-it-all in the middle of a crowded restaurant. *I am invincible! Who can stand in my way now?*

He looked at the *New York Times* and laughed. He owned most of the stock in all but one oil company in America, but that would change soon enough. *You think gas prices are high now, just wait until I am done! You'll beg, no, you'll pay anything to get your precious oil!*

The penthouse suite was quiet and the room was a perfect sixty-eight degrees. His limbs were tight from the long, taxing day, but he didn't show it. He was always tense and just a little scared whenever he killed someone. That was what made killing fun. The feeling, the rush, was like nothing he could describe. What was the word for it? Power? No, it was more than power. It was a creative act. He was God, and he created and uncreated at his will. He could still see the eyes of everyone he had killed, the spark of life as it was extinguished forever.

A hot bath waited, and it was even in a jetted tub. He grabbed a bottle of 1945 Mouton. The price tag was more than two hundred thousand dollars per bottle, but you couldn't put a price on excellence. Taras popped the cork and poured a small amount in a wine glass. As he swirled it around, he breathed in its scent. The wine was even better than Taras had expected, and it went well with the book he was reading, *The Art of War*.

He liked the book, but it angered him at times. To think that this Chinese guy thought he was some kind of war expert. He found flaws in the book, and mocked the author's simple ideas and how he presumed to know the true secret of warfare. Taras, the Red Dog, was the god of war. He was a master of fear and influence. So he told himself, and so he believed.

* * *

I SAT ALONE IN the hotel bedroom and closed my eyes. I had this gift, as Solomon called it, where I could dream the future. A few years ago, my wife and daughter died in a supermarket bombing. I lived through it and felt the pain of losing them, only to find that it was all a dream, or a *glimpse* as I called it. My dreams were real, a look into what would happen if I did not stop it. I couldn't control the dreams. At times they would come in flashes, and sometimes it would feel as if I was out for a month or longer. Tonight, I was going to try to think of Detective Kirk Weston, try to will myself to find him. I had my doubts, but it was worth a try.

The room was dark, and I turned on a baseball game to put me to sleep. How it ever became the American pastime was beyond me; might as well be added golf to the list.

I could see Kirk's face in my mind. I looked into his eyes and thought of how he had put his life on the line for my wife. He had been kidnapped by The General, along with my wife and daughter, and he had tried to rescue K and Sam even after he had been beaten half to death.

Come on, Mark, just think about him…see him in your mind. Feel him! It was getting late, and I was very tired. I didn't think it would work, and I wondered if my doubt would affect the outcome or if it just happened on its own. I still didn't know the full extent of my so-called power. All I knew was Detective Weston could be trapped in that mess of an airport, and I was his only hope!

* * *

CHAOS HAD WORKED IN a group for so long that it felt a little weird to be alone on this adventure. But it was time to do something drastic, time to step it up a notch. The Manhattan Mall was bustling with people, as it should be. The weather was warming up, and summer was coming on quick, so everyone was getting ready for the warmer weather. The killer looked at the brand new watch. It was almost lunch time. The Swiss sure did make a good timepiece. Chaos liked the feel of the finer things in life, and spending a few grand on a watch was one thing this killer had no problem doing.

Most good plans involve many people working together to accomplish one, simple goal. This plan was not like that at all. This was a one-person-gets-in-gets-out-and-makes-a-point kind of a plan. But it was perfect, nonetheless.

That spot will work perfectly. The food court began to fill up as weary shoppers stood in line to get a bite to eat. *No wonder they're all so fat! Try eating something good for you, ever try that?* Chaos was thin, but well-built, and the person who thought Chaos was weak or too thin to be dangerous would be mistaken. Dark brown hair and a smooth complexion would make even some say the killer was good looking.

Chaos clutched a brown paper bag that looked like it was what was left of a sack lunch. Inside the bag were two pounds of plastic explosives and a twenty-minute timer. The killer walked up to a trash can next to Arby's and dropped it inside.

What a good citizen, keeping the forests green, and all that crap. Go Green, what a joke!

The mall was big, so it took Chaos almost ten minutes to get to the parking lot. After waving down a cab, the killer asked the cabbie to hit the expressway. Time to get some writing done. The newspapers would want an inside look into the bombing.

* * *

"THIS IS TERRIBLE!" THE CBS news anchorwoman looked

shocked and even a little upset at what she was reporting. "It appears a bomb exploded in the Manhattan Mall just twenty minutes ago. The scene looks like sheer pandemonium out there, and we still don't know if this apparent terrorist attack is the only one, or if there are more bombs to come."

Taras looked up from his late breakfast and toasted the television with his glass of orange juice. He liked to see Americans suffer. It bothered him that he had nothing to do with the bombing, and he wondered who was behind it. *A shopping mall at lunch time. Very nice.* The story unfolded with the usual media coverage. They killed it, kicked it some more, and then got a panel of experts to give their opinion. In addition, to make sure you were still watching, they brought up 9/11 and showed pictures of the last ten bombings to get everyone in a tizzy.

The bomb had taken out fifty-six people, four of them children. Taras tipped back the last of his OJ and let out a yell of glee. Good for them. Not that impressive, but not bad.

Getting upstaged again? You're the Don of the Russian Mafia and the most powerful person in the world. And no one knows it!

The voices in his head gave Taras a headache. It was as if a lunatic lived in his skull and demanded to be in control. He had seen what was possible if he released him, and didn't like it. Then again, maybe he wasn't sure how he felt about it. Sometimes it was a good feeling. He would have to keep his feelings in check if he was going to—

A knock at the door brought the madman back to reality.

"Knock, knock! Guess who?"

Taras opened the door and a tall, thin woman stood in the doorway. She had on a black dress that fell just above her knees, and high heels. She smiled and threw herself into his arms. Taras kissed and hugged his brother's wife. *She doesn't even know it's not you!* The dark eyes of the Red Dog looked out from Taras's head. *It is me. It has always been me!*

"I've missed you so much! The beautiful blonde kissed her

loving husband back and stared up into his dark eyes.

"I couldn't wait to see you. The flight was so long, and I hate to be away from you for that long." She sighed, and as she looked into his eyes, something made her stop. He seemed different somehow, but she brushed it off with a shrug and smiled up at her husband.

Taras smiled as he pulled his brother's wife closer. He had always loved her. He'd promised himself that one day she would be his, and now here she was. She was a flight attendant with American Airlines, and she hadn't seen Taras in more than a week. "You look ravishing!" Taras said.

Her smile could light up the room, and it did just now, making his heart thump in his chest. "Well, you don't look too bad yourself. I guess you will do." Taras and his wife of ten years liked to meet up in different cities and make mini vacations out of it.

Nayda grew up in upstate New York and met Taras in her second year at Princeton. Her parents loved Taras, and being from Russia had given him instant extra brownie points. Nayda's parents came to the US from Russia when she was just a baby. She could still remember her father telling her bedtime stories about the old country. After the wedding, they had had a baby girl. Nayda loved her baby but the Red Dog hated the poor thing with every fiber of his body. He tried to hide his feelings, and did so successfully, until he found out Nayda could not have any more children. Knowing all of this and experiencing it somehow through his brother's eyes made it feel as if he already knew everything about Nayda.

"And what would you like to do today, my love?" Nayda rolled her eyes and pushed Taras onto the bed.

"How about we go see a movie, then go downtown and shop. Oh, I want to get a new dress for the party this weekend!" The Red Dog wanted to scream at her to stop babbling and shut up He hated shopping and didn't want to go to a horrible party with all her arrogant, snobby, stuck up friends.

"That sounds wonderful, you look wonderful!" He was

glad he only hated his wife half the time. Taras loved her and could not live without her, maybe that was why he hadn't killed her yet. "You hungry? I made scrambled eggs."

Nayda laughed and looked at her husband. "You and your breakfast. I would love some scrambled eggs!"

"Coming right up."

Taras scooped the eggs onto a plate and put two pieces of bread in the toaster. He looked over at his beautiful wife and thought about his daughter's face. He could still see the look of terror as he—

You are a monster! I hate you! He could feel the Red Dog inside him moving around in the back of his mind. He was up to something. He did not trust it, and then he thought of Nayda's lips on his and how they felt. If it wasn't for *him*, he would never have Nayda in his arms.

CHAPTER NINE

THE SMELL OF BURNT rubber and smoke filled my head as I looked through the rubble that used to be the Dushanbe airport baggage claim. Isis pulled a chunk of metal off a pile of broken cinderblock and waved me over. Blood caked his face and one eye was swollen shut, making him look like a boxer after twelve rounds. Something exploded behind me, I jumped, and my heart hit the roof of my mouth. The noise all around us screamed for attention. Police cars, fire trucks, and ambulances blared, and then there was the undertone of people crying and yelling for loved ones in about five different languages.

Detective Weston was under a mass of debris, hanging on to every breath with fierce determination. It was so real, as if the thick black smoke was right there in my eyes burning them, and yet it wasn't real. I was laying in a queen size bed in a hot hotel room with the lights off and a faint smell of mold hanging in the air. I woke with sweat dripping from my nose and called Isis, in the next room. We headed over to the airport at the blessed hour of three in the morning.

We reached the bombsite, and we both gasped when we saw the mass of burning cars and rubble scattered everywhere. I was amazed at how the fires and destruction in a few short hours had grown as if the bomb had unleashed a hungry monster. I pulled the Bug over to the south side of what used to be the baggage claim area.

Isis jumped out and ran toward a burning, upside-down sidecar. It was all but twisted off the motorcycle. Police and fire crews still worked through the site trying to put out the fires. No one noticed a few more people running around, so we blended in with the rest of the rescue crews and local people who were helping out as best they could. Most of them were looking for loved ones, and by the cries and wails filling the air, I had a bad feeling that many families tonight would be missing someone they cared about.

"I think I found something!" Isis dug frantically, tossing chunks of concrete to one side as she called out Kirk's name.

A family station wagon lay on its roof, still smoldering from the blast. It reminded me of toy that a boy had tired of, so he stuck a firecracker inside just to see it explode.

"I see him, Mark, he's here!" Isis looked up as I bent over to see where she was pointing. I could see a hand, about four feet below where we stood. It was lodged in between the car and the concrete. It was impossible to move very fast. I grabbed a chunk of metal rebar and began to pry up the largest piece. *Come on, hang in there, Weston!*

I dropped to my belly and stretched down to reach the unmoving hand. Almost. "I can't reach him! Keep digging!" I wanted to check his pulse, but I just couldn't reach him. I pushed again on the rebar, and it groaned like an old woman, but the wagon did not budge.

"Is he alive, Mark? Was he alive in your dream?"

"I couldn't tell, just that he was here. I think he was, but I'm not sure!" I couldn't believe I actually had a glimpse of him. *Good, Mark. Weston is dead or dying, and you're thinking about your dream ability!*

"Give me a hand, I think I saw his hand move!"

Isis grabbed the end, and on the count of three, we pushed. After what seemed like an eternity, the heavy chunk of concrete gave way. We could now see Kirk down in a cave-like hole that, by some miracle, had formed by the two cars, buried under everything else. It might have saved his life.

He looked unconscious. Who am I kidding, he looked dead! I climbed in and half fell as I made my way to his side. He had blood all over his face, making it look like he had fallen face first in a pool of red paint. His shirt was stuck to his chest and was red with blood, but most of it was dried.

I reached down and took his pulse.

He was alive.

* * *

DARKNESS CONSUMED ITS PREY as it looked for another victim. The sounds of screams, fire burning flesh, and crackling coming from someone's nostrils, made Kirk jump. He could smell burnt hair and melting metal as he ran as fast as he could. Anywhere but here! He could feel eyes on him, evil eyes of something so dark and hideous that just the thought of it gave Kirk the creeps. He could feel his heartbeat speed up, and he started to hyperventilate. The thick smoke was in his eyes and he couldn't see anything, only darkness. He had to run, had to get out of this nightmare! Sucking in big gulps of smoky air and gagging at the taste of it, he ran. But no matter how fast he went or how hard he pumped his legs, it seemed that it was gaining.

"Detective—Mr. Weston, can you hear me?" A soft voice broke into his destructive thoughts and made him feel warm inside. "Kirk, you're safe now. It's going to be okay."

Kirk slowly opened his eyes and squinted in the light. It stung his eyes, or maybe his eyes themselves hurt. The room came into focus at last and the confused detective looked around.

A picture of a mountain lake and a fisherman standing in the cool water with his fly rod held out in the perfect two o'clock position hung on the wall. Kirk looked up and into the beautiful eyes of his angel of mercy.

Isis Kanika smiled at him and said, "Welcome back."

Kirk tried his best to smile but it sent a rush of pain through his cheekbones and into his skull.

"Don't try to move. You're one lucky guy to be alive right now. We have the best surgeons working to mend you. Don't worry, in no time you'll be on your feet and back to no good!"

Kirk liked the weird sense of humor this nurse, or whoever she was, had. He always was a sucker for the foreign ones. Redheads, blondes too…well, he liked women in general, as long as they argued with him.

His head swam and the room started to spin as the morphine kicked in. His world went black again, and then the fear came back. He was running from something, nothing. It was after him but he didn't know what *it* was. He remembered what his Dad used to say. "The dark will show you who you really are." Who was he?

* * *

THE NEXT WEEK, KIRK made amazing progress in his recovery. He had two broken ribs, a dislocated shoulder, and multiple cuts and bruises. All in all, he was just happy to be alive. The surgery to pin his ribs in place and do some reconstructive work on his shoulder went just as planned. Kirk walked down the hall that overlooked the huge command center to the World Justice Agency headquarters. He still couldn't believe they had brought him here and helped him. He was still bitter about the whole kidnapping thing, but he figured that they saved his life, so that started to make up for it.

Isis laughed when he figured out where he had seen her before. The 'mystery woman' that Kirk had a photo of in front of the Merc building, linking her with a crime scene. Of course, it never amounted to anything due to her perfect alibi. "We like to run a tight ship around here," Isis said with a smile. He liked her smile, it made her whole face light up.

The place was more amazing than Kirk had ever dreamed it would be. The kind of stuff that ran back-to-back on the Sci-Fi channel. The control room had to be two hundred feet across and just as long. A huge screen made up the far wall and had over a hundred individual screens on it.

"How are you feeling?" Kirk didn't hear Isis come up

behind him.

"Good, considering. You sure got one great office here."

"Mine is upstairs, remember?" She smiled and touched his shoulder. Kirk liked how gentle she was, but something in her eyes told him she was more dangerous than she let on.

"So you monitor every agent down there? How many do you guys have?"

"We employ over three thousand. I know that sounds like a lot, but we are in every country all over the world. So, in the big scheme of things, we're just a small potato. This center controls the United States, and in each country where we have more than two hundred agents, we have another command center."

Kirk whistled. "So you think you guys are doing the right thing? You ever heard of letting the law handle it?" The idea of a single organization taking the law into their own hands scared Kirk. He thought about the public getting wind of it, and he shuddered. "You know if anyone finds out what you do here, it'll start a world war!"

"Yes, we know. The law is only good and just if it is upheld. We just keep them honest." Isis sounded so sure of herself. "Besides, one day the world will have to know. We just have to wait for the right time to tell them."

Kirk looked again at the madness and sheer power that stood in front of him. He was a cop and wanted to see justice prevail just as badly as anyone did, but this was a bit much! He would boil with rage and even considered killing when a rapist walked or got off with a slap on the wrist. Now, he saw what the country had created. The law was made to keep the innocent safe and the guilty scared. *Well, you've got a reason to be scared now!*

* * *

A DARK FIGURE STOOD outlined against the Hollywood skyline. Her dark hood made the killer look like the angel of death itself. Checking her watch, Chaos looked up the deserted road that overlooked the beautiful city. Sometimes she would talk to herself. Most of the time no one noticed, or they just thought she was speaking into a Bluetooth. Her dark gray pullover hid her dark hair and if you looked at her at a glance, you might even think she was a guy.

Come on, you better not keep me waiting.

The headlights of an oncoming car lit up the night sky and made Chaos jump. The spot she had picked was outside the city, about a two-hour drive, and had a view that was breathtaking. She had liked the spot from the first time she had seen it more than four years ago. Blue, white, and silver lights sparkled, making the city sparkle like a diamond. It was everything New York was not. In fact, she rather hated the Big Apple. Such a silly name, the Big Apple! What did it even mean? She took one last look, turned toward the car, and prepared herself.

She shoved her hands in her pockets as the dark green Ford Explorer pulled off the road and parked under a large maple tree. An overweight man opened the door and peered out as he shut off his lights.

"You're late." Her manner was gruff and commanding.

The middle-aged man stuttered as he got out of his SUV. "I, um…sorry. You see there was—"

"Never mind," She couldn't believe a man of his age could still be as dorky and unimpressive as he was. "Do you have what I want?"

He wore a white t-shirt with a Microsoft logo in bright blue. His jeans were baggy, and he pulled on them every few minutes to keep them from falling down. "I have it right here."

The manila envelope he handed her was bulging. She sighed with open disgust and took it from his hand. He almost dropped it, which made Chaos even madder.

The contents satisfied the killer and she thanked him with a handshake. "Where's my…uh, money?" He asked.

Chaos turned around and stared at the man with a confused look. "Money? Oh, money!" She threw back her head and laughed. The thought of paying this chump made her want to gag, but business was business.

A small, black, leather briefcase sat like a lonely cat in the dirt four steps behind Chaos. She turned, picked it up, and handed it to the man in the white T-shirt. He smiled and took it like a puppy that just got a meaty bone.

"And please don't disrespect me by opening it to count it in front of me."

He nodded, as if that was common knowledge. Opening the door to his SUV, he tripped, almost dropping the briefcase. Chaos muttered under her breath and moved toward the edge of the lookout.

The late spring evening air was warm and had a hint of lavender as it drifted past the mysterious killer's senses. She looked out over the edge and wondered how many people had died at this very spot. It was a great place to jump, with the rocky edge and all. The landing didn't look much better.

The chunky man climbed back into his SUV and drove back down the hill from where he had come, most likely from his Mom's house where he labored day after day to become the most powerful toon on *World Of Warcraft*, or something just as stupid.

Nice night for some fireworks.

Chaos turned and looked after the Ford as it drove down the hill, rounded the corner, and disappeared out of site. She waited for the man to lean over and open his prize to see all his glorious money. She knew he wouldn't be able to resist, no one could.

"Kaboom."

Seconds later, a cloud of fire rose from around the corner and cracked with a sonic boom that made even the killer jump a little. She smiled and wiped her mouth. She loved to burn money. She even liked knowing that there really was one hundred thousand dollars in that suitcase.

Not anymore!

* * *

"MR. WESTON, MY NAME is Mark Appleton. I see you're

getting to know your way around the place." Kirk looked at me with a judging smile and nodded. "It looks like you're feeling better. Shall we walk." I could tell from his body language that he was still uncomfortable with the whole situation, so I started down the hall and he followed without a word.

"I am an up front kind of guy, Mr. Weston." I wanted to put him at ease, but he seemed determined to make it hard.

"Kirk, you can call me Kirk. Makes me feel like my Dad to be called 'Mister.'"

I nodded and moved on. I needed his help with the Red Dog case and we needed to move fast. "I need your help catching a very bad guy. He's known by the name of The General. I suspect you know him?" I wondered how much he knew and if he had gotten anywhere with his own investigation. He looked at me and shoved his hands into his pockets. "I know this whole thing is a bit much for you to take in all at once. Believe me, I still haven't figured it all out myself."

"You were recruited?" Kirk asked.

"Yeah, I joined the Agency a few years ago. I was an architect before that." He seemed to soften a little with the news. "Taras Karjanski is on a rampage, and we suspect he's planning something big, and soon. You have been following him and investigating him for the last year, isn't that right?"

"Yeah, I lived just up the beach from his villa in Bali. I tapped his phone and bugged his house. He has been planning something codenamed *Dreamcatcher*. I haven't figured out what it's all about, but I'll tell you whatever I know. I want this guy worse than you do."

I took Kirk down to the conference room and we talked for a few hours. He had learned about the legend of the Red Dog, and I took notes as he spoke. The General/Red Dog was a killer, and a good one.

It worried me a little that he knew about operation *Dreamcatcher*. I couldn't help thinking it had something to do with me. He was linked to more than twenty killings in the past year alone, and those were just the ones he was suspected to have been involved in personally.

Kirk acted like a caged animal, and he paced and fidgeted as he spoke. "You're not in prison here, you can leave anytime you want to. I just hope you see the importance of keeping this organization a secret."

"I know. It's just that I have a beef with you guys, with the kidnapping and all." His voice turned gruff and his face flushed red.

"I understand." Isis had filled me in on the whole kidnapping thing. I shook my head. It was not the greatest idea to pick a fight with a man with nothing to lose. "However, I do believe if we work together, we can bring this guy to justice."

Kirk looked at me and I could see the wheels spinning in his brain. I figured he would agree and then use the time spent here to build a case against us. But at this point, I was willing to take that risk.

"Okay, but we do it my way, with my rules!"

"Done." I stuck out my hand and Kirk took it. We shook on our deal, and I smiled. He had no idea what he was getting into. Life was going to get a lot more interesting for Kirk Weston!

CHAPTER TEN

YOU MAY THINK I'M just dreaming that i am buried alive. That, soon i'll wake up in a cold sweat and find out it was my future i was dreaming of, and this terrible place was all in my head. For just such an occasion, i have a test i run to make sure that i'm in the real world.

In a glimpse, I cannot have another glimpse. I have anywhere from one to four a week, and when I'm in a dreamlike state, I don't ever have a dream within a dream. And sad to say, I've had a few since I've been in this tomb. Believe me, if I knew why this was happening to me, or how I ended up trapped in a coffin without the benefit of already being dead, I would at least have some peace about it. However, that memory is lost to me. From what I can tell, I have been trapped in this casket for one, maybe two weeks now. Somehow, I am getting just enough air to breathe. Not sure how that is possible, but here I am, breathing, and so far, even though it is thick, stale air, it has kept me alive.

I shut off the recorder for a minute and wondered who would find it or if anyone ever would. I hoped Isis or Big B could use the information to find the person responsible for my death. I ran the scenario over and over again in my mind, and each time, I ended up dead. Losing air, and with no water, on top of being stuck who knows how far underground. It doesn't take a genius to work out the equation. *All roads lead to Rome, dead man walking, out of time, all debts called in...*

The question that tugged at me and clamped down on my heart was if they knew who I was, and it seemed they did. *Do they know where K and Sam are? Do they know where I live, and are K and Sam okay?* I could see their faces in my mind as if they were standing right in front of me. My eyes stung as they filled with tears, but I brushed them away, I had to be strong and leave them with something more than a recording of a dying, blubbering man.

Not many people would have the resources to find out who I was, let alone believe that an agency like the WJA was more than a story in some book. *They knew everything about me. My ability to look into the future, cases I had worked on.*

"Stop it, Mark, you worry too much, and at this point, there isn't much you can do about it." The sound of my own voice startled me, and if I had had the room to jump, I would have.

The air! They want me to starve to death and with no water I won't last much longer. Could that be a clue? Did this person grow up in poverty and as an act of revenge, he is starving me to death, trying to make me feel what he felt? Obsessive!

I snapped back to the situation at hand. Clicking on the recording device again, I spoke into the thick blackness.

"K, I love you more than life itself. You hold me together when I'm so lost that I can't even see past the day in front of me. You have kept me going. You found me, believed in me, and loved me without reservation, which I have to admit, I did not entirely return. I'm so sorry, K. I don't deserve you, let alone your love. Please forgive me for holding back part of my heart. It's all yours now, every piece!" My heart ached in my chest and holding back tears, I softened my voice, thinking of Sam.

"Sam, I love you so very much. You will always be my little girl, and no matter what, I will be looking out for you. You be a good girl and remember that no boy will ever love you the way I do. I love you, baby girl."

I couldn't go on, there was too much to say. How was I going to give her advice for the rest of her life in the time I had left? Maybe this was for the best, the danger that loomed over them would be gone. They could go on in safety, knowing some monster wouldn't be waiting for them in the darkness. I was a danger to my own family! What a thought. Maybe I was the problem!

Was I giving up? Am I giving up? I think so. I think I'm all out of ideas and strength. My body was so weak, and I was so thirsty, and now thinking of K and Sam, all I wanted to do was weep and then die. I didn't want them to remember me as I am now, weak and worn out and void of any hope. I had kept my voice strong for them, but now I was done.

Giving up? How can I give up? I am dead already!

* * *

THE MALL BOMBER SPEAKS OUT

THE WASHINGTON POST RAN the breaking story on the front page. Kirk looked up from his black coffee and stared at the headline.

"Oh, bugger."

"The person called Chaos sent our own Pete Ross a letter this morning. The following was to be printed or Chaos said a bomb would go off in a school right here in Manhattan."

To whom it may concern,

The bombing in the mall was just the beginning for this wretched country. I want it to be known that Chaos is the only way to bring true freedom to pass. The time to act is now. The time to panic is now! If you don't believe me, then just try to stop me. I am Chaos, and I am here to bring to light what is hidden. The world needs justice, and no agency can stop what has to be done.

With all my hate,

Chaos

Kirk threw the paper down on the table and cursed. The world was going to hell in a hand basket. His ribs hurt, and just about every other part of his body, as well. He shuffled to his feet, stuck two pop tarts in the toaster, and refilled his coffee. He found himself in yet another hotel, but this time, the tab was on the WJA. It was a bit nicer than he was used to, and if it wasn't for them saving his life, he would be down at the precinct right now telling them all about the ever-so-secret World Justice Agency. The bombing and how they rushed to help him nagged at him, turned over and over in his mind like an itch you couldn't reach right in the middle of your back. So close, yet so far away!

He got a call informing him of a mandatory meeting in two hours at the Merc building. The only thing that scared the daylights out of him was how open they were with their operation. Either they trusted him completely, or they were dumb as a box of rocks!

He figured they'd kill him if he decided to turn them in. No way they would open up their books to him and then let him walk away without some *accident* taking his head off before he could breathe a word about who they were. Then there was the part of him that loved what they did. Taking the bad guys off the street, standing up for the little guy. It was every cop's dream to be able to see the street scum taken down for what they did. But there was no possible way to do it like this and get away with it. Not for long anyway.

The pop tarts jumped from the toaster and landed upside down on the counter. Kirk burned his hand juggling them before dropping them on a plate to cool off. *Looks like you're getting yourself into many hot situations these days!* Grabbing the paper again, he studied the note from the crazy called Chaos. Then he saw what only he would see and anyone else who knew who the World Justice Agency was.

The note was for them!

* * *

TARAS WALKED WITH HIS wife down Fifth Avenue and wandered into store after store, Saks and Mexx, to name a few. The smell of hotdog vendors and the storefront lights annoyed Taras to no end. He was doing a wonderful job of pretending he was enjoying himself; however, it took all of his will power. *Why do I even put up with this? Just leave her and go hang yourself after a good glass of wine!* That at least would have a satisfying end.

His wife was trying on a big hat that looked like it belonged on an eighty-year-old woman in the South on Easter Sunday. She wore a huge grin that made her face light up. She was a beautiful woman, and he loved to look at her. Plus, the fact that he stole her made him feel alive…he felt like telling her just to see the look on her face!

"Oh, look at this, hun, don't you just love it?" Nayda giggled as she put it on and spun around so he could see.

"Wonderful, my love, you look amazing. You should get it!" Taras grinned and held in the urge to slap it from her hand and spit on the miserable thing.

"Oh, you think so? It is a beautiful hat. And it would go with my new dress, don't you think?"

Taras nodded.

"You're the best!" She threw her arms around his neck and kissed him. "Now all I need is a pair of shoes to go with it, oh, and maybe some earrings and a bracelet!" She rushed to the register to buy the hat and Taras looked up and down the street, searching for an escape.

People from every part of the world stuffed themselves onto the sidewalk. They swarmed like killer bees and bumped into him, then plodded on as if they didn't even notice him. Stupid drones! They all were so horrible! *Shut up, man, all you do is hate and look down on people. Try to be happy for a change. You never know, you might like it.* This inner voice did not speak up often, and its comment fell on deaf ears, as a heart that was growing harder with each passing day was dead to any input other than its own voice.

The city was alive with color. Green leaves filled the trees, and the sound of birds could be heard in the distance. He breathed in deep as the smell of car exhaust mixed with food wafted down the street from the street vendors. Then, another smell drifted up the street, and this one was not so pleasant. The sewers and bums that hung out in the alleyways gave the city a nasty smell and made it look like a junkyard in spots. Most of the drones passed on without a second glance and never looked into the dark alleyways where they knew people of a lower class than themselves lived.

Taras daydreamed about killing them all, and it brought a smile to his face. Maybe he would! The only thing that kept him going was the fact that, in time, this blasted city, this blasted country would fall to its knees, and he would be the cause of it all.

* * *

I MET KIRK WESTON at the Merc building and escorted him down to the main lobby. It was huge, and I always enjoyed the glass floor with fish swimming around under your feet. I looked to find my favorite starfish. It was in its usual spot, stuck to the underside of the clear floor, and I thought I saw a smile on the small face.

Solomon was a brilliant man, and the design of the building was amazing, from the pillars of stone carved by hand to the two hundred-year-old wooden doors that opened to his office.

Kirk was quiet, and as I watched his movements, I could tell he was uncomfortable, but not as much as he had been. I hoped he would come to understand who we were and what we were trying to do. After Kirk checked in, we walked to the large conference room where Solomon and Isis were waiting. Big B was going to be late, so we started without him.

Solomon stood at the head of the oval, stone table and brought up a holographic image that hovered in the center of the heavy table. It was a photo of a large, dark-skinned man who reminded me of a mobster in *The Godfather* movies.

"Mohammed Dior. Until a few days ago, he was one of the most ruthless oil tycoons in the world. He had ties to the Taliban and is suspected to have been involved in the attacks on the Twin Towers and countless others. A bombing in Baghdad last December that blew up a bus parked in front of the American Embassy, killing one hundred and twenty-three, was linked to him." Solomon flipped to another picture. "We all remember two years ago in Alaska, we lost over half of the pipeline in that one. Again, Dior. His attacks brought the price of oil up at an alarming rate, and they've risen each year since, making him one of the wealthiest people in the world."

The next photo showed the dead body of Mohammed Dior lying next to a heavyset man with a hole in his forehead. From the photo, it looked like it was in a restaurant or café.

"He was shot and killed by a professional in the middle of the lunch hour at a popular café here in New York." My mind began to run through the news accounts and newspapers, but I didn't remember seeing any story about it.

"And yes, as you've guessed, there was no news story or anything other than a blurb on page five in one newspaper. The FBI and CIA believe it was Taras Karjanski. We also have information that he is still in New York. If we are going to get this guy, we need to act fast. Any and every lead is being looked in to, but so far, he's a ghost." Solomon sat down and we all looked at each other.

Come on, Mark, think! How can we find him? Kirk raised his hand and held up a copy of the Washington Post.

"Did you all see the headline this morning?" Solomon pulled up a copy of the paper on the hologram in the center of the table and nodded. "I think this note is directed at you guys."

I had seen the paper earlier but didn't pay much attention to it. I scanned it over once again and looked at the detective. "If you look at the wording, the words *World, Justice, and Agency* all are in it. I think this Chaos person is trying to talk to you."

Solomon looked over the note and made a quick phone call. I was impressed. For Kirk to pick up on that was a good sign.

"Very good, Detective. We will be looking into this further. In the mean time, Taras Karjanski is top priority. You two will be working together, and I am sure we can wrap this up in a timely manner."

We discussed our options and the only thing missing was where to start. Kirk spoke up and said, "I have a guy that might be able to help us. Ever hear of a kid named Mooch?"

CHAPTER ELEVEN

THE DARK FEELINGS THAT surrounded the Red Dog's mind made him shudder. He tried to shake off the feeling, but couldn't. Sitting on the edge of his bed with his head in his hands, he sobbed. Shoulders jerking up and down, a mournful groan filling his mouth, he let out everything he couldn't talk about, or even allow himself to think about. The dark thing in the back of his mind, the passenger, the evil conscience, bellowed for him to stop, but sometimes you just needed to cry.

After a few minutes, he calmed himself and stood up, wiping his face with the back of his hand. If someone ever found him in this state, it would be the last time they would ever see anything. Taras didn't see his tears as a weakness, but a way to keep a hold of the small part of his sanity and his true nature that was slowly slipping away. He didn't know why he had these irregular bouts of tears, and he didn't even know why he was sad. He wondered if it was his way of rebelling against what he was becoming. Or maybe it was the penance he had to pay for who he was and what he had done.

His wife was gone, on her way to Rome. He wouldn't see her for a few days. He smiled when he saw the morning paper. Bomb in a mall. He found it amusing, yet he couldn't help feel a little jealous; however, he would never admit that to anyone, not even to himself. Now this amateur was sending the newspapers notes and threatening to kill more if they didn't pay attention.

The letter made Taras grin like an idiot, because he knew that was why he was so much better. He didn't need the recognition and the fame. He didn't need a personal fan club to make him feel like a man. He had a plan and a set goal in mind. This Chaos was out of control and subject to passions and feelings. He felt free again.

The poor, helpless rat of a detective was dead and the WJA was running around like a chicken with its head cut off. Then again, it closed out a cat and mouse game that he had rather enjoyed. He'd miss the little pest, always lurking over his shoulder and thinking he was so smart. *Not so smart now, are you?*

Taras grabbed a quick breakfast of corn flakes, two slices of whole-wheat toast, and a large glass of orange juice, then took a cab to the airport. The airport was crowded and this time, he didn't waste time taking a plane with all the other boring people. He had a G5 waiting with his own pilot whom he had known for years. He was an Arab who defected to the States when he was fourteen. The schools in California taught him everything he ever wanted to know, and now he was a very successful pilot.

The morning air felt good as it ran through Taras's hair. He walked with determination as he crossed the tarmac toward the waiting plane. A warm breeze filled with the scent of jet fuel and sticky buns from the airport's cafeteria made Taras a bit hungry, and now his small meal didn't seem like enough.

"Morning, my old friend. You look well." The dark skin and jet-black hair of the man standing in the doorway of the G5 reflected the sunlight.

"Abdul Azim, you are looking trim and fit. The wife must be a bad cook, yes?" Taras liked Abdul Azim as much as he could like another human being, and that was saying a lot. He didn't like people at all, and most of them he loathed.

"Taras, only you call me by my birth name. Most of my

friends call me Abe. Are you not my friend?" He looked down at Taras from the top of the stairs leading to the sleek white G5 with a twinkle in his eyes.

"Well I'm not just a friend, I'm your brother, Abdul Azim." He laughed and embraced his friend. "It is good to see you again. What has it been, three years?" Taras looked for a glimmer of doubt in Abe's eyes, but Abe didn't even look twice at his face to consider the possibility that Taras was not who he thought he was. Grinning with all of his teeth showing, Taras put the thought out of his mind. He was Taras, and more to the point, he was the Red Dog!

"Four." Abe said and held up four fingers.

"Four? Too long. What do you say we get out of this God-forsaken country." Taras waved a hand back toward the city with a wave of disgust.

Abe nodded and patted Taras on the back. "The smell of America always makes my stomach turn." He spat out the side of his mouth and laughed.

They climbed into the cockpit and, after a briefing with the tower, were soon off the ground and on their way to Equatorial Guinea. Taras acted as the copilot so the tower would let them pass through. The small country on the west coast of Africa was producing close to one billion barrels of crude oil a day. Taras wanted to get acquainted with one of his newly acquired refineries.

* * *

"EMILY DOBSON, I CAN'T believe it's you!" The tall blonde smiled at Emily as she rummaged through the never-ending colors of lipstick and lip-gloss.

"Uh, yeah," Emily didn't remember the blonde or her way too bubbly personality.

"Marsha, from York Prep." Marsha, or whatever her name was, stood looking at her with a classic confused expression on her intelligent face.

Emily faked that she remembered her new—or was it old?—friend. "Yeah, Marsha. How are you? It has been what...?" Marsha stood five-foot-five and had her hair dyed so blonde it was on the border of being all-out white. She was skinny, as anyone in her class had to be, and had about eight pounds of makeup on, finished off with cherry red lip-gloss.

"Like, ten years! Wow, you look so good. I mean, *wow!*" The blonde stared with an open mouth and looked Emily over.

"Thank you, you look good, too." Emily Dobson could act on the spot; it was one of her many strong points. "You still live here in Manhattan?"

"Me? No way, I'm here visiting my Mom. She just had to see me. I live in Santa Monica. I'm in a commercial, you know, the one for that new chunky soup." Marsha shifted on her feet and turned her head, as if that would help Emily remember the commercial.

"Right. Well, good for you." Emily wanted to run from the store, but this energetic girl was determined to spend the day gabbing it up in the makeup aisle. "Well look, here's my number if you ever want to grab a cup of coffee sometime. I really have to go!" She scribbled a number on a scrap piece of paper, pushed it into Marsha's hand, and started to turn away.

"Oh, right. No problem. Thanks, I'll call you." The blonde took the paper and smiled as she turned and walked off to look at the newest music from Fergie. Emily could hear her singing softly something like, "Big girls don't die," or, was it, "don't cry"?

Emily sighed, grabbed the Revlon *Hint of Rose* lip gloss, and went to pay. She still couldn't remember Marsha or much about her high school experience. Emily had blocked out her childhood, and other miserable memories. High school was terrible and not worth one tear or the time wasted to remember it or anyone there. Marsha was case in point of that. *Good, quality stock, that one.*

Besides, she had much bigger things on her mind at the moment. Her new fantasy was a man named Mark Appleton. He was someone she thought about a lot these days, and, in his own way, he was quite good looking.

Emily Dobson liked to sit and think about what she was going to do when she had Mark in her hot little hands. Killing him would be too easy, she thought. She imagined thousands of different ways to torture him and how she was going to make him beg for death, but she would not give it until she was good and ready. Emily had many things rolling around in her head as she walked the mall looking for the perfect outfit to wear when she met him. She was going to meet Mark for the first time, and she had to look spectacular! *Just wait, Mark. Soon, you and I will be together. Just you and me!* The thought of it made her feel giddy inside. Emily could feel butterflies in her stomach. *Not now, Emily, you are much braver than you were in High School.* She could remember the days when she was scared to even talk to a boy.

The day she saw a boy named Frankie McDonald in Jr. High was one she would never forget no matter how hard she tried. He was the most popular boy in school. His good looks and the easy way he carried himself made her heart melt. He was too good for her, and he had made her cry.

Now who's crying? He would jump at the chance to be with her now. She had it all—money, power, and looks. Her long, dark hair was layered and colored a deep mahogany with a splash of brown. She had big brown eyes and a smooth complexion. The plastic surgeons had outdone themselves. Even her family wouldn't believe the change. She could think of what her mother would have said. "You think too much of your looks. Beauty is only skin-deep." Yada, yada, yada. At five-foot-nine, she blended in with the crowd in the mall. No one looked her way, except for the occasional college girl as she passed by. They envied her and even hated her. If it wasn't for the way she dressed, every man in the state would be at her doorstep.

Emily liked to dress conservatively and didn't like to draw attention to herself. Then again, sometimes she would, just to show them that she had it, and more.

Dream on, girls. You couldn't afford it anyway!

* * *

THE BRIEFING WAS LONG and way more information than I needed. Taras Karjanski was on our top priority list, and Kirk and I were on the case. He didn't quite trust me. I could tell when someone had that look. I had a way of reading people. Of course the, "I don't trust you," might have been a giveaway, too.

Isis was going to run all our intel along with the detective's source. He was adamant on using his own contact, so we obliged.

The story of the bombing in the mall was brought up, and it was clear the Agency was a target. Solomon was working on it, and so far, the FBI along with the CIA had a taskforce going full throttle to solve the case.

I wanted to help out, but at this point, it was out of my reach. Solomon had many more agents that I thought were better qualified to handle it than I was. Besides, I was the rookie, the new guy.

The World Justice Agency was under attack from all sides. The FBI and their taskforce were covering up and hiding from the media every case they thought we had a hand in. We still left calling cards, but that was just to keep them on the trail. We were walking a tightrope, and we had to keep silent but we also needed to prep the public for our introduction that was sure to come in the near future.

Then there was Taras Karjanski. He was of the Russian Mafia and had more information on us than even the FBI did. We needed him alive, and we needed him now. He could prove to be the one wild card that the Agency would grow to regret. They had had a chance to catch him when K was kidnapped, but let him slip through their fingers. But then again, they had no idea who he was or the level of evil he was capable of back when he was known as The General. Kirk broke into my thoughts from the passenger seat in my black and silver Shelby Mustang.

"So, is this the new one?" He motioned to the car and

opened the glove box.

"Yeah, I like that they went with the old design. It makes it more appealing to the old school car guys, like me." I'd sold my Ascari KZ1 because it drew too much attention. Not that the Shelby didn't, but in most cases, it fit in with my age and the whole mid-life crisis thing.

"I've always wanted one of these, only the original, not the remake." I liked the detective; his rough nature made me think of a big teddy bear. I always knew where he stood—no games, no surprises. If he had a problem with you, he'd let you know. "They must pay you pretty well to afford this thing."

I couldn't help myself. I laughed and answered with my usual smart aleck response. "And who said crime doesn't pay?"

Kirk grunted.

"Taras Karjanski has dropped off the grid so we don't know where he is or where he's going. You have any ideas?" I hoped Kirk had something in his head that would shed some light on the lost terrorist.

"I think I might. We need to get to Detroit. I have an old friend we need to visit."

"Then you are in luck. We can take the next TAXI."

"Don't you think flying would be faster?"

I didn't respond. He was in for the ride of his life. In an hour flat, we would be standing on the doorstep of Mooch B. Striker, the Third.

* * *

KIRK HATED BEING IN the passenger seat. He always drove, and any partner he'd ever had was not allowed to even think of touching the wheel, or the radio for that matter. Now, he had a partner he didn't know, not to mention he was cooperating with an organization that was breaking the law. And besides that, he didn't even believe in what they were doing. Well, he did agree that it had to be done, but not this way! He felt compelled by their kindness in saving his life, but he had a secret plan. The only way he would catch Taras and this Red Dog was with their help. He needed them and they apparently needed him as well.

Bringing down the biggest vigilante group that the world had ever seen would be his early Christmas present to himself.

Mark seemed nice enough, a little over the top, but he could be a little over the top at times, as well.

The streets were crowded, and the horn was the weapon of choice as people crawled through New York. After an hour in the car, they came to a run-down building and Mark pulled the car into the alley.

"You aren't going to kill me back here, are you?" Kirk asked.

Mark laughed and shook his head. "Nah, too easy."

At least he has a sense of humor. Someone has to. Kirk felt a slight shaking as he sat looking down the dark alley. He could see the ground open up as a ramp leading below ground appeared before them. The underground parking garage was lit with wall-mounted lights. Kirk saw a few other cars parked in the twenty or so spaces. All of them were expensive and looked to be in pristine condition. *Hmph, some job.*

"You ready for the ride of your life?" Mark had a grin on his face that Kirk didn't like.

"Sure, it better be good, with the hype and all." Kirk looked around making a mental note of everything he saw. The garage had a small office with a single door and window off to the right. A short, stocky Italian looked at Kirk with a half smile.

"You the cop?" He didn't wait for Kirk to answer. "Well you aren't anymore, so no funny business." The short man spit when he talked, and some of it stuck on his chin like wet spider webs.

"Whatever. You just stay on your side of the room and we will get along just fine." Kirk stood up straight and pulled his shoulders back. The last thing he needed right now was a crazy little Italian going off on him.

"Come on you two, play nice. Now, would you mind telling our new friend here about all the wonders of the TAXI?" The little man's name was Mario, which seemed to fit like a glove. All he needed now was a little red hat and overalls.

"Okay, the TAXI is our way of getting around. In between cities across the world we have underground tubes, if you will. The tubes carry you in this," he said as he punched in a code on the keypad on the wall.

Kirk liked big-boy toys and this just about pushed him over the top. The wall split in two, revealing a pod that was equipped with a five-point body harness and a gel-like padding on the bottom.

"Now, after you suit up, I'll go over the rest. Hurry up, too, I got a tee time in an hour!" Mario grunted through a thick accent. As he waited, he pulled out a fat cigar and lit up. A ring of gray smoke wafted toward the ceiling like a miniature cloud.

Kirk followed Mark back to a changing room where six suits hung behind a glass case. "Now, Mr. Weston, this suit will save your life. Without it, you will be crushed under the G-Force you are going to experience. The suit will pump pressure points all over your body so that the blood will circulate in a somewhat normal fashion."

The suit was soft, like a synthetic woven cotton. Tiny lumps were imbedded in the fabric all over it, and it was to be pulled over the head, so anyone wearing it looked like Spiderman or maybe just a freak in a dumb suit.

"You gotta be kidding me? You want me to wear this?" He held up the suit like it was a pink dress and scowled.

Kirk could tell by the look on Mark's face that he wasn't kidding. "Fine, but no pictures, or I'll kill you!"

After they were suited up, Mario explained how the TAXI worked. Kirk just stared and tried to act like it was just another part of the job. *No problem. I'll jump in that pillbox and shoot myself across the globe, underground. Why not?*

After Kirk was strapped in, the lid closed, and the air sealed him in, he let out a sigh. Mark was in the one right behind him. He seemed to like all this high tech stuff. The two pill-looking devices hooked together like train cars. The countdown sounded and Mario pushed a red button. *Of course, it had to be a red button, what next, a red phone to make important calls?*

The sound of air sucking and the pressure of the air pushing in on the tiny capsule made Kirk wonder what he had gotten into. *You dumb cop, now you are going to die in a tunnel somewhere between here and Detroit.* The smell of bananas and cream filled the cabin. Kirk smiled and closed his eyes. He loved bananas and cream.

Soon he was asleep and speeding his way under the ground at speeds unimaginable. It sure beat waiting in line at a stuffy airport. The trip took forty-eight minutes and thirty-two seconds.

So much for taking the relationship slow!

Chapter Twelve

THE PRESIDENT OF THE valco energy company sat and stared at the two men standing in front of him. His blood vessels looked like they were going to pop right out of his forehead. Taras Karjanski looked over at his friend and partner, nodded, and Abdul Azim pulled out an AR15 Strikeforce and pointed it at the now sweating president.

"Are you ready to listen, or do I need to put a few more holes in your head?" Taras spoke in clear, solid tones, but didn't raise his voice. He knew how to control his temper. He just hoped Red Dog was sleeping, or on vacation.

The president almost fell over as he got to his feet. He had four bodyguards at the door, but for some reason, they didn't come into the room to aid their boss.

"What do you want? I am just a businessman, please don't kill me!" The fat man spit all over as he spoke. The smell in the hot, humid room would make a rat gag. The dingy office was littered with papers and old cigar butts. The back window was busted out and flies buzzed around like it was an amusement park.

"I'm going to speak slowly so you are sure to understand. You work for me now. I am your new boss. I'm God to you! You understand? This factory will be painted and so clean that, when I come back in a month, I can eat off the floor!"

Taras walked over to the terrified man and shoved his finger in the squirming man's face. "One month! If I see a speck of dirt, I will use your fat, wet body to mop the floor! You got it?"

The man nodded and closed his eyes, expecting to be beaten. Taras wished he could find a man with some backbone. He had killed the only man who had ever given him a run for his money. Kirk Weston... it just wasn't the same without him.

"Let's go, Abe." Taras opened the door to the small office and a body fell onto the floor. The bodyguard's neck was opened up, and blood flowed out as he stared into the air with dark lifeless eyes. The fat man screamed like a girl and Taras laughed. *That was funny. This fat pig just made his day!*

The plant was dirty and stunk like burnt rubber and sewage. Taras couldn't bring himself to even look around anymore. He wanted to have an operation that was efficient and clean. He was only asking for the best, and that was what he planned on getting.

"Can you believe that guy? This place better be spotless when we return. I hate a dirty place of business."

Abe nodded and opened the door to a black BMW. They had a few more stops to make. The hot, humid air was suffocating and sticky, and sand was everywhere...sand and dirt. Even the water was murky and lukewarm, and Taras refused to drink it, opting instead for bottled water. He opened a fresh one and took a long drink.

Taras sat in the back of the BMW as Abe drove down the broken pavement. He looked out at the dusty landscape. The city wasn't far, and he wanted to get something to eat before he starved to death. *I hate this place, and I've only been here a few hours. What a hole!* But money had a way of making you go places you normally wouldn't go...and do things you wouldn't normally do. For Taras, he liked being the boss, but it was the fear he thrived on. America was soon going to feel that fear. The thought brought a smile to Taras's face.

* * *

EMILY DOBSON COULD SEE Mark and Kirk walk from an

office building and get into a yellow cab. She was always one step ahead of them, and this excited her.

Detroit was balmy, the spring air was leaving, and the pollution came in its place. Detroit used to be a city of lights and action. It had a certain allure of a bad boy city and a place to party. Every year, the city lost more of its luster, and even the old movies that used to boast of the city as a bad boy hang out had disappeared. Now, it was just another city, trying to attract new business and survive.

Emily sat on a Harley fat boy with ape hangers. She wore leather chaps and a half helmet with her hair stuck underneath. The cab headed north and she was right behind it. She was a pro at the art of tailing. The trick was to be noticeable. Most cops or FBI would get a car that blended in, and by doing so, they stuck out like a cowboy in Macy's. The bike was seen, and then forgotten about. The driver wasn't even looked at because everyone just drooled over the chrome on the bike. She was an experienced rider, and if it came to it, she could hold her own against anyone. *Where are you going, my little friend? Are you going to see your old friend Mooch?*

The neighborhood changed into a charming little community of houses and perfect little lawns. Sycamore trees lined the streets and one house even had a white picket fence with a fresh coat of paint on it.

The cab came to a stop in front of a small, green house. The yard was in need of mowing, and the fence had a broken gate. The neighbors had to be ticked off by their unsightly neighbors. But then, everyone has a neighbor like that.

A tall, blond-haired man stepped out of the cab and looked her way. She smiled and pulled right up to the curb and shut off her bike. Her heart was racing a thousand miles a minute. She couldn't believe this was happening. She was standing right in front of Mark Appleton!

* * *

"HELLO, I'M MARK, AND THIS is Kirk Weston." I had seen the Fat Boy tailing us and kept an eye on it from the time we got in the cab. For a moment, I thought we were not the only ones who knew we were here.

"Hello, I'm Emily, Emily Dobson." She was medium build, and when she pulled off her helmet, a pile of deep mahogany hair fell over her shoulders. She was a striking woman. Kirk was taking in everything without a word.

"You must be looking for Mooch. I'm his girlfriend!"

I tried not to, but I raised my eyebrows. From everything I'd heard from Kirk, Mooch was the class nerd with an addiction to potato chips and soda. I couldn't help thinking this woman was a little out of his league.

"Oh, you don't say." Kirk had a smile the size of Texas on his face. He was thinking the same thing.

"Well, come on in. Are you friends of Moochie's?"

This time, we both laughed. "Moochie? Oh, he won't live that one down," Kirk said. "I can't wait to see his face when I call him Moochie!"

The house was trimmed with white around the windows, and a cat was looking at us with disdain in its eyes as we walked up the steps and knocked on the door. Emily Dobson pushed the door open and walked in. We followed as Kirk chuckled under his breath. I shot a glance at him and he looked back with a scowl. He was back to his grumpy old self in a heartbeat. Good, I needed him to be on the job.

This house was made up like an old hen's coop. The knickknacks and lace under everything had an *I live with my Mom* kind of feel.

The lady of the house wasn't home, and Mooch was holed up in the basement. I could smell the salt from Doritos and old pizza as we descended the stairs. I'd had a nice talk with Kirk about keeping quiet about the Agency, and we had come up with a good story to use as a cover on the ride over.

The basement was cluttered with books, magazines, empty pizza boxes, and Dr. Pepper cans. Mooch sat hunched over a computer and had four flat screens lined up on his desk. He looked up and stared at the two of us like we had just come to ruin his party.

"Hey Moochie!" Kirk laughed and charged the startled geek. "Glad you found yourself a girlfriend. What are you, like thirty now?"

"What's all this?" Mooch stood and started backing into the corner of the cramped basement. "Detective Weston, why are you here? In my basement!"

"Easy, we just need your help on something. This is my new partner, Mark Appleton. He's part of a joint task force we are on to try to catch a killer."

I nodded and let Kirk handle the small talk. Mooch seemed to relax some, but by the look on his face, he didn't look like he trusted me.

"So where do you know these guys from, honey?" Emily wrapped herself around Mooch and looked up at us.

"Uh…this is Kirk Weston—he's an old friend—and his partner, what was it? Mark?"

"Yes, I'm Mark Appleton. Now, we apologize for the impromptu visit, but we really could use your help." I looked at Mooch and then back at Emily, trying to figure out where the attraction was. Mooch, he was a nerd, and well…Emily was not.

"Well then, I'll leave you guys to talk shop. I'll be upstairs making lunch. You'll be hungry, I'm sure."

"Thanks, hun." Mooch kissed Emily on the cheek and watched her as she left the room. "Pretty hot, huh?" He had a stupid grin on his face and he winked at us.

Kirk laughed and motioned for Mooch to sit down. Mooch was thin and had a scruffy beard, and long dreadlocks hanging like ropes from his oversized head. He had a slumping, slick way about him, but under all the hair, he wasn't a bad looking guy. He reminded me of a lizard.

"Look, we need to find a guy named Taras Karjanski, otherwise known as the Red

Dog and The General. My agency lost him, and Kirk here says you are well gifted in the PC world." I hoped this wasn't a waste of time. Every minute that passed left a killer and madman on the loose.

"Well, I am the master of disaster, if I may say so myself. But I come at a price…"

Kirk grabbed his shoulder and growled. "How about I lock you up and forget to visit! No internet, no personal computer!"

Mooch twisted free and looked at me for support.

"How does twenty thousand sound?" I offered.

"Now you're talking. See, you could be a little nicer!" Mooch glared at Kirk and sunk into his high-backed chair.

"Shut up!" Kirk slapped the back of Mooch's head, which made dust fly through the air, and Kirk got a sideways look from me. I couldn't help but laugh. It was like two married people, and the annoyed look on Kirk's face made it all worth it.

After we logged on, Mooch explained the web site and inlaid traps on the Karjanski's family web page. "We can get in some serious trouble if we get caught. This is like, totally not cool." Mooch said.

"Just do it." Kirk mumbled.

Mooch typed and brought up a page with a ten digit password that had a timer on it. "If I don't get it right in twenty seconds it will automatically…" Mooch typed in codes like true hacker. "Got it!"

I looked at the voice encoded speech bar that appeared on the screen. "Okay, now what?" Mooch looked at me for the next move. I couldn't think of anything to get us by this block in the security.

Kirk looked over at me with a smug look on his face. "Ask me nicely."

"What?" I didn't have time for games, but the detective seemed to like playing them. His ego needed to be stroked about every other second. "Fine, what does the dead detective have?"

Kirk rolled his eyes and pulled out a digital recorder. He hit the play button and the voice of The General Karjanski came on, reciting the exact code to get by the security screen. "Who da man?"

"I won't even ask." Kirk liked to be the tough cop, it was the façade he was used to. And with what he'd probably seen in his lifetime, I couldn't blame him. I also could see that way down deep, he had a big heart. It was just *way* down.

The dark red screen had a background that looked like blood sliding down a wall. On one side, as Mooch explained, was a list of people who were logged on, and on the other side was a chat box. Kirk looked at the names and said, "I don't see him logged on. I say we log on as the Red Dog and go fishing." The gamble was that Red Dog wouldn't try to log on while we were there. If he did, then he would know he was being hacked, and change all the security, making it all but impossible to get back on.

"Give it a try, we don't have anywhere to go, and we need a lead."

Mooch entered the screen name Kirk gave him and within seconds we got a hit. The screen name **Blackmamba22** popped up and said, **RD, you're late for a very important date.**

"Kirk, you need to be Taras, what would he say?"

"Get up, let me type." Kirk sat down and looked at the screen.

Reddog: Never late... you're just early.

Blackmamba22: Then, I will be on time next time.

I wondered if we could track the user **Blackmamba22** and find out where it was coming from. Mooch must have read my mind because he slipped over to a second computer and started a trace. He looked over at Kirk. "Keep him talking."

Reddog: Do you have what I want?

The answer came back after a long pause that seemed like forever. I wondered who we were dealing with and hoped he bought our chatter as the real deal.

Blackmamba22: I think you will be happy with the merchandise.

Reddog: For your sake, I hope so.

Mooch waved his hand and turned the screen he was working on so we could see. The map he had pulled up was in Africa. Before we could say anything, the user **Blackmamba22** logged off and only one other user was left online. I nodded to Kirk to try to engage the other person in the private chat room. Mooch started another scan and the **Reddog** started to engage user **Hottie669**.

So far, Kirk seemed to be getting away with his alter ego. I hoped we weren't pushing our luck. If anyone logged on while we were on, I was going to abort the chat room madness.

Reddog: Did you need something?

Hottie669 did not answer. The room went silent, other than Mooch and his excited typing. I felt the hairs on the back of my neck stand up on end. The feeling of panic washed over me like a warning bell.

Hottie669: I already got it!

"Abort! Kirk, log off, now!" I looked over at Mooch who looked white as a ghost. He was staring at the screen and looking at an address. It was an address in Detroit, it was the residence of...

"You boys looking for me?" Everyone froze as I spun around just in time to feel blazing fire shoot through my shoulder. The force of the impact twisted me around and sent me crashing into the computer desk. Papers, food, CDs, and everything else on the desk went flying. The lights went out, and I could hear the sound of Kirk grunting and Mooch screaming like a girl.

I felt sharp trails of new pain claw their way up my neck and into my head. It was dark in the room except for the glowing monitors and flashing equipment. All I saw was thick, choking blackness. Then, I could feel my body falling. It felt like a never-ending hole in the floor. Then, all went quiet.

Chapter Thirteen

THE DINER, OR RESTAURANT if you wanted to call it that, was run down and dirty to say the least. The plaster was cracking and falling off the walls. Taras could see into the kitchen and saw a whole pig hanging from a hook, gently swinging back and forth. It reminded him of back home in Russia, when they would go into a small town near where he lived and shop in the open-air market. *Ah, the good old days!* Meat was open to the air with large black flies buzzing around sides of beef, pork hindquarters, and various other meats. If you wanted a pound of beef, then the butcher would carve off a slab, wrap it in brown paper, and hand it to you.

Times change. Now everyone was running around scared of the Swine Flu or Mad Cow Disease. No one seemed to wonder where all of these deadly diseases went after all the hype had been kicked out of them by the government and the news media. Funny how West Nile was killing so many of our old, and we were on the brink of an epidemic, but now, not a word of it, not so much as a peep. That was the thing with the Americans, they were already programmed to fear. They were taught from a young age to fear this or that. Taras knew that, in the end, this predisposition would make his job a lot easier. He would step in and take over where the media had left off.

Abe sat in silence and looked at the menu, looking for

something that sounded good. The choices and what might end up on your plate could in some cases be as different as night and day. Taras sighed and decided on the grilled chicken with a side of yams. The waiter was black as coal and had a smile that showed all his teeth. They looked like keys on a piano.

"You like the chicken? And for you, sir?" Abe looked up and smiled.

"I think I might try the pork. Just make sure it is cooked through." The thin African smiled and hurried off. Taras grunted and looked around the room with disgust. He thought about his meal, and about his childhood. This was not the time or the place to be thinking about either. The food was likely to be filled with God knows what, and his childhood, well, he didn't have good memories of that subject. But it was hard to tell your brain to stop thinking about something once it started.

South Africa was much different than most people think. At once, the thought of open plains of tall wheat-like grass comes to mind, with a lone lion resting underneath the shade of a tree with a funny top. One city Taras thought of was Joburg. He had been there a few times and was impressed with the modern architecture and just the feel of the great city. This dump was nothing compared to Joburg and it reminded Taras of his home. When he thought about his home, it always made him sink into a bad mood. The streets had potholes the size of Volkswagens, and many of the businesses had paint peeling off the walls and rusty metal bars bolted over the windows.

The food came with a dingy glass of water after more than twenty minutes. *This place gives me the creeps, what a dump!* The two men ate in silence as the three-bladed ceiling fan spun above their heads with jerky movements and a squeak and grinding sound that worried Taras a little. Taras had thoughts of his own rolling around in his head, like a marble in a gas tank. The things he thought about would sometimes make him shudder in horror. However, he couldn't help it.

The only other place they had to go was an oil refinery project in Angola, where he had a new interest in progress. He smiled at himself as he thought of the days when a great lord or warrior would fight at the palace gates and take over the throne. Times had changed, but he was still reaching for the throne.

"We leave tonight," Taras spoke without looking up from his chicken. "There is someone I want to meet!"

The true oil tycoons had dropped in number over the last few years with OPEC and the United States pushing for change. Taras Karjanski had his own methods. He would turn them to his side, or they would die. Death had a way of making people do things—things Taras wanted them to do.

The game of chess was just about over. The pawns were almost in place, and with the king in jeopardy, he would pronounce checkmate in short order. The only sad part was that he was the only one playing, so how could he lose? It made the game a touch boring, but he took heart. He had someone in mind to bring into the game to add the level of excitement he so desperately wanted.

After he finished his dry chicken and over-cooked yams, he pulled out his billfold and grabbed a twenty and a small piece of paper the size of a business card. He would leave a tip to go along with the meal. Abe stood up and walked to the door as Taras placed the white, blank card on the very edge of a full glass of water. Abe was not completely finished with his meal but was used to moving when Taras did. No use rocking the boat for two bites of pulled pork.

The food was terrible and for that, Taras would have his revenge. The black BMW pulled away and disappeared down the street. The waiter glanced at the twenty and took it as he cleared off the table.

Just like a play on Broadway, the card was bumped and slid into the water, causing an invisible vapor to rise into the air. With the aid of the ceiling fan, the powerful poison was dispersed through the air and went throughout the building. The patrons and anyone else exposed to the gas would be dead by morning. It was a nerve gas that would cause the infected body to reject oxygen, and they would suffocate as their lungs gave out.

Fun times in Africa, and more to come. Hold onto your hats, boys, the Red Dog is in town, and he's hungry!

* * *

MY BRAIN JUMPED TO life as I snapped out of my glimpse. Kirk was typing and Mooch looked at me like I was on drugs. I smiled and wondered what I must look like when I zoned out. I think it was only seconds but in my mind it could be any length of time. Time was different on that side, slower somehow, as if I was put on slow motion in my glimpse, or even paused as the rest of the world flew on at breakneck speed.

I looked up the stairs and reached for my gun. I needed her alive, and whoever she was, I wouldn't get any answers if she was dead. The gun slid into my hand like an old friend, and I clicked the charge to stun. I'd had the gun handmade right from the lab floor in New York. It held small, dart-like charges that could be programmed to explode a millisecond after impact or just send a shock to incapacitate the target.

Kirk felt the silence coming from my direction and he looked over his shoulder and acted just as a trained cop should. He played along and continued typing and looking at the screen as if nothing was going on. I was impressed once again by the detective's attentiveness. He didn't miss much and was always on the lookout for danger.

"Guys, you've got to see this." Mooch didn't seem to be aware of the changing situation. "The signal is coming from this very house!" His eyes grew wide as he looked from Kirk and then to me and then to the gun in my hand.

"Get down, Mooch!" Kirk yelled as he shoved Mooch with one hand and drew his own weapon with the other.

Emily came down the stairs faster than I thought she would. She had her gun drawn and fired before anyone had a chance to defend themselves. I was partially hidden from her line of site, and I fired, hitting her in the chest. She screamed and hit the floor. Kirk rolled toward Mooch, who was struggling to his feet.

My reflexes kicked in, and I jumped up and dove for Emily. She was shaking and lying on her back still holding onto her gun. She surprised me by kicking up with her boot. Connecting with my jaw, I heard a crunching sound and could see stars as I fell backward. She was strong for a woman, I would give her that. I turned and aimed at her again only to see her bolt up the stairs and out of sight. *How did she recover so fast? The last time I was hit with a stun dart, I was shaking for a few hours.*

I looked over my shoulder to see Kirk holding Mooch, who had blood bubbling from his chest and mouth. Kirk nodded at me with a grim look on his face. I took the stairs two at a time. The staircase seemed longer than it had when I came down them earlier. The living room was empty, and I could see the front door swinging shut as Emily ran toward her bike.

You want to play. Fine, you picked the right guy! Now I was getting angry. Sprinting from the house I looked around a quick second as Emily fired off a shot in my direction. I ducked out of habit and saw a Buell sitting in the driveway. I hadn't noticed it on the way in, but then, Emily was definitely a distraction. I was so focused on her and wondering who she was that I must have missed the bike sitting in the driveway. I ran up to it and smiled. The key hung from the ignition like an invitation. As I started it and squealed out of the driveway, I hoped I'd been trained on a motorbike sometime in my life, because as far as I knew, this was the first time I had ever ridden one.

Emily, or whoever she was, blasted down the road, her hair flying in the wind behind her. I twisted back the accelerator and the bike lurched under me, throwing me forward. I held on with everything I had. A calm feeling came over me like a cool spring breeze, and I knew I was in for it. The Harley banked a corner and turned right onto a side street. I was right behind her and found myself enjoying the chase, the ride, or maybe both.

The feeling of being in control and knowing what to do at every corner was hard to explain. As Solomon said, he gave me reflexes, and very good ones!

I ran through my memory bank trying to place a news article or event that could shed some light on who this Emily Dobson was. It didn't make any sense. What did she want with me, or was she just some crazy girlfriend who was hell-bent on killing her boyfriend?

I glanced down at the speedometer, and my heart jumped. It read ninety miles an hour, and it felt like I was flying. Leaning hard right, I could feel the pavement brush my knee. But I made the corner and was gaining on the Harley. *What does she have to do with this twisted up case? Why was she trying to kill us?*

My mind raced as the landscape blurred past me. I tried to focus on the situation at hand and put my deductive skills to rest for a better, safer time to ponder them. Time to give this chick a run for her money! The mind is a funny thing. Here I was, riding a motorcycle for the first time, and doing quite well I might add, and I was thinking of how she fit in, what did she want, and did the Dodgers really force all their players to take steroids? *Okay, Mark...road...crazy chick...me...going really fast!*

Dropping low on the powerful bike, I opened up the throttle. I couldn't believe the power coming from the bike; it felt like I was strapped to a rocket. The light up ahead turned red and Emily didn't even slow down. Her Harley screamed through the intersection as a Honda minivan slammed on the breaks and started to spin out. *Great! Just what I need. A crazy woman and busy streets!*

I was closing in on her, but now a mass of cars were slamming into each other, making the intersection a death trap. My instincts kicked in. Through the mess, I spotted a bus stop bench on the sidewalk that had been toppled over by the Honda while the van slid across the sidewalk into some bushes. "You've got one shot at this," I told myself. The time it took to make up my mind was only seconds, but everything seemed to be in slow motion. The only thing not in the slow-moving gel was me and crazy girl up ahead. I swerved onto the sidewalk and people jumped from my path. I was going well over a hundred now, and when I hit the bench, it acted like a ramp,

I was airborne.

Clearing the minivan, I hit the ground hard, making all the air in my lungs burst out with a grunt. I recovered from a near tailspin and was back on the road after my would-be killer.

* * *

EMILY CURSED WHEN SHE saw Mark Appleton make it through the intersection unscathed. She had had that Buell built from the ground up as a gift for Mooch, but he was too chicken to ride it. So there it sat in his driveway for a month. Now she had it on her tail, and it was closing fast.

Stupid, stupid, what was that? It was like he expected her to come down the stairs. Mooch was too smart to have left him in play. He had already done enough damage! "Fine, you want to chase me? Let's see you follow me now!"

Emily was an experienced rider and had even raced competitively in college. She knew the custom Harley because she had built it with her own two hands. The cold metal felt good next to her skin, and the wind in her hair made her smile with satisfaction.

There! The parking garage. This would test out his nerve. *See if he can follow me through this little wonder.* Skidding to the left, she burst through the crossing gate and started up the spiral garage. The gate attendant yelled in her direction but was almost run over as Mark sped past him through splintering debris.

Emily was not only confident, but she was very well organized. She had gone over every escape plan and had driven this very route no fewer than ten times in the last two months. She could hear Mark's deep-throated engine, and with a swift jerk of the brakes and a lean to the left, Emily did a one-eighty with her gun drawn. Mark blazed around the corner and ducked as she sent two shots crashing into the side of his bike. Before he could recover, Emily hit the gas and raced toward the top of the parking garage. She cursed out loud. She'd missed!

Tires screeched as she raced through the garage, and as the bright sunlight hit her in the face, she squinted, halted, and laid the bike down. The sound of the Buell could be heard coming up the ramp. It was time for the second act.

Emily slid under a tan Chevy truck and aimed her pistol at the opening where Mark would be coming from in just a few… the Buell flew through the opening and went into the air. Mark hugged the bike like a trained professional and landed five feet beyond where Emily's bike had come to a rest, but caught the front tire and flipped over the handlebars.

Pop—pop—pop!

Bullets slammed into the fuel tank of the bike and threw Mark farther into the air just as the bike exploded. Emily jumped from her hiding place, grabbing the handlebars of her Harley, and hopped on. Mark was only dazed. She couldn't kill him. She needed him alive.

Another day, my friend. Keep an eye out! Spinning around, she floored the Harley. The parking garage stood a floor higher than the one next to it. Emily had placed a metal ramp in the corner just for this contingency. She hoped she'd make the jump. Too late to turn back now! She just about ran Mark over as she flew past him. The Harley hit the ramp at seventy and ate the air up like candy. But someone had moved her ramp on the other garage. She leaned into the bike and could see that her landing was going to be close. The Harley slammed to the ground, sparks flew, and Emily was almost thrown. Amazingly, she controlled the bike, raced down the garage, and disappeared from view.

That was total Chaos! *Take that, Mr. Appleton!*

CHAPTER FOURTEEN

TWO CRANES HOISTED A large shell for A reactor. The construction site was more than two hundred thousand acres. The round, metal cylinder was welded stainless steel that made a perfect tube of hard mass. Taras Karjanski overlooked the site from his perch high above in a dark helicopter. He thought all the workers looked like ants on the ground. He remembered burning them with a magnifying glass as a kid.

Much to his displeasure, the plant was only about half finished, and it would take another three years to complete. The refinery would double as a nuclear power plant. The underground operation was to build nuclear bombs beneath the cover of the power plant.

"Bring me around to the main entrance. Is Joseph here?"

"Not sure, he's supposed to be," Abe yelled over the drone of the blades cutting through the air.

Taras nodded and looked at the refinery as it towered above the relatively flat landscape. The swing from the Middle East and its oil power had begun. After the discovery of a massive underground oil reserve running through Africa, the world rushed to claim its part of the trillion dollar industry. The Middle East was rumored to be drying up, which was causing a war of mass proportions over who would control the last, few, precious drops of oil.

Taras Karjanski was the first to pounce on the opportunity, but for entirely different reasons. His plan was coming together without a hitch. If only it didn't cost so much!

The chopper landed with a soft thud, and Taras was greeted with a smile from a black native who wore a bright yellow hard hat. "Welcome, Master Karjanski. This way, please."

Taras ducked with a hand over his face and followed the black man through the dust cloud produced by the rotating helicopter blades. It was hot and dry. Even the heat thought it was too hot and blew dust in protest. A four wheeler waited for them, and soon Abe and Taras would be able to sit in comfort after descending underground to the main construction office.

The place made Taras feel like God, or more aptly, like the devil. His mind raced as they drove deeper and deeper underground, thinking of all that would one day be his.

The lights of a building shone up ahead. The sunlight from above had disappeared and was replaced by a thick, black shadow. The air cooled almost instantly and felt wonderful. Even though it had a stale taste to it, Taras still preferred it to the sweltering heat. The building was brand new, with metal walls more than a foot thick. The windows were thick glass mixed with an alloy that made the material transparent, but hard as steel. The underground caves and tunnels had a tendency to collapse, so every structure was reinforced to withstand a possible cave in. They made their way to the front door and got off the four wheeler.

"This way." The black man took off his hard hat and walked up the metal stairs, wiping sweat from his forehead with a dirty, gloved hand. Weird lighting filled the office even though no fixtures were visible. It looked like the ceiling was glowing, as if from a magical source. A skinny, white-haired man stood up from behind a plain, metal desk. He smiled with an awkward look and held out his hand. "Welcome to the future, Mr. Karjanski. I hope your stay in our great country has been acceptable." His voice shook slightly, and he cleared his throat to cover it up.

"Less then accommodating, but I hope to have a better experience here." Taras could see the look on Joseph's face fall. Taras was about to drop a bomb on his day, anyway, may as well get on with it. "I am here to protect my investment. Not with money as of yet, but with sheer force. You understand?"

"I believe you have made your point." Joseph St. Clair was a powerful man in his own right, but in this power struggle, he wasn't sure where he would end up if he took The General head on.

"The shares and stock numbers show that I own fifty-one percent of this project and you are owner of the rest. I propose we make a deal. You work for me and finish this plant, and you supply the money to do it. I need a man I can trust to make this work." Taras sat down in a metal chair and clasped his hands in his lap, as if he was in his own living room.

Joseph had a fair complexion, but it was rising to red. He tried everything to keep his rage in check, but it wasn't working. Taras had killed his partner and friend, and now he was pulling a power play, and the thought of it turned his stomach. "I will do no—"

"Before you answer, I have something I want to show you. I am a bit of a photographer, and I think these pictures might interest you."

Abe stepped forward, opened a briefcase, and pulled out a plain, manila folder. He handed the photos to Joseph who looked through them and fell back into his chair with a pale look on his face. "You...Please!" He stuttered as his face turned white with fear and shock.

"I find your mood is better, and this, I can work with." Taras had the demeanor of a lion. He sat and his eyes lit up as he looked at his prey. "Your wife put up a fight, but as you can see, she won't be calling you on the phone anytime soon. Her screams were not for you as she died, but for your only son, Julian is it? Well, anyway, he is safe, for now. If you finish the plant, you will be allowed to visit twice a year. If you try any funny business, I will pull him apart, limb from limb." As Taras said this last part, his eyes hardened. He leaned over the metal desk and caught Joseph in his deadly stare.

Joseph looked devastated and lost all power over his emotions. The black man who brought them on the four wheeler had lost his white grin and looked at the two in horror. "Please, I'll do whatever you want, just don't kill my son, please!"

"I have sent your wife to your house in a trunk, I hope you will find the time to put her back together and bury her with honor. I will permit you a week off to take care of her. Now that we are in agreement, I expect the details of our arrangement will not leave this room."

Joseph nodded, and the black man cursed and looked down at the floor. He never even saw the bullet as it crashed into his skull. Taras smiled and looked at the end of his gun. It was smoking, which made him happy. He bent over the body. The smell of iron and blood made him chuckle. It was so sweet, like a sleeping baby. He looked up at Joseph. "He couldn't live, you know that. Only you will know the truth, and if you tell anyone about this conversation, I will kill them and your family, down to your grumpy old aunt!"

Taras felt good. The meeting went better than he had hoped, and after a tour of the facility, he was going back to the States to finish some old business that needed his attention. Taras's mental chatter erupted, and his ever-dwindling conscience yelled. *You are a killer. You aren't even human. Can't you feel that? Answer me! I hate you!*

Try again! You love me or you would have killed me a long time ago!

* * *

BLOOD SPILLED FROM MOOCH'S chest as he labored to breathe. Kirk pressed his hand on the wound and talked in soft tones to his friend. *Friend? Wow, I guess he was a friend.* He had known Mooch for years, and through it all, he liked the guy. The event had caught Kirk off guard. The last thing he had seen was Mark sprinting up the long stairs after Mooch's girlfriend.

What did she want to kill Mooch for? Was it just a thing between them, or was he a target, as well? Mooch coughed and spit out a mouthful of thick blood. "It's going to be okay, man, just hang in there." Kirk had called 911 and he cursed them for taking their sweet time.

Mooch looked up at Kirk with a blank stare in his eyes. "I'm dying, man, please don't let me die!"

"Don't talk that way, Mooch, the paramedics are on their way, just hang in there." Kirk knew his buddy was a goner. His lung had been hit, and Kirk could feel Mooch shivering and hear his ragged breathing. He didn't have much more time.

Kirk was shocked and scared at the same time. *What happened? Why did she just shoot him?* His fear turned to anger, and before the cops got there, Kirk hotwired a car one block up and took off. It didn't take a super detective to follow the trail of destruction to where Mark made his stand with the female killer.

By the time the ambulance got there, Mooch was all but dead. His eyes looked up at the sky with dead nothingness in them as they placed him on the stretcher and in the back of the ambulance. The parking garage had two wrecked cars on the way up and smoke billowing from the roof. Kirk spotted Mark walking back down the ramp. He pulled over and let him in.

"You okay?"

"Yeah, she got away. Mooch?"

"No," Kirk shook his head without looking at Mark.

Mark muttered something and looked up at Kirk. "I'm sorry about your friend."

The rest of the ride passed in silence. Kirk thought about the case and had a feeling this woman was somehow connected to the Red Dog. It was not just a coincidence that they were interrupted when they had the first real lead on the case. He didn't voice his theory just yet, but in the deep places of his mind, he wrestled to make a connection.

The sidewalks were filled with shoppers and businessmen

who milled about, talking on their Blackberries and iPhones. Detroit was a big city, and much of it was poorly planned. The roads would make someone without a good sense of direction completely confused. And no one wanted to be lost in Detroit. Kirk had lived in Detroit for a long time, and even he would get nervous if he got caught on the wrong side of town.

He remembered the TAXI drop-off point, and turned the car down a small side street, looking over at Mark. He noticed a wet stain was leaking through his shirt. His shirt was tattered and looked burnt as well. "You okay?"

Mark looked up with a start. "Uh, me? Oh yeah, I just got blown off my bike and shot at, but most of the damage happened when I met the concrete. Tough customer." Mark managed a weak smile.

Kirk laughed. "Still a smart aleck. So what do you want to do about the psycho woman?"

"I have a feeling we won't have to do much of anything. I think she'll find us. She had a chance to kill me, but she didn't take the shot. I think she wants something we have, or maybe she just wants to kill us in her own way."

Kirk thought that over and nodded. "Could be an old score."

"Well whoever she is, we've got to put her on hold for now. Taras Karjanski is in Africa, and with the coordinates we got from Mooch, we can be within thirty miles of him in less than an hour. I can't chase a crazy woman around and lose Red Dog. But don't worry, we'll catch her. For Mooch."

Kirk sighed and relaxed a little. He sat rigid in his seat and had a death grip on the steering wheel. He couldn't get the picture of Mooch pleading with him out of his mind. *I'll get her, Mooch. You can bet on that!*

* * *

I FELT BAD FOR Kirk. Even though he played the tough guy, I could tell he was broken up over Mooch. Everyone else Kirk knew thought he was dead, and the only person in the world who knew otherwise was now gone. I wasn't exactly a close friend, in fact, I was forced on him due to the case. I picked up my cell phone and dialed. Isis would need to come into the field on this one, now that Mooch was out of the picture. I had been planning on taking him with us to have a code breaker onsite.

"Isis?"

"Hey, Mark, I heard. Tell Kirk I'm so sorry." Isis was an understanding person, and I could tell she liked the detective. She was drawn to strong men, and I couldn't blame her for that.

"I need you to meet us in Africa. We got a lead. I'm sending the location over now." I loved the weird techie stuff the WJA had. The portable device in my phone could upload files or photos in seconds from online or from my PC at the office. I'd picked up Mooch's IP address and uploaded everything on his hard drive. He had some info I didn't want getting into the wrong hands.

"Okay, I'll meet you there, and be careful. This guy is bad news and shows no mercy. I also sent a clean up crew to dispose of the computers and secure the house."

"Good, and don't worry, we'll be careful." I promised.

After I hung up, I called home and talked to K. I had been gone a few days, and I missed K and Sam immensely. K laughed and told me she loved me. I still couldn't decide if I should tell her what I did for a living. She was a very loving and patient woman. I knew it bothered her not to know, and the not knowing had gotten us into a few arguments over the last year or so. "How's Sam?"

"Good. She's doing great in her classes. Almost has her reading down and is starting to do some addition. She's one smart kid, just like her dad." K was always good at putting me at ease.

"I have to go out of town for a few more days. I was hoping to be home this weekend, but it doesn't look like I am going to make it."

"Be careful, and keep out of trouble, okay?" I could hear

the stress in her voice, but she masked it so fast, I wondered if I'd just imagined it. If she saw my arm and the burnt shirt, I think she would have a different tone in her voice, but I shook off the feeling and tried to think about protecting her and not my feelings.

"I will be careful, and you keep my side of the bed warm for me. I love you, K."

"I love you, too. Hurry home."

"I will—bye."

I hung up my cell and sighed. It was so hard to do this and I felt like I was lying to her even though she knew I had to keep secrets. I felt convicted and pulled into my mind what I was a part of. I thought about the future and could see the very thin line I walked. If we took over the government in one fell swoop, I think it would work and be a good change. But, if the people found out about us in a bad light, then all mayhem would break out.

The thought of the agency going bad plagued my mind as well. The power it gave us was boarding on supernatural. I knew Solomon would keep everyone in check, but I wondered who would keep him in line if he lost it someday.

I knew one thing: this had to be for a reason. A goal and a time frame had to be set to enforce a plan, or all would be in vain. I didn't know if Solomon had one, but I planned on finding out as soon as I got back.

Much of my thinking was a little obsessive, but I knew what Solomon was thinking. He wanted me to lead the WJA into the next century, after he was gone. The decisions I made fell heavy on my shoulders, and every person I killed, no matter how much they deserved it, haunted me. Not only in my dreams, but also in my waking dreams, my glimpses.

"What's the dark warrior thinking about now?" Kirk jolted me out of my worries, and I smiled through my fears.

"Oh, the usual, bad people, the fate of the world. You know, normal stuff."

"I see. I was thinking that I need a burger. Oh, and a coke.

You game?"

"Come to think of it, I am starved."

"Drive-through or dine in?" Kirk was acting more pleasant than his normal grumpy self, which meant he was not himself. I gave him some leeway. He had lost a friend today, and I had a feeling he didn't have many. "Let's go in, wouldn't want to take the TAXI on a full stomach."

"Good point. What do you want to do about your, uh… appearance?"

I looked down at my shirt, the blood spotting it here and there, and grinned. "I think the safe house should have something I can wear. Guess we will be going through the drive-through after all."

Good old Burger King. If I had the choice between Mickey D's or BK, it was BK all the way. The stuff at Mickey D's would kill you if you ate it too much. Besides, I thought the fries at BK were much better anyway.

CHAPTER FIFTEEN

THE WASHINGTON POST RAN the second note ON the front page. They were told if they didn't run it, a movie theater would be bombed, and not an empty one.

The headline read. **Eeny Meeny Miny Mo**

Dear World,

The time has come to right the wrongs and to bring Justice back into alignment. The CIA, FBI, and other Agencies have tried to find me, and, to my displeasure, have fallen short in a laughable way. This is my message: Listen or die! Drink, drink the water of life, and you will not feel the grip of death. Try the bottle and feel safe to find that you have sealed your fate!
Now, catch a tiger by its toe…

With all my hate,
Chaos

The paper went on about the city's water treatment plants shutting down to search for any poison or contamination that may have been put in the drinking water supply. Every brand of bottled water was pulled from the shelf, and mass panic washed over the city. The city's water was shut off until further testing could be conducted to confirm that it was safe to drink.

Chaos had the city in an uproar. She was getting exactly what she wanted—chaos!

* * *

SOLOMON SAT IN THE large conference room and looked at Big B, Jamison and Captain Jordan. Captain Jordan was ex-marine and special ops. He had joined the agency a few years back after he was left to die in Iran with three of his men. The military didn't see the need to risk more lives on a rescue mission for so few at the cost of losing more trained soldiers.

The men in the room were silent as they looked at the notes from the person called Chaos. "Men, I believe they are talking directly to us." Solomon pointed out the highlighted areas on an overhead, floating, 3D hologram projection system. "As you can see, the words *World, Justice* and *Agency* all show up in order, and in both letters."

"This last one is addressed, 'Dear *World*. The time has come to right the wrongs and to bring Justice back into alignment. The CIA, FBI and other Agencies...'"

The captain looked up with a scowl on his lined face. "What are they trying to tell us?" He chewed on the end of his ballpoint pen and looked around the room with dark brown, pinpoint eyes.

Big B cleared his throat. "They don't seem to be asking for anything, they just want us to chase them. I think it's a big game to them." His huge frame all but crushed the poor office chair he was sitting on, and it creaked and moaned in protest.

Solomon ran his hand through his white beard and paced the room. "This is my fear: they are going to bomb places in the name of the WJA, and try to make us look like terrorists. They want us to try to stop them before they can do it."

The screen switched to another set and Solomon used a laser pointer to show them the new information. "We just uncovered this. I hope it will help identify the killer or killers." The picture was of a hooded person that came from a cell phone camera. It looked like a woman or a small man. It was from the back, and it was the only photograph they had. The image zoomed in, and the computer was able to turn it from side to side creating an image of what the computer thought the bomber might look like.

"This is our bomber. This was taken by accident and ended up on the internet, which is where we found it. The bombing happened a few minutes afterward. On the mall's surveillance cameras, you can see this person leaving the parking lot a few minutes before the explosion. I want this person found. We need to move quickly!"

Jamison was ripping a piece of paper into tiny shreds when Solomon looked at him. "You have something on your mind?"

"Well, I think I do, my fellow agents. I say we play their game, but we play it and win!"

The room grew silent as they waited for an explanation. "Try this on for size: I say we send a letter from our friend Chaos to the paper and see what they do. No one will know it is a fake except Chaos. The paper will run it and we can send them a message that we are on to them—tit for tat, as they say!"

Solomon sat down in a black leather high-back chair and leaned all the way back. "I think you might be onto something. We can start controlling the situation and possibly cause them to make a mistake, draw them out of hiding."

The rest of the group nodded in agreement and worked on a letter that would send a message and, provoke Chaos to anger and, possibly, a mistake. It was time to drag a large net and see what they could catch.

The next day a new letter ran on the front page with the threat of bombing a church on Sunday at mass if they did not comply.

The headline read. **If He Hollers, Make Him Pay**

Dear World,

You think you are so smart, well I am on to you! I know what you are trying to do and you will not get away with it. One day, at the top of the hour, I will be waiting. Show yourself or die!

Fifty dollars every day...

With all my hate,
Chaos

* * *

EMILY DOBSON LOOKED AT the morning paper and flew into a rage. She threw her coffee mug against the wall, shattering it into a thousand pieces, cursing and screaming at the top of her lungs. She could feel her face flushing with heat.

"They will pay for this! Who do they think they are? They can't speak for *me!*" She paced her hotel room and muttered under her breath.

Okay, they want to play? They'll get the game of their lives. One day, at the top of the hour...okay, the day is today!

* * *

CAPTAIN JORDAN LOOKED OVER at Big B and shook his head. The man was over six-foot-seven, weighed well over three hundred pounds—and most of it raw muscle—but he was scared to death of flying. Big B sat with white knuckles gripping the chair he was strapped to, and a half grin on his face. He looked all but happy and Jordan wondered how long the seat arms would hold up under the giant's death grip. The small, black helicopter swung north and headed toward the Adirondack Park to the town of Day.

The top of the hour was noon or midnight, but they hoped Chaos would pick noon. That is, if he even showed up. The small town only had a few hundred people who lived there year-round. The beautiful mountains and lush hills drew many campers to the Adirondacks every year with high hopes of good weather and long nights. The Great Sacandaga Lake sat south of the little town and gave a spectacular view of evergreens. The lush undergrowth made the earth look like a green carpet.

The chopper glided through the mountain air and touched down a mile outside of town in a clearing. The team wanted to keep their presence a secret for as long as possible, and the woods provided good cover.

Jamison was the first to jump from the helicopter. He grabbed a black duffle bag on the way out. Each member had a bag with necessary equipment, as well as weapons of their own choosing. Without a word, they each assembled their rifles and got ready for the fight that was soon to come.

Captain Jordan had a shaved head and a few scars on his face. He was stocky and well muscled, but quicker than he looked. He lit up a long, skinny cigar and sucked in deep with his eyes closed. After he'd drained most of the cigar, he blew out the last of the smoke from his lungs and grunted.

Jamison was the sharpshooter and stood six feet. He was of a slender build with a head of thick, black hair. Big B was in charge of ground cover, and he had infrared and heat sensing gear. Most of his fun would take place a half mile outside of town and involved a mounted computer-controlled super-weapon. From a laptop, he could control two fully automatic, silent submachine guns. The bullets could penetrate any metal or stone with pinpoint accuracy, not to mention the ammunition was auto-locking.

Jamison was shocked that Solomon himself would venture out to meet this psychopath, but he'd insisted. With the backup they provided in the woods, Solomon had nothing to worry about in town, though there was always a risk.

Jamison and Captain Jordan looked at each other and stepped into the thick woods. Dark shadows covered the ground like a thick fog, making the midday sun seem unimportant. Jamison silently made his way through the trees and over logs and rocks like a panther. He was completely at home in the woods. Captain Jordan was slower, but his skill in combat would be useful in the upcoming conflict.

Jamison couldn't help but wonder what this Chaos person wanted with them and the WJA. *Is he an ex agent? Or maybe FBI?* He had a hard time believing the FBI would bomb a building just to make a point. No, this was a rogue agent or worse.

They covered the ground without much trouble and soon had the little town in view. The cobblestone streets and the old time storefronts screamed *tourist town*.

At one time, the town had been a logging camp, and it had turned into a camping spot over time. Now, it stood alone, but still thrived in the summer with the lake to draw boaters and fishermen. The winter proved no less profitable with cross-country skiing and a modest downhill ski resort nearby. All in all, the entire town had been renovated and looked almost brand new. Investors and bankers had moved in with a healthy flow of cash and had made this sleepy, little town into a mountain paradise.

The meeting with the group or person called Chaos was a meeting of the minds to hear Chaos's demands. The WJA had to stop the threats and the possible bombing of schools and libraries.

A small outcropping up ahead put them about a thousand yards out, which was plenty of room for Jamison to get a clear shot. He set up his sniper rifle as Captain Jordan swung around and took another angle on the small town. Jamison was soon part of the woodland landscape, branches covering his body. There was only a small glint of light coming from the rifle scope as he scanned the area. In the middle of the town was a fountain with an oval pool surrounded by stone benches and a food court. He could see Solomon sitting on a bench with his back toward the wooded hillside where Jamison lay in wait. With the, "All clear," sounding in his ear, he answered back, "In position." The Captain was in his location, covering the only road in or out of town. Big B had the whole town covered on his perch high above, where he had a clear view of the courtyard and all possible exits.

"Got a possible target approaching, no heat signature to lock." Big B scanned the woman as she sipped on a soda and took a bite out of a hotdog.

"Got her," Jamison said as he looked through his scope and saw a slender woman walking towards Solomon. She sat down next to him and took another bite of her lunch. The lack of a heat signature worried Jamison. Everyone had one, unless she was wearing a suit that masked it.

The woman had long dark hair and a mini skirt with thigh-high black boots. Jamison took his finger and clicked the safety off, waiting for the signal from Solomon. They had an implant in his ear and as soon as they spoke, everyone on the team would hear it. The tension was thick and Jamison felt a single bead of sweat run down his back. *Come on, say something!*

Finally, the woman spoke in a clear, calm voice. "Hello, Solomon."

CHAPTER SIXTEEN

I FELT LIKE THROWING up, and when I looked over at Kirk, he was bent over a trashcan doing just that. The TAXI was something you just didn't get used to, and every time you rode it, you felt dizzy for fifteen minutes or so afterward. I didn't know if it was the drugs, or the G-Force your body had been through. Either way, it was a rush, and not always in a good way.

"You okay?" I asked.

"Yeah. Holy crap, that thing makes you feel like you were tossed in a blender." Kirk stood up and grabbed the wall for support. "You get used to that?"

"Nope, you just learn not to lose your lunch." I could feel the heat in the room as it reflected the air outside, and from the feel of it, the day was going to top the one-twenties. Africa was hot, dry, and dusty.

The sight of Isis made both of us jump, but she was a cool fresh breeze in this miserable place.

"You boys okay? I see the TAXI has you over a barrel." She was amused with our discomfort, you could see it in her eyes.

Kirk strained a nod and tried to brush off his churning stomach. "I'm okay. I had a late lunch, no problem." He was green but put on a weak smile in spite of how he felt.

Isis laughed and rolled her eyes. "Hm, I see. Well, let's get going. Karjanski is booked on a flight out of here in fewer than six hours. We need to get a visual on him before he gets on that plane."

I unzipped my flight suit and changed into a pair of slacks and a button-up shirt. I liked blue shirts on most days, but I felt like black today. Even in the heat, the shirt breathed incredibly well. Egyptian cotton was my favorite fabric, and in this heat, it was the only way to go.

Kirk looked over at me and pulled on a white t-shirt and a pair of well-used blue jeans. The shoulder harness and a silver .45 completed the look. "What?" He looked at me sideways and spit on the ground.

"Nothing, just a little obvious, don't you think?"

"Hey, I really don't care what these local bimbos think, I never leave home without this baby, and God knows I have enough trouble *with* it, let alone without it."

I turned and finished up by tucking a small weapon in my arm holster. It was an air-powered gun without any metal parts, so it went through metal detectors without setting them off. The rounds were made of tiny darts filled with a toxin that would knock out a full-grown man in half a second flat. Perfect for non-lethal force and for tight quarters. I could shoot it without even pulling it out. The strap around my wrist was hooked to my middle finger. With a flick of my wrist, it would fire, and no one would even know where it came from.

"So." Kirk was leaned over tying his boots up as he looked toward the door. "What's the story with Isis? She married?"

"Uh, no. I think she's single, but she is a little out of your league, if you know what I mean. No offense." I couldn't believe he was thinking about Isis at a time like this. We were on a manhunt and he was gawking at the scenery!

"Yeah, well, she's hot, and everything else a guy could want." He stood up and ran a hand over his smooth shaved head. "Well, all but the killing assassin thing."

I was getting a little impatient with the killing remarks

coming from Kirk, and I had a good idea what he thought of our group. "You know, if you lived in my shoes for a week, then you wouldn't be saying that." I knew I was being overly sensitive, but I needed to know that he was on board. "Besides, I know there are a few criminals you've put away that you wouldn't mind seeing dead."

Kirk looked around for a defense and shoved his hands in his pockets. "Okay, sorry. I didn't mean to get you all rattled. I just need some time to get used to this whole 'taking the law into my own hands' thing. Not that I've never done that on my own, but just not to this extreme."

"Well, next time you have a gun shoved in the face of someone you love, then come talk to me about our justice system." I really didn't want to have this conversation right now. "Anyway, we need to be sure that Karjanski doesn't escape. We might not have a chance like this again. He tends to leave a trail of dead bodies, and I have a feeling he isn't here in Africa to hunt elephants."

Isis came into the small changing room and broke in. "I've been thinking about this guy Karjanski murdered in the café. The killings are not random, he is killing for a reason, and I think it has to do with the oil refineries he owned."

"What refineries?" Kirk had a funny look on his face, and I had a feeling he knew more than he was letting on.

"Mohammed Dior was the president of OPEC. Something else is going on here. Dior and his bodyguard were killed in the middle of a crowded restaurant. That's a pretty bold move unless you have a really good reason."

I ran through the options in my mind. He was after the oil, like the rest of the world, and did not mind killing for it. The list of senators and congressmen on the board of OPEC was kept a secret from the rest of the world, and on paper, we didn't even hold a seat in OPEC, but America ran it from behind the curtain, like we tried to run everything else.

"He is going to take over the world's oil supply!" I blurted it out without realizing I had even been thinking it.

Nevertheless, once it was out, it made sense. "His killings and murders are just to throw us off. He wants us to think he's some two bit serial killer when the whole time he is setting up the game board. In one move, he'll control the world's oil reserves and hold everyone hostage!" It was falling into place in my mind, as if a light bulb lit up, and I could see what he was thinking.

Isis looked at Kirk who was rolling the thought over in his mind and said with a low voice. "The files I went through on his PC had to do with a few congressmen in the Senate. He also had a map of Africa and the Middle East. Forget the murders, we need to follow the money right to his next hostile takeover!"

With the new information, we sat down, and in a half an hour, we had a good idea where he was going next. The congressman on his PC was Nicholas Carver from Mississippi. The two others worked at Mr. Carver's law firm. Isis used her laptop to hack into a satellite to locate the oil refineries here in Africa.

"Okay. There are six refineries in Africa. One isn't too far from here, and the others are within a day's drive. OPEC board members own them all, or their partners do, and I would bet anything Karjanski is going to try to take them over." Isis turned the laptop toward us and pointed out where they were on the map.

I ran the scenarios and had to come up with a decision. "Okay, the bad news is we can't follow Karjanski and check out the refineries at the same time. I think we can get a tracking device on him at the airport and let him go. With that, we can always pick him up later. I doubt he is going anywhere we can't follow. Worst case, we draw him out by hitting one of his refineries." Isis pulled up a map of the area and the layout of the airport. "We go in through baggage claim and get a tracker in his luggage." I pointed out where we would set up.

"No good," Kirk said and shook his head. "I did that and just about got killed for it. He goes through everything, sometimes dumps it, and just buys new clothes." Kirk had a point. He would be looking for something obvious.

"Then we can use the floater." Isis said. "He'll need to be within five feet to set it, but I think we can pull it off." She paused. "Why he's flying on a public airline when he has a private jet sitting on the tarmac?"

"He is taking public transportation for a reason," Kirk said. "He is looking for his next victim. His profile shows him picking up women on planes or in clubs and killing them after he tires of them. He might be looking for someone you can't find by taking a private jet." I gave Kirk credit. He paid attention and could read people better than most.

"Okay then, either way we need to be careful. Isis, you will have to be the one to get close to him. He doesn't know what you look like. Kirk and I are somewhat compromised." I was going to be on high alert. I didn't want anything to happen to Isis, but at this point in the game, we had to take risks to get this guy.

Kirk asked about the tracking device, and I pulled out a bottle of perfume from a backpack I had slung over my shoulder. "This perfume has microscopic transmitters in it. When it is sprayed on someone, it sticks to their clothes, skin or whatever else it comes in contact with. Once it's active, it will send out a signal for about five days. It should give us enough time to get our recon done here and catch up with him later." I looked at my watch and noticed that we didn't have much time. "We should get going if we're going to catch him before his flight." We headed to the car that was waiting for us outside. It was one the agency ordered for us, and, true to form, it blended in.

The car had sat in the hot sun, so it was less than comfortable. It was an old station wagon without air conditioning. I took the wheel and rolled down the windows to get a breeze going. Kirk sat in the back with Isis and they went over a plan to figure out how to get Isis close to Karjanski. She was a beautiful woman. With that and her way of making men fall all over themselves just by flashing a smile, I didn't think she would have any problems.

The airport was an hour away, so that gave us a few hours to get ready. The African sun shone down on our car as we drove through the vast countryside. It was rather beautiful and, in its own way, pleasant even. The heat was dry, and when your body accepted it for what it was, it didn't seem so terrible.

I looked across the brush and saw a lone lion sitting under the shade of an acacia tree. The city would soon cover the raw nature with its own expanse of life of tall buildings and people wandering in and out of their air-conditioned offices. It was the nation of surprises and the world watched as it discovered underground rivers of oil that reached far beyond those of the Middle East. Soon Africa would be controlling the world's oil supply. Soon all eyes would be on Africa.

* * *

TARAS KARJANSKI LOOKED THROUGH the local newspaper and smiled as they reported on the murder of a local executive. *What is this world coming too? Murders, rapes. The violence that runs deep in people's hearts!* Abe had taken the jet over an hour ago with a pat on the back from his old friend and an envelope with ten thousand dollars in it. He liked Abe and thought maybe one day he would make him a partner.

Not on your life!

The airport was somewhat crowded but Taras was looking for something other than a Cinnabon or a taco from Taco Bell. He had the urge, the unmistakable desire to kill. It had been over twenty-four hours and the hunger seemed to be getting stronger. His thoughts would run to relive every murder and play each gory event over and over in his mind. *Stop. You need to focus on the plan. This is not who you are, you are not a killer!*

His eye followed a tall, slender woman, as she smoothly walked through the crowd with a black travel bag in tow. Her tan skin and black hair had him hooked before he even realized she was heading his way. *What luck, this should be easy!* She

looked Middle Eastern or even Egyptian, but whatever her
background, Taras knew he had to have her.

The woman ordered a cinnamon roll and sat down at a table
not three feet from him. He could smell the shampoo in her
hair and he looked over at her without any reserve. She smiled
and took a bite of her sticky bun.

"Hello." She made the first move. This was surprising!
Taras blushed. He was staring and worse yet, he was caught
staring. Or had he caught her?

"Hello, I am Taras, you must be…wait, let me guess.
You're a princess from a far country, or a queen, maybe?"

Isis smiled and answered. "My name is Shelly. You must be
Russian from your accent?" Shelly smiled and her face radiated
as if she were an angel straight from God himself.

"Very good." He could see her dark eyes scanning his
and he made his own sparkle like gemstones. "Where are you
headed?"

"New York. You?"

"As am I." This was going better than he had planned. He
wanted desperately to grab her and pull her close, then kill her
right there in the middle of the airport. He shook off the feeling
and then had the urge to run and get out of there before he
made a scene. He would never forget what happened next. She
reached into her bag and pulled out a bottle of perfume. The
scent made his senses rise in excitement. He breathed in deep
and filled his lungs with the sweet smell. It made him a little
dizzy, or was it her?

"Sorry, I hate flying. I get all gross and with the stale air in
there, I need to drown it out with something." She batted her
eyes at him ever so quickly, and his heart fluttered with each
flip of her long, beautiful lashes.

Taras was churning inside as his instincts took over. "It is a
wonderful scent, and it fits you perfectly."

"Thank you. Do you mind watching my bag a sec, while I
go freshen up?"

"I would be delighted."

He watched her every move as she walked to the bathroom across the food court. She was cool and confident and had a dangerous way about her that Taras found intoxicating. He took her travel bag and looked around before he opened it and pulled out a silk blouse. He felt the fabric and breathed in the smell of it and quickly shoved it back into her bag. *Oh, I love you so much, Shelly!* Shelly, even the name made him smile. It was simple, yet perfect.

A few moments later, she returned with a smile and thanked him. "Well, maybe I'll see you on the plane. I need to get a magazine and some motion sickness tablets."

"I will save you a spot. I have a first class ticket. If you like, I could save a seat for you."

She smiled, showing all her perfect white teeth and said, "I can't wait."

With that, she disappeared around the corner leaving him reeling with excitement. This was just what he needed. He was a good guy, he liked people, and they liked him. She was a beautiful woman and looked successful. He wanted to get to know her, and the flight home would give him plenty of time to do just that.

Taras couldn't feel the tiny microchips as they filled his lungs and stuck to his clothing and skin. He was deep in thought about his new friend and the possibilities of the day ahead of him. He would be enraged by the time his flight landed in New York and the beautiful woman he longed for never showed up. He would walk the plane three times looking for her before giving up and cursing under his breath. The woman, like the saner of his two fighting personalities, had disappeared. The Red Dog was slowly rubbing out Taras Karjanski!

CHAPTER SEVENTEEN

EMILY DOBSON FINISHED HER hot dog, absently looking at Solomon as she chewed. Her nerves were running on high, but to look at her, she appeared to be calm and in control. She finished chewing and took a sip of Pepsi from the half-empty twenty-four ounce cup.

"Hello, Solomon."

He looked at her and a bewildered look came into his eyes. Her age and looks would make her the last suspect in any investigation, let alone in one to find the mastermind behind multiple bombings and misguided letters.

"I assume you are Chaos. Is that what I should call you, or do you have a real name?" He looked composed, and to anyone looking at them, they appeared to be two tourists talking over lunch.

"You may call me Em. My mom used to call me Em, but that was a long time ago. I won't waste your time or mine. You called this meeting, now get to the point, or I'll be on my way!" Em's eyes lowered and her calm demeanor changed at once.

"What do you want? And I guess it would be pointless to ask why you are doing this?" Solomon said with a hint of disdain in his voice.

"You should already know the 'why,' and the 'what' is… well, I want one thing: I want Mark Appleton!"

Her answer shocked Solomon, and by the look on his face, she was getting the reaction she wanted. "This is my offer. Think carefully before you answer. I want Mark handed over to me, or I will take down the World Justice Agency, one bombing at a time. I know who your agents are and what you are trying to do. Your answer will determine what I do next and how many people will die." She liked being in control. It was the only thing that made her feel like more than just a woman. Her words were casual as if she were talking about her favorite ice cream, but they cut deep. Solomon seemed confused and looked her in the eyes as if searching for a human deep inside, not knowing that she gave up humanity a long time ago.

"What will happen if I refuse?"

Emily laughed as if amused, then responded. "I will bomb one building every day in the name of the WJA. The papers will blame you, and I will tell them everything about your little agency, down to your little hideaway in the Merc building. The FBI will be on you so fast it will make your head spin, and with that, the WJA will go down in flames!" Then she smiled.

The answer was not what Solomon had in mind. His eyes fell, and he sighed deeply as Em took another sip of her soda. Her mind was racing as she pushed a button on a remote device in her pocket. An F16 would be there in fewer than three minutes, and the answer she expected was on its way. She knew he would never give up Mark and that this meeting was a trap, right down to the last sniper, half a mile away.

Solomon looked up and shook his head. "I am sorry, but I cannot do that. I believe you should come with me, or my men will shoot you before you can even blink." He grabbed her arm to prevent her from running.

***

SHE WAITED FOR THE sound of the rocket as it bore down on the little town. Her body was relaxed, and as Solomon gripped her, she could see a flash of worry cross his face. She was not scared, and that was not part of his plan.

"I am afraid I will need for you to come with me, instead,

Solomon. I have a little surprise for you." Before he could respond she grabbed him around the midsection and rolled off the bench just as a bullet crashed into the cobblestone just above her head. Solomon toppled over and landed on top of her as she pushed the button a second time, causing an explosion right underneath them. The ground cracked and gave way. They fell about ten feet down under the street and landed on a small pontoon boat that waited on the underground waterway that led to the lake beyond.

"Sorry, old man, you messed with the wrong chick." She plunged a needle into his neck and injected a tranquilizer into his bloodstream. He fell limp, and she pushed him off of her as she hit the remote start. The small engine roared to life.

Seconds later, a ZWR 45 rocket slammed into the center of the small town, ripping through the cobblestone streets and exploding in a flash of light and an ear-piercing screech. From Big B's vantage point, he could see the mushroom cloud rise into the sky, and he frantically scanned the hillside for his team. A rush of wind shot up the mountainside like a typhoon and knocked him down as trees, pulled up by the roots, flew by his head.

The gift shop and food court shattered like a wine glass in fire, and the town burst into a million pieces as the hot ball of flame tore through the streets. The helpless people, who stood licking ice cream and throwing pennies into the fountain, were incinerated before they even knew what had hit them. Boaters on the lake, enjoying the morning sun, watched in horror as the place where the town of Day once stood burned and disappeared before their very eyes.

Emily could feel the heat and rush of wind as it licked at their heels. The boat raced through the underground waterway and they were soon out on the main lake where, within minutes, a helicopter would pick them up. Her captive was just what she needed to draw the famous Mark Appleton to her side. She had lost him once, but this time, he was going to be hers.

Hers to kill!

* * *

FIRE AND THICK, BLACK smoke filled Jamison's eyes as he climbed down toward the town, or what was left of it. He checked in with Big B, who told him he couldn't get a response from Captain Jordan. *What's going on? She just blew up a town! And for what?* The area where Captain Jordan was set up was just to the south of the aftermath. Jamison wiped his face and pulled his shirt up over his nose so he could breathe. The heavy smoke made it hard to see, and the woods around him were filled with hot spots and flames. He called out for the Captain, but only heard screams as people ran around looking for their loved ones. He was amazed that he could hear them almost a mile away, and above the roar of the fire.

Jamison ignored the sharp pain coming from his shoulder. A chunk of wood from a tree or maybe a piece of a building had dug itself into his shoulder when the blast knocked him over. The rocky cliff to his left had saved his life, acting like a shield to protect him from most of the flying debris and flames. He choked on the fumes from something burning nearby, maybe tires or oil, he didn't know. Captain Jordan had found a spot close to where the tree line ended and had been hiding in some tall grass behind an old barn that had been torn apart from the blast. The spot where he was supposed to be was burnt beyond recognition.

"No sign of him, I think he is dead!" Jamison spoke into his microphone and tried not to sound as scared as he was.

Big B looked through the thermal lens of his binoculars and scanned the hillside for any sign of the captain. "I can't see anything, there are too many fires, all I see is red!" They both knew Solomon could have never survived, when Jamison, who was a half mile away, was injured. Solomon had disappeared, and they assumed the worst. "We better get out of here." Big B's words made Jamison sick to his stomach, but he knew they could do nothing more here.

"Start the chopper, I'm on my way up."

They flew high above the devastation and looked for Solomon and the Captain. After an hour, they gave up and headed back to the Merc building.

When they reached the offices two hours later, the place was in an uproar. Solomon was assumed dead, and a whole town had been bombed off the map. Jamison called a meeting, briefed everyone who was available, and gave them all assignments to work on. "I want this woman caught! Use any means necessary—I want her! Solomon is to be assumed dead, but until we get a body, I am going to hope he somehow made it out alive. Come on, people, let's do what we do best."

The meeting broke up with the conference room emptying out in hurried hushes. He knew what everyone was thinking, but he couldn't bring himself to dwell on the thought. The WJA was under attack!

* * *

MUCH OF WHAT KIRK was thinking, he could never act on. He wanted to belong, and be a cop again, but this agency, this stupid agency, was changing his mind about everything. He tried to keep an open mind about them, and now with Isis filling his mind, he had feelings that were buried so deep, he couldn't even remember what to do with them. It had been so long, and he was definitely out of practice. He finally decided to just wait and see what happened.

Kirk had a side of his personality that was, well, against authority. He'd never been one to go with the flow and usually was just totally rebellious. He'd occasionally wanted to grab the thug and ring his neck just like the next cop, but these people didn't do it for revenge or hate. They really loved their country and wanted to change things. Granted, he didn't think killing off murderers and the wicked people on the earth was the best way to go about it, but it was a start in the right direction.

He looked at Isis and admired her long black hair, how it shone in the morning light. He looked away when she caught him staring at her, but she said nothing and just smiled.

Come on, Kirk, man up. Just get to know them. Get to know her!

The helicopter made a thumping sound as it glided across the African sky. He could smell the dry air and see the scattering water buffalo as they ran from the mysterious sound up in the sky. They had left the airport with Taras tagged and his signature sent to Isis's laptop. Much to Kirk's surprise, the plan had worked extraordinarily well. "So how much farther? I'm baking like a stuck pig here!" Kirk was gruff and blunt. Isis smiled and pointed down to what looked like a huge construction site.

"Just down there is the first one. We're going in as the Agency for Environmental Protection. They have random inspections out here, and with these, we should be just fine." She handed Kirk a badge and a picture ID. Isis was a professional, and with her experience in the company, Kirk could see why she scared him a little. She was always one step ahead of him, and that was the story of his relationship with her. He didn't like being the guy in the passenger seat. She had a way of disarming him, making him feel unsure of himself.

They landed on the designated helipad and waited for the rotors to stop before they got out. No need to eat dust without a good reason. The main site was deserted except for a guard. They smiled as he led them down to the main office where the foreman was. The ride felt like they were going into the throat of a giant monster with a gaping hole for a mouth.

Joseph St. Clair sat up when he saw them and rose to greet the three with a worried look on his face. "So, what brings you to my humble construction site?"

"We are with the AEP, and we're here to take a tour of your facility. We also need to see your environmental impact report." Mark sounded professional and Kirk decided to remain quiet through this phase of the investigation. He wasn't good at pretending to be something he was not.

The foreman looked nervous but obliged, sending for a jeep so they could all ride comfortably. The conversation ranged from their environmental impact report to washout areas, the proper procedure for disposing of waste, and many more boring things along those lines. Kirk nodded to make it seem like he was on the same page as them. He did, however, tune most of it out, and took the time to map out where they were, making a mental note of the exits and number of guards onsite. His detective mode kicked in when he spotted blood on the handrail leading up to the main office door. He looked around and could see fresh drag marks leading to the back of the building. He tensed and his hand touched the butt of his Glock. He didn't like the look of this.

As Mr. St. Clair started the Jeep, Isis continued her questions. "Have you had any visitors or unauthorized personnel onsite?" Isis wrote in a notebook as she asked the fidgeting man one question after another. The Jeep rumbled along the dirt pathway and began a long decent underground.

"No, no, everything's been running just the same, you know, business as usual!" His voice betrayed him. St. Clair looked straight ahead and changed the subject.

Kirk had a thought. He knew it would be risky and dangerous, but in his mind, this questioning was getting them nowhere. He pulled the .45 from his holster and pointed it at the back of the man's head.

The Jeep lurched to a stop when the driver saw the weapon pressed to the back of his boss's head. "No one move, or St. Clair gets it!" Isis and Mark glared at him and held still, trying not to act surprised. "This is how this is going to go. We are Mr. Karjanski's partners, and we want to take a look at our investment, you clear?"

The frightened man shook his head up and down like a puppet. "Good, now you do know Taras don't you? Taras Karjanski?"

St. Clair nodded.

"Then you know that we will do whatever it takes to get what we want, you follow?" Mark caught on, put a gun to the drivers head, and relieved the driver of the weapon on his hip. Isis sat in silence as if she were the ringleader of the whole thing and wanted to see how her subjects worked under pressure.

"Now, Mr. St. Clair, we realize Mr. Karjanski was just here, and we apologize for the inconvenience of our visit, but we need some more information about our little deal." She drew the last word out to drive the point home.

"Please don't kill my family, they're all I've got, please let him go!"

"Let who go!" Kirk demanded.

"My son, please!"

Joseph St. Clair sobbed in his hands and spilled everything.

Isis had the driver take them back to the main office. After threatening St. Clair again not to ever mention them coming by, they left and headed for Dior's power plant. It was getting ugly, and now with this new lead, they had a good idea what was going on. Taras Karjanski was going to buy or steal as many oil refineries as he could. With this power, he could own the world if he wanted to.

Kirk didn't like his options. On the one hand, he was running with an elite group of assassins that were on some sort of crusade. On the other, he didn't think anyone else in the world would be able to stop Karjanski. He had to decide if he was all the way in—or out.

Make up your mind!

Chapter Eighteen

THE FBI BUILDING IN the heart of new york city was humming with activity. Agent Carson had one thing on his mind, and it was not the oil tycoon murdered in a café in the heat of the lunch hour. The special task force that was set up to track down the World Justice Agency had grown, and now he'd been put on the force against his will. He had better things to do than chase some vigilante agency around.

The bombing in Day, New York, made headlines and had the country buzzing about terrorists and how the government was not doing enough to keep the people of the United States safe. The FBI held a press conference to let the American people know that it was an accident and that no one was under attack. Turns out , some crazy redneck was making a missile in his garage, and it went off, blowing up most of the town. He was arrested and charged with involuntary mass manslaughter. Unfortunately for Bob Blackwell, he was the perfect scapegoat. He had what we would call pyromania. In addition to this disorder, he had a brilliant mind and liked to research dangerous things on the internet, such as how to build a rocket or your own bomb. Between his home lab and his need to set things aflame, the FBI decided his incarceration would serve two purposes. Everyone would be safer with him in prison, and it gave them someone to blame for the bombing and destruction of the town.

Carson didn't understand why the FBI was covering up for this World Justice Agency. The public was capable of digesting the information and responding like mature adults. Although, the last thing they needed just then was all the militia banding together and joining the WJA, or worse, competing with them. It gave a whole new name to organized crime. Not organized to make money but to…to what? Kill? Seek justice?

Carson hurried into the meeting and sat down in the back. He wanted a real case, not some ghost trail to find a rogue vigilante group that some agents on the Task Force didn't even believe existed. The Senior Agent was Captain Jacobson. He was talking about the note they received from this person called Chaos.

The world had seen Chaos's letters to the Washington Post, but the FBI had received a separate note. This latest one talked about the bombing in Day, New York, and said the WJA was behind it. Their first real lead was this Chaos person. Maybe an ex-member who was disgruntled or an insider who was looking to make a name for themselves. Any way you looked at it, the FBI would take just about anything new on this case, no matter where it came from. Carson wrote down every word of the latest letter as Captain Jacobson went through it on the overhead screen.

Dear Feds,

The World Justice Agency is pleased to announce the latest of many cleansings to come. The bombing of Day, New York, was totally successful. If you think we are joking or messing around, then I hope this will change your mind. You will stop your investigation into our whereabouts, or there will be more killings and the country will call for blood. Your blood!

With all my hate,
Chaos

The room was silent as everyone copied the letter and thought about its contents while trying not to get emotionally involved. As an agent, that was one thing you had to master. Leave your feelings at the door!

"This group, up until now, has only killed those they considered the guilty. And so far, we haven't been able to find any reason to mistrust them. Most of the members on this task force have had a hard time going after a group who was helping us, in its own, backhanded way. However, this bombing changes everything, and most of us in this room feel it is time to end the WJA, once and for all. I believe if we do not get a handle on them in short order, we will have to go public with it."

Carson raised his hand and hoped that his proposed statement wouldn't get the captain riled. "The WJA has their own way carrying out justice. It has been just and fair, and, as you said, no innocents have been killed until now. Could this Chaos person or group be setting them up and doing this independently of the WJA? The thought of the WJA bombing a whole town just to make a point wouldn't stop the FBI. It would just ignite us to ramp up the investigation. Chaos knows that."

"It's possible, but, in my opinion, and with the evidence we have so far, we think the agency has gone too far. The power had to go to someone's head, and something like this was bound to happen eventually. Besides, whether it was them or not, we believe their existence is causing more harm than good."

The director took off his glasses and shut off the overhead screen. "The group is evolving, growing like a child. They are coming into themselves. This happens to every great empire, down to the smallest street gang. They get too big, then they start to fall apart, and the original ideals and dreams of the founders are redrawn by new members who want more power. Soon the group is far different than it was originally intended to be."

The meeting went on with questions back and forth, as everyone tried to understand just what the WJA wanted. Agent Carson was lost in his own thoughts as he drew small circles on his note pad. He had gone through the file on this organization, and with everything the FBI had on them, they were still far from anything solid. The leader was unknown, as well as the location of WJA's headquarters. No one knew any members who were involved or how far their grasp reached. The only lead was this self-proclaimed Chaos, who in his opinion was causing just that—Chaos! Nevertheless, Captain Jacobson was right. They had to be dismantled before they wielded too much power. The American government would not stand by as the law was twisted by any person or organization.

After the briefing was over, Carson walked back to his office, sat down, and closed his eyes as he leaned back in his chair. His office was modest, and he was not much for clutter or knickknacks. He was all business, but had a good sense of reality and could read people better than just about anyone. He'd gone to college in DC, gotten his Master's in Criminal Psychology, and became the FBI's lead profiler. He was new to profiling a group, let alone one that was invisible. This was the hardest thing he had ever attempted. But he knew the group would reflect its leader. He needed to focus on the leader of the group. His or her traits or personality was subject to the group. Like a father rubs off on the rest of the family, so the same would be true with the WJA.

Going over the things he knew, he began to put together a picture of this leader. WJA was well funded, which meant either rich ties or great sales skills to bring in money. Technology and intelligence. Might be someone ex-military, or even FBI or CIA. In order to keep their group secret, and foresee what the FBI would look for, he was leaning heavily towards ex-FBI.

He needed to think, to burn off some stress. The gym down in the basement was open, and a few hours on the stair climber would clear his head. He grabbed a dark blue duffle bag with his workout gear and took the elevator down to the basement. His girlfriend was coming over to make him chicken and pasta tonight, so he made a mental note to clock out at a decent time.

The gym was empty and the lights were off. The gym didn't get much traffic between 8 a.m. and 5 p.m. Carson liked the silence so he could just concentrate on the weights and his body. He didn't mind the empty room or the smell of cold metal. His back and arms were already screaming because they knew what was coming. It was their turn, and it was going to hurt.

Half way through his pull-up routine, his workout ended when he heard a beep from his cell phone. Looking at the caller ID, he didn't recognize the number. Flipping his phone open, he saw he had a new text message. He almost dropped the phone when he saw that it was from a dead man. *How in the world is Kirk Weston still alive?*

* * *

SOLOMON FOUND HIMSELF STRAPPED to a cold metal table in a basement or a dungeon of some kind. He could smell the stench of something dead in the room and could hear water running. It sounded like it was dripping down the walls like a trickle from an underground spring. The single bulb that hung from the ceiling made him blink as it turned on, blinding him. Then, he heard the voice of a woman as she entered the room and looked down at him.

"How are you doing, Solomon?" Em looked different somehow. Her hair was darker and shorter. *Did she cut it? Maybe she was wearing a wig before.* "I hope you'll forgive me for holding you in such a place as this. I needed a location where no one would find you. Now that I have your attention, I'm sure we can come to some kind of arrangement."

Solomon tried to speak but he was gagged. He hadn't even noticed the gag until just now. He was stripped down to his boxers and both hands and feet were firmly strapped to the metal table. He was too old for this, and he had definitely underestimated his enemy. She had planned to take him from the very beginning, of that he was sure.

"I know what you're thinking. I am a psycho, you never thought this would happen to you, blah, blah, blah. But, here you are!" Em took out a camera and set it up on a tripod at the foot of his metal bed. She flipped her hair and looked at him like she wanted to make sure he approved of her new hairstyle. "You ready to be a star?"

A little red light clicked on and Em stood in front of the camera like a trained reporter. "My name is Chaos, and as you might have guessed, I have your beloved leader and friend, Solomon." She stepped out of the way as the camera took in all of his shame and the poor condition he was in. He was too scared to be embarrassed. The table covered with sharp instruments in the corner caught his eye, and he could see that they had been used before.

"I want one thing, and one thing only. Mark Appleton. I'll trade Solomon's life for Mark's. I must have him! I will contact you with further details. If you think I am joking or that you can come here and rescue this pathetic man, then think again!" With one quick movement, Em had a sharp knife in her hand and plunged it deep into Solomon's thigh. He screamed through the gag and jerked away, but the knife remained. She pulled it out as blood oozed from his leg, and just before he passed out, she stabbed again deep into the other leg. Hot searing pain ran its fingers up Solomon's body, and as the crazy woman finished her demands, he blacked out with her voice ringing in his ears.

"You have forty-eight hours before he bleeds to death. I will give you my location and terms in twenty-four."

* * *

TARAS KARJANSKI WAS STILL pissed off at the dark haired woman who had blown him off in the airport. He had a mind to track her down and show her what she was missing, but thought otherwise of his impulse.

He was glad to be back in his apartment, After a long shower, he pulled on a pair of sweats and a t-shirt. He was getting close to his goal, but he had a loose end that needed to be tied up before he could finish all that his evil little heart desired.

Picking up the phone, he ordered room service and dinner off of the expensive menu. He felt like a steak and a bottle of wine. He loved good wine, and even if he hated America, he loved a good American steak. Something else he loved, he mused, was the feeling of freedom. He thought about Kirk Weston, and how he'd been so easy to kill right in the middle of his lame investigation. He felt free not having the pesky detective on his back all the time.

Watch yourself, you need to be careful! He was getting tired of his own thoughts, and with each murder or devilish act, he heard his own voice less and less. He was free to do and go where he wanted. The police and the FBI would never find him or catch him. He was going to be world famous in a few, short weeks. Who could stop him now?

Maybe I will kill someone just to show I can, and then see what they do? He was getting the urge, and tonight would be just as good as any other night.

The steak came and the wine followed. He drank half the bottle and finished the entire steak. He wanted to go out. The clock showed two minutes to midnight.

Perfect.

The hotel lobby was empty, except for the guard sitting behind the counter, watching a game on a small television. He waved, and Taras walked out into the summer air and looked up and down the street. He was on the hunt, and it felt good. All this business was wearing on his emotions, and he didn't like pushing the desire down. He felt so alive, so free!

A cab stopped and he climbed in. "Where to, Mister?"

"Anywhere. A club, with lots of people, and expensive. I feel like blowing money tonight." He handed the cabby two thousand dollars and smiled. "You be my ride for the rest of the night. I will pay you that amount for each stop. One condition: you can't quit on me."

The driver smiled and drank in the sight of the money with large, greedy eyes. He agreed and drove out to the center of Club Lane. New York City had some of the most exclusive clubs in the world, but if you had enough money, you could get into just about any of them.

The neon lights and signs made the Red Dog feel like singing. He was going to party like there was no tomorrow because, for someone tonight, there wouldn't be!

CHAPTER NINETEEN

THE BLACK BUILDING, COVERED with hanging lights and glass, made The Posh Club a hot spot for celebrities and up-and-comers. From the street, it looked like red, yellow, and blue lights were embedded in the building, the colors flashing as if from thousands of mirrors. Taras Karjanski made it in without much problem, since he paid the door attendant well over what the normal bribe would be. The big, bald man let him through with a nod.

The place was almost dark. Black light filters clouded the lights, and fog rolled across the floor from dry ice machines, giving the room the look of a rock star's stage. Here, everyone was the rock star. The club was three stories with an open floor and overlooking balconies. It had everything a girl or guy could want in a club—dancing, a full bar, loud music, and private rooms for those who could afford them.

Taras went to the end of the bar next to the main stage where a beautiful girl was singing with a full band backing her up. The place was classy, yet urban in its own right, and crawling with women! He liked it right away. The lighting would do fine for what he had planned.

What are you doing! Are you crazy?

Shut up! I am the Red Dog, I will do what I want! His mind sprang back and forth as he looked around the room like a spider choosing its prey. With each second that passed, he grew more and more anxious. *This is not the plan. You're going to screw everything up!* A tall woman sat down next to him and shot a smile his way. She looked strong and confident, she reminded him of someone. The woman in the airport. Shelly!

"May I have the pleasure of your name?" Taras leaned down, reached for her hand, and kissed it as he bowed his head.

"Well if you're going to ask like that, then I guess you may. I'm Heather. I saw you come in and was thinking to myself, that man looks like he knows what he wants." Her eyes sparkled as the stage lighting bounced off her glorious eyes.

Taras smiled with all the passion he could drum up. He was only thinking about the sweet sound of her neck snapping in his hands, and had to concentrate to keep from smiling like an idiot. "I do, and you may be just what I am looking for."

"May be? Well, maybe I'll be on my way then, after you buy me a drink!" She laughed and Taras nodded to the bartender who made up a Bloody Mary.

Interesting choice. It's as if the world has looked on and picked you for this very evening. She had on a simple black dress that hit her just above the knees, and a designer necklace with a diamond encircled by white gold. Taras liked how perfect she looked, just right, not over-done and not swanky.

"Do you have a name?" She looked at him with her dark blue eyes, and he could see he was falling in love with her with every second that passed. "You can call me Taras, Taras Karjanski." He didn't mind telling her his real name; she wouldn't be able to tell anyone about him, anyway. Not after he was done with her.

"Is that Russian?" She brushed a strand of unruly hair from her face and looked at him with curiosity. Taras liked the color of her hair, it was like a smooth cup of coffee, so rich and dark, and her skin was like milk.

Taras was pleased with her response as well as her appearance. "Yes, and how did you know that?"

"I had a teacher in collage that was Russian, it sounds like a

Russian name, and your accent gives you away, too!"

He smiled and took her hand, pulling her to her feet. "Come with me, my dear. I have something I want to show you."

Leading her to the front door, she giggled and followed him. The cab waited on the street as he had instructed, and the small cabby opened the door as they approached. Taras smiled, and they got in the back seat.

"I thought you would be in a limo or something?" She sounded disappointed, but Taras blew it off with a wave of his hand.

"Normally I would, but tonight, I have something special planned. Tonight, I have a show for everyone, and you my dear are the star!"

He could smell Heather's perfume as they drove. He wanted to hold her to tell her that everything would be all right, but he held back. He knew what he was thinking, and he knew what he wanted. "Heather, may I kiss you?"

She giggled and nodded. He felt a rush of excitement rise inside him, and with the speed of a cheetah, he grabbed her by the neck and pushed through to the seat. The cab driver swerved and skidded to a stop. "What are you doing, sir?" The driver craned his head around with a look of confusion on his face.

Taras pulled a gun and pointed it at the drivers head as he spoke. He was breathing hard and Heather was gasping for air and kicking her legs like a wounded deer. "You move, you die, understand?" The driver nodded. "You were paid, and you will be paid much more if you play along. If you go back on our deal, then I will be forced to kill you!"

"Please, I don't...Please!" He ran a chubby hand through his greasy hair and shook his head back and forth.

"Here's the deal. You drive and mind your own business, and you live with over fifty thousand dollars in your pocket by the end of the night. You don't, I kill you and hunt down your family and kill them, too, one by one!" Taras didn't realize it at first, but he was panting and screaming at the cab driver. He calmed, and pulled Heather toward him, his arm still around her neck. She was sobbing as he placed the gun down on the seat next to him. "Please don't kill me. I don't want to die!" Her frantic kicking and fighting slackened, and she slumped in her seat as if the air had been sucked from her along with her hope of escape.

The Red Dog was silent and quick as he pulled out the long sharp, knife that he had used to sheer sheep back home in Russia. He slashed her throat with his left hand and beautiful Heather was dead before she even had time to scream. Blood splattered across the cab and hit the driver in the back of the head. He whimpered but didn't look back as he sobbed in the front seat.

Twisting her neck, he felt it snap like a twig, and then he felt happy again. It was like a warm cup of your favorite coffee on a rainy day; he felt good inside. "Drive cabby, back to the club!"

The cab driver spun the cab around, floored it back to the Posh Club, and stopped in front of the now crowded building. Taras stepped out and dragged Heather's body by her right arm from the car and up the red carpet to the door attendant. The huge doorman reached for his gun but thought better of it when he saw the one Taras had pointed at him.

"Got a gift for you, doorman!" Dropping the woman's limp body on the ground like a trash bag, he turned and walked back to the cab. "Drive!"

The screams from onlookers filled his ears like praise from millions of fans. He was beginning to like the spotlight. He didn't want to hide anymore. He didn't want to sneak around. He was the Red Dog, and the world would bow before him, or he would kill them, every last one of them!

* * *

NEW YORK WAS HOME now, and I was glad to be back. The trip to Africa had unlocked something in the case that made the capture of Taras Karjanski even more important. The tracking device had a few more days left on it, and it showed that he was back home, as well. I was deep in thought when I felt something in the pit of my stomach. It was happening again.

I looked around and saw a long, dark hallway leading down into a deep pit. It was man-made, but looked to be hundreds of years old, maybe an old slave tunnel or part of the Underground Railroad. I could feel the humidity make me sweat instantly, and guessed I might be in the South. I had my weapon drawn and was ready as I descended into the dark, musty air. Pulling on my sunglasses, I clicked on night vision. I could see an old, wooden door at the end of the hall with a new lock on it. I was alone, and from the response on my COM stat, I was off the grid.

Where am I? Why don't I have back up?

I could sense the presence of someone or something watching my every move. I looked around for any clue, so when I was here in real life, I would have the advantage. I was getting better at knowing if I was experiencing a glimpse or not. The hard part was controlling them. They came and went on their own, without my approval.

Coming up to the wooden door, I saw that the lock was open. I turned to thermal vision on my glasses and looked through the door. I saw two heat sources. One standing, as if waiting for me, and the other lying on some sort of table. I approached, and opened the door, thinking I was ready for whatever was waiting for me.

"Hello again, Mr. Appleton."

I was not prepared for who I saw. I remembered the crazy woman I'd chased through the streets on a hot rod bike. I just about lost my life in that battle because I'd underestimated Emily Dobson. I did not plan on making the same mistake again.

"Emily, I see you've been up to no good." She had a shotgun pointed at the head of the person lying on the table.

"That's far enough. Drop the gun or he gets a face full of lead, and I don't think he can afford to lose any more blood." I stood in shock as Solomon looked up at me with a washed out pale face. There was a pool of blood dripping from the table and it made a puddle on the floor. He looked weak, and it took everything inside of me not to rush over to help him.

"What do you want?" I lowered my gun and looked at the mad woman who held my boss and friend hostage.

"I want you, Mark. I want to watch you die!"

* * *

I WAS BROUGHT BACK to reality when Isis came into my office with a worried look on her face. "Solomon is missing, I know"

She nodded and said, "We just received a tape that I think you need to see. We have it set up in the conference room down the hall."

My head was spinning. Going in and out of a glimpse was like dropping from an airplane and then expecting to carry on as if nothing happened. Why did I have these dreams, or glimpses? I could never remember having them as a child. Then again, I didn't remember much of my childhood.

The small conference room was set up at the end of the hall on the same floor as my office. The Merc building had office space on most of the floors, and I was on the fifth floor, along with Isis and many others who worked for the publication.

Jamison and Big B sat waiting for me, and I looked around for the captain. He was missing, and from the look on Jamison's face, I knew he was dead. The team was back together, but I wished it was under different circumstances. "Everyone okay? Jamison, you look like you've been through a war." I scanned Jamison and Big B to see if they had any serious wounds. They both looked beat up, but outside of some scratches, they seemed well enough.

"Yeah, Chaos, aka. Emily Dobson, blew up an entire town. We thought Solomon was dead until we got a tape this morning. Take a look." I was not surprised, and deep inside, I wished that every once in a while what I saw when I blacked out would turn out to be just my imagination.

Kirk came in and sat down without a word. The television

was on, and Isis hit the play button. The screen was black and then Emily showed up with a short, dyed dark brown haircut. She was smiling and began her threat. When I saw Solomon, I gasped along with everyone else in the room. I knew it was coming, but wasn't prepared to see it live. He looked terrible, and with his body stripped and all but naked, it was hard to watch. We all kept our eyes open, but only to glean any information we could to help him. When the knife went in the first time, Isis closed her eyes and let out a scream. I had a feeling this was my fault somehow. She was after me. I had to set things right.

After the tape was finished and the screen returned to its original, black state, I looked around the room. "I think you all know what has to be done. It's me or him, and I can't let him die for something I may have done." I told them that no amount of arguing would change my mind. I was replaceable, but Solomon was not. Big B cast his eyes down and folded his large hands in his lap. He knew what I was going to do, and he knew that, if Solomon were in my position, he would do the same for me.

"Mark, you can't. She'll kill you!" Isis had tears in her eyes, but the rest of the room knew that it was the only way.

"I've seen where he's being held, and in my glimpse, I was there alone. I think I can get him out, but I have to do exactly what she wants. I have seen her, and she is not going to stop unless we do it her way." I was afraid, but my fear was being smothered by my anger. This was now a waiting game, and we were at the mercy of a woman who we knew almost nothing about.

Fear comes over you like an earth-shattering wave; you can't stop it. I have learned to just ignore it and press on in spite of the nagging feeling that my wife and daughter might lose their husband and father.

"Isis, run anything you can on Emily Dobson. We have her fingerprints from the scene at Mooch's house. Run them through everything we have. Big B, can you get me an emergency medical kit that I can take with me? And Jamison, set up a satellite that we can use, so if I go off the grid, you can still track me. She knows how we do things and what we will do before we do it. We've got to get out of this box and get back the element of surprise."

Kirk stood up and started out the door.

"Kirk, you think you can track Taras? I am going to put you and Isis on it. You know him better than any of us here, and I can't be both places at once."

"I'll do my best. You be careful."

The next twenty-four hours would mean life or death for myself or Solomon. We would have one shot at this, and from what I'd seen, it didn't look good.

CHAPTER TWENTY

KIRK WALKED INTO THE sports bar, sat down, and ordered a Budweiser. He had called Carson, set up a meeting, and hoped his old friend would show up. He didn't know what he was going to say or even what he wanted. Carson was an old buddy, and Kirk knew he was on the task force looking into the WJA. In the beginning, Kirk wanted to bring them down from the inside. But now his viewpoint was different, and he was starting to see the good they were doing.

Kirk sipped on the cold beer and looked at himself in the mirror that hung behind the bar. The stubble on his head was starting to show like pepper on mashed potatoes. He was fit and tough-looking with his tattoos, and his few scars proved he was not someone to mess with. He looked at life through the eyes of a critic and a pessimist. He liked to make people show their true colors. All people were evil deep down inside. He thought it was only honest to be yourself. *Doesn't everyone always say to be real and true to who you are?* Well, he was just that, and not many people liked it!

"Whatever. They are the ones with the problem. Let them stew in their own juices." He grumbled.

"My God, it is you! How the heck are you?" Carson wore a dark blue suit and a clean white shirt without a tie. He was shocked to see Kirk and the look on his face proved it.

Kirk stood up and grabbed his old friend's hand. "Good. You look like you lost some weight. The bureau is doing you a service, I see."

Carson grinned. "They've got a gym in the basement. And I see you've trimmed down as well. Gym or starvation?" Carson sat down and motioned to the bartender for a beer.

"Ha, funny you should say that. Okay, I won't keep you in suspense. I was kidnapped but made it out with my life and a small lump sum of money. So I went out of the country to regroup, and wouldn't you know it, I was assumed dead. Now, I can't say I minded or even tried to stop the rumor. I was sick of the cop thing, and I really didn't have any reason not to make a fresh start."

Carson looked at him with a million questions running through his mind by the look on his face. "Okay. So you're back in the land of the living, and you called me. Your old boss know you're alive?"

"Nope, and I want to keep it that way. Outside of you, not many people know I still exist." Kirk looked down at his drink and wiped the condensation off the bottle. He was having trouble knowing what to say. He wasn't even sure he knew what he wanted to say.

"Come on, spit it out. I know you didn't come back to life just to have a drink with me. We weren't that good of friends. Come to think of it, you always were a pest and a grump." Carson took a swig from his beer and wiped his mouth with the back of his hand.

"Yeah, yeah. And you were too pretty to be a cop. The feds suit you better. I do have something that might interest you. First, I need to know everything you have on a group called the World Justice Agency."

Just as Kirk expected, Carson's mouth dropped to the floor. He regained his composure and looked dumbly at Kirk. "Not sure what you mean." He turned away for a moment but realized that was a classic tell, and turned back to look Kirk in the eyes.

"Cut the crap, I know all about your task force, and I know you're on it! Now this is important to me, and it won't leave this room, I swear." Kirk made the sign of the cross and nudged Carson.

Carson sighed and thought as he grabbed a pretzel from a bowl on the bar. A football game was on and he looked at it for a few moments before deciding how to answer. He wondered what Kirk Weston was running. He was a good cop, back when he was a cop, and he was a digger, he would never give up until he found it. Carson didn't know how Kirk knew he was on the task force, but at this point, it would do no good to lie to him about it. Weighing his options, he decided to take a risk and maybe in turn, Kirk would give him some information that might help him with his own investigation.

"Okay, I can't tell you much, but what I do know is that they are in a lot of trouble. This recent bombing was the last straw. Up until now, they have done things that the FBI could look the other way on, but they're growing in power, and now they're killing innocent people."

"What bombing? You mean the Day bombing?" Kirk cursed under his breath and took a big gulp from his Bud.

"Yeah. I won't even ask how you know that we suspected them. We have a note from them admitting they did it. I have worked up a profile on the leader and we think we might be close to getting a name soon. You understand, I will be in a load of trouble if anyone finds out I'm talking about this?"

"Look, they didn't bomb that town, it wasn't them. Think about it. The other things they have done have been specific and calculated. No innocents killed—ever! Not this bombing, it doesn't fit the profile." Kirk wanted to let it all out, but first he needed to feel out Carson. How much did he really know? Could he trust him?

"That is one thing that's been bothering me. It's out of character. But by the way you're talking, I think you might know more than I do about them." Carson leaned back on his bar stool and crunched on another pretzel.

Kirk grunted, tipped back his beer, and slammed it on the counter in frustration. "I'm involved with them. I know where they're located, how they work, even who the leaders are! My plan was to infiltrate them, then bring them down on my own." He stopped and looked at Carson. "Look, they may be misguided and going about this in all the wrong ways, but they're doing what they think is right. I need you to do me a favor."

Carson just nodded because he was too shocked to answer.

"I need you to turn the investigation in a different direction. We know who bombed that town. It was Chaos. I can feed you information on her and lead you to solving this case. But you've got to give me more time."

"Her? *Chaos* is a woman? How do you know that? Is she here in New York? How do I know you won't turn on me and disappear?"

Kirk held up a hand and shook his head. "Yo, hold up, I will tell you what you want to know, but you've got to stall them. Turn the focus to Chaos and work the profile. They wouldn't and didn't bomb that town or the mall. They have nothing to do with this Chaos person."

The conversation went on for twenty minutes more, then ended with a handshake. Kirk had known that Carson was an honest guy, and that he would do the right thing. But Carson was also a goody two-shoes, so when he waved at him from the cab, he hoped he'd made the right decision.

* * *

EMILY DOBSON SAT IN front of five monitors with four computers humming like a small engine on an aircraft. Two monitors played surveillance of the White House and Pentagon she'd accessed by hacking into a satellite marking the movement of key people in governmental power. She liked having the world at her fingertips, and she used it like a game at her command.

The underground room, where she'd created her command center, was attached to a main house that sat on the ocean,

overlooking beautiful palm trees and crashing waves. It was a
three-story house with a white painted porch wrapping all the
way around it. The porch swing moved back and forth on its
own as the sea breeze slipped by.

Emily liked to be hands-on, and in most cases, she worked
alone. She had hundreds in her company, but she only trusted
them about as far as she could throw them. Hence the cameras,
alarms, tremor alerts, and self-destruct emergency button that
would turn the coastal house into a ball of fire.

The company was running at full speed and everyone and
everything was falling into place. She thought over her plan.
How sweet it would be to have her revenge. She had waited
years for this day, and now it was finally here. Mark Appleton
was on his way to the meeting place she'd dictated. He had no
idea what was waiting for him.

The other three monitors had different scenes splashed on
their screens. One showed a live feed of a construction site and
an aerial view of everything that was going on. The other was
flipping through the stock market and running a program that
her top analyst had created. It cheated the system by selling
and buying at the last millisecond to earn millions a day on
the stock exchange. Not only was she making millions every
day, but her company was growing in numbers, and with each
scare tactic she initiated, she cashed in like no other company
could. The water scare forced people to boil water and even cut
down on showering or watering their lawns. Her water-bottling
company and her water-cleaning device, which could be used
in city water mains, was making even more money than her
original calculations had predicted. The bacteria was unknown,
and since she was the only one who knew the antidote, she was
an instant billionaire.

*I'm brilliant. Cause a need, and then fill it. What could
be simpler?* However, it was not just the money that appealed
to her. It was the control. She wanted to be in charge and to
see and know everything with a click of a button. Women had
been pushed down for far too long, and even in the new age of

women's rights, she could still feel the looks and thoughts men gave her. As if they were so much better than her!

Her big plan would knock the socks off anything she had done so far. It was risky, and in the end, it would be a blood bath. But if she pulled it off, it would make her wealthy beyond her wildest dreams. Not to mention powerful.

After going over a few, last minute details, she walked up the narrow hallway leading to the main house. The room was sealed off, and, without a retinal scan and fingerprint identification, it was impossible to get in. Mark would be at the cave in less than an hour. She was only a few miles from it and had time to grab a bite to eat. Solomon would be dead, or close to it, by the time Mark made it to the cave entrance. She would watch his face and enjoy his pain. She knew all about pain, what it felt like to lose a loved one. Now it was his turn.

Ready or not, here I come!

* * *

AT THIS POINT IN the evening, the taxi driver had forgotten all about the fifty thousand dollars. He didn't care if it was a *million* dollars. He was splattered with blood and the madman who sat in the back of his cab didn't seem like he would be stopping his killing spree anytime soon.

The third woman was only nineteen. Taras Karjanski had made her stab herself over and over before he tired of the game and ended it himself. The inside of the cab looked like it had been painted red, and each time Taras slipped on the bloody seat he would laugh so hard that he would fall over holding his side. *He's going to kill me, too—I just know it.* This man, or whatever he was, wouldn't let him live. Not after what he'd witnessed tonight. He had to think of a way out of this horrible situation, but nothing came to him. He was shaking so badly, he could hardly hold on to the steering wheel, and he had soiled himself on top of everything else.

"What are you looking at?" The madman screamed at him and kicked the back of the seat. "You just drive and mind your own business and you might live. Now, for the main event.

Take me to Central Park. I hear there is a *Red Dog* on the loose tonight!" With that, he laughed and laughed, sounding more like the devil than a man. His eyes were wild and bloodshot, and he was panting like…like a dog. He was red from all the blood, and as the driver looked in his rear view mirror, the crazy man was now on his back with his shirt off, rolling around on the blood-soaked seat like a pig in a muddy pigpen.

The Red Dog was back.

* * *

TARAS KARJANSKI STUMBLED FROM the cab like a drunk. He was dizzy, but his brain was clear and focused. It was like he was in a dream, yet he could control the story. The cabby squealed the tires and left without the money that Taras was waving at him. *Fine, don't take the money! You were a crappy cab driver anyway. Shaking and crying! What a crybaby!*

He held the sharp, curved knife in one hand and balled his other fist, cutting into his palm with his long fingernails. He noticed he had cut his leg and blood was oozing from the wound. After seeing the blood, he cut the other leg so he could rub more of it on his body. He was dripping with sweat and blood as he scrambled into the bushes and got down on all fours. He waited.

Looking at the knife, he tossed it away and tore his pants off like an animal. He drooled as he crawled through the woods and hunted his next victim. He could hear the sirens of the NYPD and wondered what they were looking for. *Maybe for me? No, that cabby was too scared. He knows what I'll do if he tells.*

Sniffing the air, he could smell the faint perfume of a woman. He picked up his pace and saw what he was looking for. On a park bench under a street light sat two lovebirds kissing in the lamplight. He licked his lips and looked at the pair with pure hate in his eyes.

Nice night to die! Kissy, kissy!

He studied the pair for a few minutes as they kissed and

talked like best friends. Looking down the paved trail and into the woods, he could see that he'd be alone with his next victims. This time, it was not the woman he was watching. He'd had his fill of them tonight. Now he wanted a fight. He wanted to feel the surge of power as he clawed with a man for the prize of the fine female. The wolf inside cried out, and with a leap, he bounded for the couple like a rabid dog.

The two stopped and looked at the thing coming toward them on all fours. It took them a second to realize the danger they were in, and by the time they did, it was too late. The Red Dog jumped on the man, knocking him backward off the bench, and they tumbled to the ground. The woman screamed and ran for cover as her boyfriend hit the pavement. The Red Dog bit down on the man's arm and could feel the skin break as his teeth sank in.

The man cried out, and, stronger than Taras had expected, threw Taras off. He scrambled to his feet, but he didn't run. Getting in a football stance, the two hundred-pound man charged the crazy dog-man, and hit him with both fists in the chest, sending him flying through the air. Righting himself, the Red Dog smiled at his opponent and jumped on his prey with everything he could muster. He dug his nails deep into the man's eye sockets and could feel the eyeballs rolling around his fingers.

You want to feel the power of God. I will ascend. I will be like the most high!

Screams came from somewhere behind him, and he figured the woman was running for help. He had a few minutes to enjoy the fight before he finished off the pathetic man. A blow to his head brought the Red Dog back to the match at hand. The football player crushed his fist into the side of his head, but Taras didn't let his grip on the man's eye sockets loosen. With a quick movement, he moved to the man's back, wrapped his arms around his neck, and grabbed his head. The sharp twisting movement and the loud snap made the football player buckle and fall to the ground. He was dead. His neck was twisted back and his body was curled up on the dirt as the Red Dog howled up at the half-moon. He couldn't hear anything but the sound of his own heartbeat and the faint screams of a woman in the background. He could remember every scream. Each time he killed, it made him stronger. He lived off their fear. He loved the sound of their voices in his head.

In fewer than five minutes, the scared girlfriend was running through the doors of the police station with a story no one could believe. When they arrived at the scene and found the body, the officer in charge covered his mouth with his hand to keep from vomiting.

CHAPTER TWENTY-ONE

ISIS FOUND SOME INFORMATION from the fingerprint of Emily Dobson that was recovered off of a glass in Mooch's kitchen. I was a little surprised to find that Emily was her real name. In cases like this, most criminals use an alias, or even change their fingerprints to keep from being identified. One thing Taras Karjanski and Emily Dobson had in common was their lack of fear of being caught. Emily used her real name, left fingerprints, and didn't wear a disguise. Taras killed without caring what DNA he left behind. He started out careful, but he was getting sloppy. I hoped it would lead to his downfall, and that I would be the one to bring him in.

Isis handed me the file that covered all the known information on Emily Dobson. "She has been linked to multiple bombings. In 2006, she set off a bomb in Moscow in a crowded train station, killing forty-three people. Then, again in 2007, with a much bigger bomb. This time she picked a school in Egypt and blew up every bus in front of the school as the kids were loading. Seventy-two killed. The FBI believes she has been behind many more bombings, but can only find circumstantial evidence, so they cannot arrest her. The FBI had her in custody in 1997 on a drug trafficking charge, but didn't have enough evidence to hold her. She was released that same day."

I flipped through the file and noticed that her husband had been involved, but had since been killed in an accident involving a bomb. "So, she disappeared for three years and resurfaced as Chaos. Does the FBI know that Emily and Chaos are one in the same?"

"I do not believe so. I found the information on Mooch's hard drive. The FBI database didn't have much on her outside of her arrest in '97 and possible connections to bombings, but no concrete proof."

"What was Mooch doing with a file on Emily. If he knew who she was, why was she his girlfriend?" Isis shook her head as we walked toward my office.

"I have no idea. Maybe that's why she killed him."

"Could be he researched all of his girlfriends. He was a white hat hacker. I wouldn't put it past him to run a background check or something."

Isis excused herself and met up with Kirk who was waiting for her to set up the tracking program to find out where Taras was. I tucked the folder under my arm, and after closing up my office, took the elevator down to the parking garage where my silver Mustang waited.

Big B was down in the main control room were Jamison had pulled up a satellite link with a live feed on my location. I was in contact with Emily Dobson via a cell phone that I'd found left on the dashboard in my car. *How original.*

Emily gave me a location on the coast, so I expected to be spending some time in the car. I gave Big B the location, and he entered it in his computer. "Looks like a deserted house. No one seems to live there, and no mail is delivered there, either."

"That means it's the right one. Sometimes the unlisted ones stand out more than if you went under your own name and had a nice personalized mailbox out front. Do you have a fix on the tracking device in the car?"

"Yup, but if she's as smart as I think she is, it will be worthless. I have a feeling the house is in a dead zone, so we will try to track you via satellite."

"Sounds good. Keep me up to date as much as you can on what Kirk and Isis are doing. Taras is as slick as a snake and more dangerous."

"Will do."

"Thanks, and don't worry about me. I've seen the ending."

"Ha, lucky you. Just watch your back." The trip to the coast would take a few hours, and it would give me some time to think. I called K and talked to Sam for a few minutes. She was excited about her new school, and in the few minutes we had, she told me everything that went on, which was quite a lot.

"And Billy told me to 'shut up,' so I told the teacher, Mrs. Johnson, and she made him sit in the corner."

I laughed, and K came on after she pried the phone from Sam's Kung Fu grip. "You won't be home for dinner, I take it."

"No, I have an out-of-town meeting, and it is very important. I might be a week or longer, but I will call you as soon as I can." I could hear K sigh and the line was silent for a full minute.

"I am worried about you, Mark, you go on long trips, and you show up with bruises and get phone calls at all hours of the night. Please tell me that what you are doing is worth it."

"K, I know it is hard not knowing, but it has to be this way, for your own safety and my peace of mind."

"Promise me you'll be careful?" K sounded scared, and I suspected she knew more about what I did than she let on.

"I promise. I love you, K."

"Love you, too."

The conversation ended too soon, but I had to get back to the plan, and if I talked any longer, I would end up with a sobbing wife, and then I would lose it!

I had everything I would need and hoped that Solomon would still be alive when I got there. It had been forty-six hours, and I knew he wouldn't last much longer without medical attention.

I knew from my glimpse that there was only one way in or out. She would be waiting for me, and Solomon would be on his own if I was captured or killed. I played the glimpse over and over again in my mind, trying to see if I'd missed anything. The room, the items on the table, the color of the walls, anything that would help me. Emily made it clear that if I was not alone, and that meant completely alone—no undercover microphones, no hidden cameras, nothing—that she would kill Solomon.

Think, Mark, why does she want you?

The sky was getting darker as the sun made its way down, making the orange and pink clouds look like a painting. The city outline in my rearview mirror was breathtaking, but all I could think about was my friend lying on that table bleeding to death. I was going up against someone who would blow up a whole town just to kidnap one man. What would she do next?

I had a feeling I was about to find out!

* * *

KIRK AND ISIS LISTENED in shock as a special news bulletin interrupted the radio playing in their cab. The cab driver turned it up and everyone listened as the horror of the previous night hit the airways.

"They are calling him the Red Dog. An eyewitness says he looked like a wild dog, covered in blood and cuts, raging naked through Central Park. Four are dead, and the police are coming up empty. The killing spree started late last night at The Posh Club when a woman who had left twenty minutes earlier with a tall man was dumped in front of the club—dead. The doorman tells us what he saw."

"This is Cindy Winters reporting from The Posh Club here in the heart of the city. I am here with Ben Washington, who is the bouncer here at Posh. Can you tell us what happened last night?"

"Yeah, man, it was crazy. This dude paid me to get in the club, and then left a little bit later with this broad. She was hot, I mean, like, fine, you know? Then they drove off in a cab, which was weird because the guy had tons of cash! Then, like ten minutes later, he pulled up in the same cab…I—uh…"

"It's okay, Mr. Washington, take your time."

"Well, he was dragging something, and he was all bloody. Then, I saw it was the woman he'd left with, and she was dead. He'd cut her throat."

The doorman starting choking up, and then the reporter came back on. "The police have never seen anything like this. The killer is now classified as a serial killer, and as of this morning, he is still on the loose."

"Thank you, Cindy. Two other women were killed in much the same way and dropped off in public places. The description of a white man in his forties with brown hair and a scar above his right eye is in all the papers, and the police have issued an APB. Anyone having any information should call the crime-stoppers hotline." The report went on to interview a girl in Central Park who watched as her boyfriend was killed by the madman. Isis looked at Kirk but didn't say anything. They were both thinking the same thing. Taras Karjanski had to be stopped, and when it came to stopping someone like him, no one would do it better than they did. Kirk was beginning to see the value of the Agency. They had the information and the means to stop this kind of crime. He wouldn't mind a piece of the Red Dog himself right now.

"You okay?" Kirk asked as he looked over at Isis.

"Yeah. I just hope we can bag this fool. His time has come and gone, if you know what I mean."

Kirk nodded. He liked Isis and the way she looked tonight made his heart jump into his throat. She was wearing an all black jump suit with tall black boots. Her hair was sleek and shiny, and a hint of light hit it from the street lights. She was a stunning woman. He couldn't remember the last time he'd had a real relationship with a woman.

"So you ever date or go out much?" Kirk couldn't help his brashness, and she smiled, which was a relief. The mood was in dire need of a change to something lighter, anyway.

"No, never can find the time. I suppose my job might be a hindrance as well. I did want to talk to you about something, though."

Kirk perked up and turned in his seat. "Oh?"

"I don't know if you remember when you were investigating the prison poisoning case, but you came to my office, and I lied to you. I had no choice as you can see, but now that you are here, and, well, on our side…you are on our side, aren't you?" Isis looked at him with those big dark eyes and the kindest face he had ever seen.

Kirk nodded. "Every day I see more reasons why you do what you do. I can't say I'm completely sold, but I'm getting there."

"Well, I was the one who was behind the prison thing. We only killed the inmates who we had researched and had proven guilty. No guards or anyone else were killed or hurt."

"I remember. You didn't have anything to do with my kidnapping, did you?"

She laughed. "No, that was Big B. He insisted that I would be compromised if you kept on the case. He is very protective of me."

"Well, he was right. I was hot on your trail, and it was only a matter of time before I figured it out. Can't say I was happy about the year you guys took from my life, but I can say it turned out for the best. And I came out with a million dollars!"

They laughed and Kirk rubbed his bald head. He had a nervous habit of doing that when he couldn't bring up his nerve. *Just do it, man. You've been bombed, kidnapped, shot, and just about killed! What, are you scared of a woman?*

"Would you like to go out for a drink sometime, you know, with me?" She looked at him and smiled.

"I think I might just take you up on that, Kirk Weston." She touched his arm and smiled. "You buy?"

"Sure, for you."

"Then it's a date. Just don't try any funny business. I'm licensed to kill!"

* * *

TARAS LAY IN BED the whole day and didn't even roll over

when the phone rang. He was exhausted from his night on the town. The flat was a mess with clothes strewn everywhere and wine bottles covering the counter and floor. He had turned into the thing he hated. He was always a clean freak and had to have things in a certain order. However, recently, he was becoming sloppy and disjointed.

He couldn't open his eyes because his whole body ached. Even his eyelids hurt. He couldn't remember what day it was, or what had happened the night before. Dreams and nightmares filled his mind as he slept. He saw a dark figure looming with red, glowing eyes, and the thing scared him to death. It just stood there, not saying a word and not moving. He knew what it was and tried to run, but no matter how far or fast he ran, every time he looked back, there it was!

At nine that evening, he got up to go to the bathroom but didn't quite make it. He vomited all over the floor. When he looked up and saw his reflection in the mirror, he vomited a second time and passed out, hitting his head on the toilet on the way down.

An hour later, he regained consciousness, and his mouth and face were covered with something sticky. He figured out what it was, but at this point, didn't really care. The shower was only a few feet away and he needed to get cleaned up. The water felt good as he washed dried blood and vomit off of his body. Skin was under his fingernails, and he could taste blood in his mouth from where he had bit into his own tongue.

That must have been one great night! You dog!

His memory returned, and he relived the events in his mind as he stood under the warm, running water. He couldn't believe how powerful he was becoming. The pieces were coming together, and everything was perfect. Now, it was time to do one more thing and the plan would be in full motion.

The phone rang again, and this time he picked it up with a friendly hello. "Why are you calling me?" Taras became instantly angry.

"No. You know the rules. If you call again, I won't hold up

my end of our arrangement!"

The voice on the other end fell silent.

"Good bye!" Taras hung up the phone with a curse.
He could always count on someone to screw up the plan.
Everything was too close to be making dumb mistakes now.
Turning on his laptop, he logged on to his secure web site. The
attached retinal scanner and voice imprint device made it easy
to get on.

His user name popped up, and he saw that three others were
on. He started typing.

Reddog: Mistakes are not forgiven, keep to the rules!

He was mad at the user and did not know what to do about
it. He needed to walk carefully with this one, and he had to
keep the peace until the next stage was in place.

DC1978: It was my fault. Will not happen again.

Reddog: Do you have the package?

DC1978: Yes.

Reddog: Wait for the signal then send back.

DC1978: Permission to open the package.

Reddog: Denied.

DC1978: Fine.

Reddog: Wait for my signal.

Logging off, he shut down the laptop. It was going to be
close, but in a few days the world would know and fear the Red
Dog!

CHAPTER TWENTY-TWO

I STOPPED THE CAR and sat on the side of the dirt road leading up to a white beach house. It stood against the horizon and looked like a hulking monster in the night sky. It had a porch that went around the front and the side, making a beautiful spot to sip tea and look out over the ocean. I was not interested in the view right now, though. I only hoped I wasn't too late to save Solomon.

I'd been instructed to throw my cell phone out of the car a few miles back and to pick up a new one at a local gas station. Now days you could get a "Go Phone" just about anywhere and load it with minutes for emergencies. Emily was smart. Smarter than I'd originally thought. Maybe I had overlooked her ability, but tonight she had my full attention.

She sent me a text message with the longitude and latitude, which led me to an old, bumpy dirt lane and the grassy spot where I was now parked. The rolling hills were covered with lush, green grass that grew a foot or so tall. It made a swooshing sound as I walked through it. The target on my GPS showed a red dot about two hundred yards ahead. I wondered if she was leading me into the underground holding tank I had seen in my dream.

"Ow!" My foot hit something, and I just about landed on my face. My gun was out, and I crouched down in the grass and looked around as my instincts kicked in. It was an old piece of metal and looked like a handle of some kind. I grabbed it and tried to pick it up. It wouldn't budge, and my back screamed in protest as I pulled. The handle was attached to something. I brushed away the dirt and weeds, and saw the outline of a wooden cellar door. My heart skipped a beat as I pulled up and the old door groaned, awakening from its long slumber.

This is all wrong! The entrance hadn't been used in years, and the steps leading down into the blackness had weeds and grass covering them. I looked for fresh footprints, but found nothing.

I pulled out my GPS and the red dot was sitting right over where I was now standing. "Well, guess this is the place." The smell of earth and water hit my face as I squeezed through the heavy, wooden door and descended. The door slammed shut behind me, leaving me in complete darkness. It unnerved me because the sound was so final. I had a feeling I was walking into a trap. In fact, I knew I was. This was the only way, though, and I was just hoping my reactions and training would somehow get me out of this alive.

I slipped on my sunglasses, and turned on the night vision option. The stairway opened up, and a tunnel led slowly downhill off to the right. I could see a ways down, and everything looked clear and empty. My mind raced as I walked cautiously along. *What does this woman want with me?* I could have done a number of things to get someone upset. My job was dangerous and put me in a position where a criminal might take offence to me killing one of their own. We were very careful, and to my knowledge, we covered our tracks well. Whomever Emily was, she had inside information on who we were, and what we were involved in.

The underground tunnel looked manmade and was getting smaller, or was it my imagination? I felt like Alice in Wonderland as I seemed to be growing and the tunnel shrinking.

I thought of the satellite that was supposed to be tracking me. It wouldn't be able to follow me underground, and I'm sure that was her plan from the beginning. I looked at my watch. The time indicated I'd been walking for over half an hour. The farther I went, the smaller the walls got. Soon I was on my hands and knees crawling through what now looked like a fox hole leading into a den. I'd left my earpiece in the car. It had lost its signal about an hour before I got to the big white house, but even though it was worthless here in this cave, I wanted it for the sheer comfort of having a device that could give some sort of contact with the outside world.

I could tell this tunnel was open on the other end from the cold air that was hitting me in the face. And the cave-like shaft I was in was like an air-conditioning unit, a pipe carrying the air from above. I saw a little gleam of light coming through a small hole where the tunnel came to an abrupt end. It was too small for me to get through, so I started digging to open it up enough to slide through.

"This is a waste of time, where am I going?" My anger was building, and this wild goose chase was taking precious time from the life of my friend. I knew I had to hurry. He would only make it a little…Whoa. I clawed through and was shocked to see a huge cavern open up in front of me. I rolled down an embankment and stood up, looking around at the gaping cavern I was standing in. A small opening was at the top of the dome ceiling and looked like a blowhole. The room was round, with bricks lining the walls, and the dirt floor was smooth and flat, as if it had been leveled and swept clean. It was some sort of meeting room with two wooden doors at each end. I ran to the one closest to me, and opened it to find that it was packed full of dirt and rocks. The one on the far end however, had a clear opening and joined another tunnel, which I entered at a jog.

Where is she taking me?

Two more huge, underground rooms and an hour later, I was back at the surface again. I breathed deep and sucked in the ocean air as I lay in the grass with my eyes closed. Finally,

I looked up and heard my Go Phone ring.

Emily Dobson's voice sounded as if she had just watched her favorite movie and was having the time of her life. "Fifty yards south, you will find a cave entrance. Take it and hurry, Solomon is fading fast, and I am getting bored!"

I didn't have time to answer before she hung up. I was at her mercy. She was in control of this cat and mouse game. She liked the control over me, and it seemed to have something to do with her pent up hostility. I had to get to Solomon!

The ground was rocky, and I figured I'd gone two, maybe three miles from where I was parked. I couldn't see city lights or even the ocean, but I could still smell it. I was out in the grasslands looking for some cave entrance.

Bingo!

A dark mouth opened up in front of me. The entrance was about six feet tall and four feet wide. I flashed back to my glimpse as I pulled my revolver from its holster. I took one last look around and walked down into the hole in the ground. I was alone, and Solomon's only hope.

A few hundred yards ahead, I could make out a door, just like in my glimpse. And now, I was ready. The woman on the other side would be alone, with Solomon strapped to the table. I saw Solomon's pale face looking up at me, and her flashing eyes filled with hate. It filled me with rage, purpose, and adrenaline. I put my shoulder down and charged the door as fast as I could. The door splintered under my weight and I burst through stumbling but keeping on my feet. When I looked up, I was looking into the eyes of a killer.

* * *

KIRK LOOKED THROUGH THE camera that was set up facing Taras Karjanski's room. It was a thermal x-ray device that allowed them to see right into his room as if there were no wall separating them. Isis loaded the weapon and pushed the cork back into the wine bottle. Kirk wanted to charge into the room and shoot Karjanski's head off, but Isis kept him in check.

This building had housed some of the world's most famous people, from Bono to the president. Isis knew the owner and wanted to keep his reputation intact by doing this with the utmost care. "You about ready?" Kirk was getting impatient.

"Hold your horses. This stuff could kill you in a matter of seconds. You wouldn't want me to drop it, would you?" Isis wore a black uniform with a white shirt. "To keep him off guard, we need to wait until he orders another bottle of wine. If we just give it to him uninvited, he'll know something's up. My contact tells me he orders one every day and this is the brand and year he favors. Let's just hope he does it soon." Isis placed the bottle in a bucket of ice and laid a white towel over it.

"He sure likes his wine, there's ten bottles lying around in there. What a pig!"

Isis laughed, "From what I hear, you're somewhat of an expert on the subject."

Kirk grunted and thought back to his apartment where he used to live in Detroit. "Well, mine was organized, in my own way. I knew where everything was…Whatever!" Isis rolled her eyes, and he could tell he wasn't convincing her. "We can't all be anal retentive!"

"Is that what I am?" Her eyes flashed, and she stood up. "I am an organized, well-maintained, structured, attentive, fabulous person! You got a problem with that?" She smiled through her fake demeanor. She had a good sense of humor.

"Whatever. You have to have everything just perfect. Jump sometimes, live a little, try new things. You know, like eating ice cream out of the box or leaving the dishes in the sink for a week!"

"I live. You should see what I can do…I mean…never mind!" Her face turned red.

Kirk laughed, and he went back to scanning Taras's room. He appeared to be talking on the phone, and then he hung up and threw the phone across the room, shattering it against the wall. *Must be his wife? Serves him right. Little wifie got you by the collar?*

"He looks like he might go out tonight." Kirk said

"I hope not."

Kirk thought about the news stories that had filled the news that had rehashed every last detail of the killings and what each might mean. Anything for a story! *The stinkin' media has to suck the blood out of everything.*

After Taras logged onto his laptop, Isis hacked into his PC, and they read what he was writing. The web site was high tech; they would have had a hard time getting in without the fingerprint Mooch had. And now he had a retinal scan! But with the dummy program Isis had downloaded to his computer, they could access everything he did when he was logged on. Isis burned up the keys as she pulled everything she could from the site. They could only surf the site as long as Taras was on.

"Find anything?"

"Something about an operation. There's no name for it, and it seems like he's working with someone else on it. ...looking for a name."

"Better hurry, he looks like he is about to log off."

Isis punched in a code, opened up another page and began to download a file that was marked "Fun in the Sun." The progress bar turned green and was at fifty-five percent, then seventy, then one hundred percent. The page exploded into a ring of fire and the screen went black. Isis gasped aloud, but kept typing. Logging off, she pulled a zip drive from the side of the laptop and rebooted.

"What was that all about?" Kirk stood behind Isis with a confused look on his face.

"That was a download of Karjanski's entire file marked "Fun in the Sun." Normally, a file with that name would not mean anything, however, it had a firewall and a roaming security drone assigned to that one file."

Kirk rubbed his hand over his scalp and shook his head. "In English, for those in the room that don't speak computer."

"I got his most important file, and I got all of it!"

"Great, what's in it?"

Isis went to her desktop, held up one finger as if to tell him he would have to keep his shirt on, and plugged in the zip drive. Blueprints, photos, letters addressed to various members of the Russian mafia, and bank account balances in the millions—no, the billions!

"Is this what I think it is?" Kirk asked.

"I am afraid so. It appears that our friend has a vested interest in oil refineries, and he has a lot of them!" Isis scanned through some blueprints, and came to one that, to Kirk's trained eye, looked a lot like a bomb.

"That is a bomb, and forgive me for pointing out the obvious, but it is also mixed in with blueprints of nuclear power plants and oil refineries. I bet you anything the blueprints are of factories he doesn't own."

"I'll check it out, but I fear you may be right. I believe he plans to blow up any factory he doesn't own, and in the process, ruin the world's economy and give him the power to decide what we will pay for oil."

Kirk blew out a long breath of air and sat down on the edge of the bed. He had heard of hostile takeovers, but this was insane!

* * *

BIG B LOOKED AT THE screen where Mark had just gone underground. He slammed his fist down on the desk and muttered under his breath. The satellite was the only link they had because any other device, a tracking device or bug, would risk Solomon's life. Mark had left everything in his car, and his phone was not moving, so Big B assumed he had thrown it out. Pulling up a cloaking program, he filtered the image, trying to see underneath the ground so he could follow Mark. Mark showed up as a little blip of color, but the deeper he went, the harder it was to follow him. It was only a matter of time before he would lose him for good.

"Now what?" Jamison didn't like being stuck in the office, not able to assist on the ground. But he also knew the power Emily Dobson/Chaos had and didn't want to risk it. Besides,

Mark was in charge, and he'd ordered the team to stand down.

"I need a map of the area. Maybe a mine or some old underground railroad was there, and if we find the tunnels, we can find out where they lead."

Jamison jumped on a nearby computer and plugged in the map of the surrounding area, searching for anything that would help them. The coastline had old houses, mostly summer homes that, in the winter, sat empty. This time of year, they would be getting busy as the cool spring air would be changing soon.

"I think I've got something. Looks like an old slave-trader hideout. The traders would move slaves to hide them from the government, and send them back to the English, and then back to Africa. Looks like three or four rooms, and tunnels leading for miles."

"Do they lead anywhere?" Big B asked.

Jamison looked over the maps and hit a few keys on the keyboard. "Nope, they have an entrance at each end, but nothing in between. He must still be down there!"

"Has to be. I'll give him another hour, then we go in."

Mark made it clear that they had to give him four hours before they did anything. He needed enough time to locate Solomon and extract him without Emily seeing them. His guess was that she would let Solomon go in exchange for himself. She had something against him and seemed willing to go to great lengths to get her hands on him.

"I think I might have something. You see the house up the road from where Mark is parked? A dead Mafia boss owns it." Jamison pulled up a blueprint and records dating all the way back to the 1800s.

"So, what's that supposed to tell us?" Big B seemed bothered and was beginning to fidget in his seat.

"Well, the Mafia used it for a staging ground for their entire eastern operation. Guess who the family was?"

"Who?"

The Valerik family, established in 1882."

"And?"

Jamison looked away from the screen and smiled. "Valerik is a Russian name for a dog."

Big B whispered almost under his breath, "The Red Dog!"

Chapter Twenty-Three

EMILY HELD A SILVER glock to solomon's head. I hesitated as she smiled and started to squeeze the trigger. "Wait!" I held up my hands in surrender and dropped my gun. It made a hollow sound when it hit the floor.

"Mr. Appleton. I've been waiting so long for this moment. You, submitting to me. And your life, not to mention your friend's life, in my hands." She had an evil grin on her face that made me want to scream.

"Please, let him go. You want me, not him!" I didn't know if it would work, but I had no choice. She wanted control, and I wanted her to think she had it. Emily had a worn look on her face, and she didn't look like she had any makeup on. She seemed tired; the bitter anger she was harboring was eating her up. It was showing now as she lifted the gun and trained it on me.

Solomon turned his head to look at me for the first time since I came into the room. He was pale, and a pool of his blood spilled off the table and onto the ground. He had no fear in his eyes, and with a blink, he closed them.

My heart was racing, and I could feel my face flush red. Before I made a move, I waited a split second for the signal. Then it came.

All I can say is it feels like a wave of heat and energy flows over you and bursts from your fingertips. My heart slowed to a normal rate, and I knew my reflexes were set to go. I reached out and grabbed the wooden chair that was on my right. It was lighter than I thought it would be, and I threw it with all my strength right at Emily. She was surprised but still managed to fire the Glock.

I didn't feel anything, but even if I had, nothing was going to stop me now. I rolled to the ground, came up with my gun, and trained it on her chest. Blots of red bloomed on her shirt. She looked down at them in surprise. Emily touched the red spots with her right hand and stared at the blood as if realizing for the first time that this was a battle she might not win. Sinking to her knees, I heard her skull thud as it hit the dirt floor.

Solomon tried to speak, but duct tape was still over his mouth. I pulled it off and freed him from the straps. He tried to sit up but was too weak. I lifted him on my shoulder and turned with one final look at the torture room, and we left without a word.

Solomon tried to thank me, but only a hoarse whisper escaped his lips. He was dehydrated, and he'd lost some weight. A half-moon was high in the sky when we surfaced, making shadows across the grassy hills that surrounded the entrance. Putting Solomon down, I took out my medical kit and dressed the wounds on his legs. His body was covered with cuts and puncture marks. Emily had used him as an outlet for her anger.

"You're going to be okay. Just relax. I'll have you back home in no time." Solomon nodded and lay back in the grass, breathing in the fresh air. I couldn't go back through the caves, so I decided to walk in the direction of the car and hope Big B would pick me up on the satellite.

Solomon looked like he was about to pass out, and I worried that I would have to carry him all the way back to the car. I knew I could do it, but I wondered if Chaos had any friends keeping watch just in case we escaped.

My danger bells starting going off, so I glanced at the surrounding countryside to see if my internal alarm was justified. Crouching in the grass, I crawled to the top of a small hill about fifty yards from Solomon. I scanned the open grasslands. I couldn't see anything moving or anyone approaching. The flicker of light from a small house off in the distance was the only sign of life for miles around. Turning, I saw a dark figure rise out of the ground. I knew who it was the instant I saw the shadow move. I reached for my gun.

Gone!

I must have put it down when I was dressing Solomon's wounds. *Bad timing, Mark!* Emily staggered from the cave entrance and waved her Glock in the air like a crazy person. Then, pointing it at the ground, she fired three times sending a flash of light with each shot. Solomon jerked on the ground with each shot, and then lay, lifeless. I screamed and ran toward her, wrapping her in a football tackle. The impact sent both of us tumbling down the cave opening in a cloud of dust and limbs.

Solomon! I saw his body as I rushed past. His head was blown to mush from the force of the bullets.

Emily was up faster then I was, and she found her Glock. The muzzle flash was all I saw. I knew I'd been shot, but I kept coming at her. She fired again and my legs gave out. I tried to force myself to get up, but all the strength drained from my body, and I collapsed. The last thing I saw was Emily standing over me laughing. Her shirt was torn open and the Kevlar vest underneath had two bullet holes in it. A trickle of blood oozed from each hole. I didn't even feel it when she kicked me in the face. I'd already blacked out, only to dream of Solomon, and his mangled body.

* * *

TARAS KARJANSKI WENT TO bed without any wine or drugs. He was still tired from the previous night's exploits and needed to be at his best for the next morning's events. He dreamed of the United States begging for mercy as he held them hostage. His twisted face smiled in his sleep, making him look like the Devil himself.

* * *

CARSON LOOKED AT THE note from Chaos and closed his eyes. The note had been delivered an hour ago, and it was still being looked over by the forensics team. He'd had a copy sent to his computer so he could review it more closely. Captain Jacobson wasn't sure it was real, and he doubted that the threat would be carried out, or that it was even possible, for that matter.

Cursing, he looked at his recent, incoming calls. Kirk Weston was running short on time. He pushed the send button to call him. Then he hung up before it could ring on the other end. *Think, Carson. Would they do this? No, this is nothing like them.* Carson pulled up the information on Emily Dobson that Kirk had sent him a few hours earlier. It was not complete, but it was a start.

He scanned the email attachment again, even though he had practically memorized it already. Emily Dobson's life was a maze of twisted events and tragedies that had turned her into a psychotic killer. Her parents had been murdered and her husband killed as well. A trail of death seemed to follow her around like a stray kitten. But he didn't believe she had the connections or the power to pull off what he now read for the hundredth time:

Dear America,

It is time to see what you are made of, and to see if you want change or if you just want to be entertained! In two days, you will have a choice to make. You will have to choose between your children and your oil. An untraceable phone line has been set up, and you will be able to call in and vote. The choice is simple: a school full of children will be bombed, or an oil refinery will be blown sky high, causing your oil prices to skyrocket. I choose the refinery, and I will also choose the school. You decide!

> *With all my hate,*
> *Chaos*

Due to the unstable nature of this woman, and her way of getting everyone worked up, a Red Alert was put into effect. Emily Dobson was a ghost. They had next to nothing on her, and the fingerprints Isis pulled turned out to be from a girl in South Dakota who had died in 1983. Kirk Weston was his only lead, and Carson didn't like having a dead detective holding him over a cliff with no hope of saving himself if he let go.

The schools in the New York area were stepping up security. Carson had read the note in *The Post* as well as in the *New York Times*. The news media was all over the story, and with their usual flair for the truth, had blown it way out of proportion. Just like Emily liked it. America was building up a panic. Carson didn't believe the WJA was involved, but the task force had a different idea. He needed more proof before he brought it up to Captain Jacobson.

Carson picked up the phone on his desk and dialed the forensics team.

"Hey Sam, you get anything?" Carson twisted the phone cord around his fingers and grabbed a pen from a plastic penholder on his desk.

"Nope, it's clean, just like the other ones. No prints or anything else I could trace."

"Thanks," Carson hung up and sighed. Kirk better hurry up with something new, or the WJA would be the next big story on the six o'clock news!

* * *

THE NEWS HEADLINE SPREADING across the airways and internet was the chaos that Chaos wanted. Late night talk shows made jokes, and Jay Leno made up Jaywalking monologues to help lighten the country's mood. But the underlying tone was that people believed this person would carry out the threat, and worse.

The discussion was on every morning talk show. If America should call in and vote, or let the lunatics make up their own mind. It was a hot topic around water coolers and in cafés across the country.

"I'm voting. I don't care what anybody says, I got kids in school and I won't stand by and put them in danger over gas prices going up a little!" The redhead waved her hand in front of the Channel 7 News camera and bobbed her head in defiance. True to form, every crazy and uneducated citizen was polled and interviewed on the subject. The talking heads on the evening news added their slant to it and told the American people what to do—in an unbiased way, of course.

The following day, just like Emily Dobson wanted, the world watched as a single number was plastered across every paper in the country.

1866BOMB01 to vote for blowing up a school.
1866BOMB02 to vote for blowing up an oil refinery.
You can also text BOMB1 or BOMB2.

The FBI and CIA had their best hackers and agents trying desperately to shut down the phone numbers or to at least trace them. Nothing worked. The trace was routed to every pay phone in the DC area, then jumped to Detroit, St. Louis, and so on. The plan was underway, and the phone lines were busy with people trying to vote on what could be the most important decision they would ever make!

* * *

THE RED DOG WALKED from his condo with a new skip in his step. The top story on the morning news brought a smile to his face. Hard to believe such a thing, but who was he to stand in the way of progress? He wore a dark blue shirt with blue jeans and a ball cap with the Under Armour logo imprinted on the front. He looked like an average dad on his way to the store for some milk and a dozen eggs.

The elevator was playing soft music that wouldn't offend anyone. He felt the weight of the .45 under his pant leg where it was firmly holstered and ready for whatever the day brought. Making his way through the almost empty lobby and out intro the bright sunshine, he breathed deep, feeling peace for the first time in a long time. His urges to kill had been satisfied for the time being, and his plan to bring America to its knees was underway. Years of planning and dedication were about to pay off.

Today, he had the door attendant bring up his bright yellow Lamborghini. It was a day to celebrate, to be happy, to be alive. The mood of the city was not so joyful. Taras began to feel the fear and hopelessness all around him, and it filled him with a sense of power. *I am God now! I can say who lives and who dies. I am unstoppable!*

The slender bellhop drove up to the curb behind the wheel of Taras's car. He got out, touched his finger to his hat, and bowed slightly. Taras slipped him a fifty and pushed past the quiet man without even looking at his nametag. Who was he? Who cared? He parked cars and carried luggage for a living, and for that, Taras believed he was just another leech he would step over without a second glance. Sliding behind the wheel, he spun the tires and sped into traffic, making a few drivers give him the bird, which only added to his glee. He was not to be messed with today.

No, not today.

The feel of the twelve-cylinder engine and the smell of leather filled his nostrils as he made his way out of the city. In a few hours, he would see an old friend. He was looking forward to seeing her again. It had been too long, and with all the phone calls and emails, it was time to see Emily Dobson, face to face, and take care of a growing problem once and for all!

* * *

KIRK YELLED AT THE taxi driver to keep up with the yellow Lamborghini but the driver's English wasn't good, and the yelling didn't help. "Stay with him! You can *speed,* you know!"

Isis looked nervous, but tried to stay calm. The world was well aware of the new threat thrust upon them as of this morning. It was clear now that Taras Karjanski and Emily Dobson were somehow tied together in a plan to hold the world, or more aptly, America, hostage.

The cab swerved through traffic, and Kirk sat back in frustration as the yellow sports car disappeared from sight and the cab got tangled up in the morning's rat race. "Now what?" It took all his self-control to keep from strangling the taxi driver.

"Let's check in and see what Big B has on Mark. If we find Emily Dobson, we find Taras Karjanski. I have a feeling that's where Taras is going."

Isis was calm and collected as usual, which calmed Kirk down a bit. The driver was saying something over his shoulder, but Kirk ignored him and watched as Isis called in and talked to Big B. The phone call lasted less than a minute, and soon they had the GPS coordinates on the last known location of Mark and Solomon. It was going to take a few hours just to get out of the city, and longer to get to where Mark had left his car.

Kirk asked Isis about her family and in a few moments had her telling him her life story. In most cases, Kirk would be zoned out or looking the other way to give the other person the cold shoulder, but Isis was different. Somehow, everything she had to say interested him. She had a way of making him feel like she was worthy of telling her his past, too. He knew she was a reserved person, and he had a feeling she didn't open up to many people.

"I was born in Egypt, a little town you never heard of, and my mother died a few days after I was born. My father was not able to take care of me, so he put me in a children's home."

"Where is your dad now?" Kirk asked.

"I don't know. I don't even know who he is. The adoption agency only has a first name. I was adopted by Solomon a year later. He took me to the United States where I grew up as one of the first to go through the WJA training program." Isis smoothed her hair and turned to look at Kirk.

"Wow. So you were molded from a kid too, huh?"

"It's not like that. Solomon loved me and cared for me. I had no memory of all the training, and when I turned eighteen, he offered me the choice. I took it without a second thought. I wanted to do something that mattered, something that would change the world. I was just a castaway, a nothing, and now I am somebody. I save people from murderers, rapists, and worse. What more is there?"

"Does it ever bother you? I mean the killing. It's not easy to kill another human being, even if it's for a good reason."

"Yes, it bothers me. I live with the faces of the ones I've killed in my dreams every night. But if that's the price I must pay to save the innocent, then I gladly pay it."

Kirk wondered if he could be as strong as this little girl who seemed to have the heart of a lion. He'd always thought of himself as a tough guy, never scared of a fight, but to know and live with the ghosts of the men you have killed was a different story. Kirk had killed and would kill again, but he only did so if he had no other option. He had never gone out to kill as a mission of justice.

The cab driver said something, and the conversation ended. They were out in the middle of nowhere with grassy hills on all sides and the smell of ocean air wafting from the south. Kirk looked at his watch and couldn't believe how the time slipped by. They were parked behind Mark's car, and up ahead, a lone beach house stood like a sleeping giant, just waiting for someone to dare wake it from its slumber.

CHAPTER TWENTY-FOUR

I FELT A SHARP pain in my shoulder when i tried to move. The jolt sent me back to the ground like a sack of cement. My eyes were swollen shut, but I managed to open them just in time to see Emily punch me in the face again. I didn't feel anything when she hit me, but I figured it was from the mixed signals my brain was getting from every other part of my body that screamed out in agony.

"Not so tough now, are you! Mark, open your eyes and look at me. *Look at me!*" Emily was quivering with rage as she stood over me with a three-foot long metal pipe in her hand. I tried to speak, but couldn't get anything out other than a gurgling sound. I looked at my hand and saw that I was strapped to the same table Solomon had been strapped to just a few hours earlier. Solomon! I suddenly remembered him and his bloody body. It hurt to think of my friend, and the father he was to me, as being dead.

Emily busied herself with a handful of sharp instruments that she placed, side by side, on a wooden table. They looked like ice picks and scalpels mixed with other torturing devices that I was sure I would soon get to try out. *Think, Mark, you've got to keep your brain working!*

It was just then that I noticed a dark figure standing in the doorway, motionless and powerful. Emily looked up from her work, and a huge smile spread across her face. "Taras!" She jumped like a kid on Christmas who'd seen what Santa had just brought her.

My heart sank when I heard the name. It had to be a mistake, some other guy named Taras. But, deep inside, I knew. Taras Karjanski stepped into the room and took off his ball cap.

"Sis! It has been too long." He stepped into the room and hugged his sister.

Sister?

"Oh, where are my manners? Taras, I want you to meet someone!" Emily was acting like she just won the lottery. Her mood gave me a little hope. "This is the pig that killed my husband! Mark Appleton, I want you to meet the Red Dog."

Taras looked down at me, and I stared back into his dark eyes. He was quite good looking, in a dangerous sort of way, and he seemed pleased to see me. "My sister has told me a lot about you. I am pleased to meet you."

My memory flashed like a movie screen as the pieces came together. Emily ranted and paced the room as Taras looked on, taking some sort of sadistic pleasure in seeing his sister so upset.

"You!" Emily pointed a long finger at me and her anger boiled once more. "You killed John. He was at the cabin the day it exploded, and you did it!"

I thought back to how this all started. I'd had my first dream, my glimpse, and then I woke up to find that I still had a family, they didn't die in a bombing, and then I knew where the evil men were and what they planned on doing. I could stop them. I could save all those people's lives.

"My brother could have been killed too, but he was running late and he saw you leaving the cabin, he saw the whole thing. You just walked away as if it was no big deal." Her lower lip was quivering now, and Taras grinned at me with something hidden in his eyes that I could not explain.

"I guess being late has its advantages, but I still got to kill that sniveling little brat who ratted us out. Pat Rotter was a worthless worm anyway; I shot him in the back of the head where you had him tied up like a criminal."

Emily took a sharp hook from off the wooden table and held it up for me to see. "You killed my husband, and after years of searching and waiting, I will kill you! But your death will not be quick as was my husband's. I want to see you die a thousand deaths and make you suffer as I have suffered."

I could remember the cabin and the three men. I wondered which one was John. In my glimpse, there had been four men. After the explosion, I assumed the missing man was Tripp Maddock/Geoff Martin. But the fourth man was the ringleader, Taras Karjanski. He had helped track me down, and now his sister was going to kill me!

"You know the best part, Mark? You were just a bonus. I had all but given up on ever finding you. I was going about my business when my brother told me he had found you. And then, when he said that you were with the World Justice Agency, I just had to laugh. You never had a chance. And now you will pay for what you've done!"

Emily turned the sharp instrument in her hand. It gleamed as it caught some light from the single bulb hanging from the ceiling. It looked like a dentist's cleaning hook, but much bigger. Emily stepped forward and stuck the hook end into my abdomen. I felt it pierce my stomach and a wave of pain washed over my body like hot lava. The last thing I saw was Emily's face as she smiled and twisted the sharp hook deep inside of my body.

A shot pierced the room.

I didn't even feel the bullet go in, but I felt my life slip away as I died.

* * *

TARAS LOOKED AT HIS sister, remembering when her name was Natasha Karjanski. She looked different now, after a little plastic surgery and implants. He almost did not recognize her, but when he looked into her eyes, he knew it was his little sis.

Mark Appleton didn't look like much, Natasha had worked

him over pretty good. He could smell blood as it dripped from Mark's body and filled the room with that familiar, iron metallic smell. Taras closed his eyes for a moment to savor the sweet smell. His sister was rambling on and on about her husband and blah, blah, blah. *Why won't she just shut up and kill him already?*

He watched as Natasha dug the sharp tool into Mark's abdomen, and he could see the color wash out of Mark's face. He was going to pass out any second, and Taras wanted him to see what happened next. With a slow deliberate movement, Taras drew the handgun from its holster and pointed it at his sister. The look on her face was worth every agonizing second he had been forced to experience with her. The shot rang out and made her jump as the bullet crushed her ribcage. Taras smiled and looked at her as she sank to the floor. She looked up at him with a confusion, and the only word she got out was, "Why?" She gurgled as blood bubbled from her mouth.

"I don't need you anymore. I guess I'll have to finish him off for you. You don't mind, do you?" He had to laugh at his sister's demise. She had waited so long to have her revenge, and just when she had it in her grasp, she failed! "You should have never taken off your vest. You never know what will happen, or who you can trust."

Looking at Mark, Taras saw he was out cold. His breathing was slowing, and with the blood loss, he didn't think he would make it even if there were a doctor nearby. *Stupid female! Don't you know how to torture someone? You have to keep them alive!*

He turned back to his sister who had drug herself over to the table where her gun lay. The Red Dog grabbed her by the hair and yanked her head back, shoving the gun hard against her neck. He pulled the trigger, sending blood splattering all over his pants and the wall. He smeared his finger in the blood that dripped from his leg and brought it to his nose. It smelled so good, it made him want to drink her blood like a vampire.

Releasing his grip on his sister's hair, he let her body

drop to the floor. Then, he untied Mark and slung him over his shoulder. He would bury him and save the next person the trouble. He would bury them all. It was the only kind thing to do. After all, he was a kind man, even sweet in his own way. Some would say that he was honorable! So, he buried Mark Appleton alive, and then threw Solomon and Natasha in a second pine box to spend eternity together. "If you can't work out your differences in that amount of time, then I'm afraid you'll never get them resolved!"

With that, Taras Karjanski left the way he had come, walked through the living room of his clean white beach house, and made himself a glass of wine.

He did love a good wine.

* * *

THE WORLD WATCHED TO see what would happen as they fell under the spell of fear cast on them by a single terrorist. Taras Karjanski was still unknown and walked where he wanted and did as he pleased, unencumbered.

The president of the United States called a press conference to address the people and try to calm their fears before the inevitable.

The small room was packed with reporters and photographers taking pictures and yelling out for an answer to their questions. The president walked out to a barrage of flashes and questions. He looked in control and sure of himself, even though he felt quite the opposite. The press secretary held up her hand and calmed the crowd. The leader of the free world was about to make history.

"Ladies and gentlemen of this great country. I stand here before you enraged and humbled by the events of the past few months. This country has survived wars, floods, and natural disasters that would put most people in the ground. We now have an enemy that is a ghost and a coward. He hides behind letters and threats in order to control us by fear. But we will not be scared. We will not be driven from our way of life because someone doesn't like it. No, we will fight, and we will win!"

The crowd cheered in a burst of energy as they felt the rush of hope surge from their leader. Holding up his hand for silence, he continued.

"This goes out to the people who are calling in and voting on who will suffer and who will not. Stop playing their game, stop giving them what they want: control. I urge you America, give him silence. Give him your answer by living, and living well. We are Americans, and we will not negotiate with terrorists."

Turning from the reporters, he left the stage without answering any questions. Nevertheless, one made it through the noise to his ears and haunted him later as he collapsed in his overstuffed chair in the Oval Office. *"Who is behind the letters? Who is Chaos?"* He rubbed his chin and cursed under his breath. He had no idea who Chaos was, and he was not the only one.

"Jill, get me the FBI and the CIA. I want them in my office in one hour. You know the drill, Defense Secretary, Chief of Staff. I want them all here. One hour!"

Slamming the phone down, he sat back and turned to look out the window overlooking Washington DC. It was a beautiful day, with the sun high in the sky, making the shadows flee for cover. He had a knot in the pit of his stomach and a sick feeling that things were about to get a whole lot worse.

* * *

KIRK WAITED IN THE dark as a soft breeze sent the bitter smell of salt through the air. Isis was next to him with binoculars, scanning the house and the rolling hills that surrounded it. He had to keep his mind on the task at hand, but it was hard when all he wanted to do was look at Isis.

"Looks vacant. I'm getting some readings of a heat source coming from behind the house, though. Could be a car. Let's go check it out."

Kirk pushed off the safety on his .45 and held it low as they moved silently through the tall grass. Isis carried a weapon she had helped create in the lab. It was a sonar gun that acted like a shotgun, but with sonar waves. It sent out a pulse without making any sound, and anything in front of it would feel the waves pulse through their body. In a few seconds it would literally crush them from the inside out. It was only designed for close range combat, and would cause permanent hearing loss for anyone on the receiving end, if they lived through the experience.

Kirk preferred his old-school Colt .45.

The house was dark, and as they worked their way around to the back, Kirk could see fresh tire tracks in the dirt road leading around the house. Isis cleared the house with her scope using the infrared option. Anyone inside couldn't hide unless they happened to have a lead-lined room. The Sonar gun also could penetrate through doors, walls and most anything without too much trouble. A yellow Lamborghini sat quietly next to the house as Kirk rounded the corner.

Kirk signaled to Isis and they walked around it, looking for any signs of life. Taras must have gone underground or somewhere other than the house, because there was no sign of him anywhere. Kirk had a dark feeling in the pit of his stomach. Something wasn't right. The house stood empty and stared back at them with an evil presence. Kirk looked over his shoulder with worry.

With a flip of her wrist, Isis motioned for Kirk to follow her inside. They would clear the house, and then call for backup to seal off the area. If Mark or Solomon were in the area, they would find them. As for the Red Dog, he was on a short leash, and the dogcatcher was coming.

* * *

CARSON LOOKED OVER HIS file, which had grown to cover just about everything anyone would want to know about the woman who was called Chaos. Emily Dobson was a busy girl. She had two hundred million dollars in one offshore account alone, and he still had six more accounts to go through. He sighed and closed his eyes, replaying the president's address over again in his mind. He was getting impatient with

Detective Weston, and with the director breathing down his neck. He could only give Weston one more day to come up with something new.

"Come on, Kirk. You're killing me here!" Picking up the phone, he dialed, and just as he suspected, went right to voicemail. "Kirk, give me a call. I can't hold out much longer. It is getting crazy out there, call me."

Fine time to be on vacation.

The fresh information on Emily Dobson had come through his Hotmail account from Kirk's email address. Kirk was doing a good job gathering new leads, but still nothing to tell them where she was, or even what she looked like. The only photo was from the mall security cameras, and they showed a hooded person from the rear. Not much to go on, and with the votes coming in, in record numbers, the entire country was waiting to see what was going to happen.

Just when Carson was about to give up, he heard his computer beep, and the "New Mail" notice popped up on the screen. He looked at the address and didn't recognize the sender. When he opened it, a photo came into view. It was a dark-haired man in a Russian military uniform. The heading under the picture said.

General Taras Karjanski, aka The Red Dog, aka The General.

The next photo was of a woman with long, dark hair and a sweet smile that made Carson half-grin. He thought this might be some kind of joke, or maybe his buddies were sending him a funny picture. Once he got one of a fat, ugly chick blowing him a kiss and the heading under it that said, "Mrs. Carson."

The name under the photo made his heart stop for one or two beats.

Natasha Karjanski, aka Emily Dobson, aka Chaos.

The pages of information that followed made him just about lose his dinner, from pictures of slaughtered livestock to the latest killing spree in New York just a few days ago. The bodies and the extensive brutality was not human. Carson scanned through them, and stamped at the bottom of the last page, he saw a symbol with the letters, "WJA" . *The WJA is helping the FBI?* He sat down and shook his head. Kirk must have gotten through to someone. The printer fired up, and in a few minutes Carson would have everything he needed to present it to director Jacobson. It was time to stop the Chaos!

CHAPTER TWENTY-FIVE

THE HOUSE SMELLED LIKE mothballs and old wood as Kirk and Isis cleared each room from top to bottom. Taras Karjanski was nowhere to be found and neither was Mark or Solomon. Kirk cursed and looked out the window from the master bedroom. on the third floor A note was taped to the glass, the red letters still wet from the blood used to write it.

They're all dead.

Isis read the note and a washed-out look crossed her face. "He knew we were watching him. How could he have known?"

"I don't know. We have to get this guy, and I mean quick. He's killing in front of everyone, and gets away. Now, Mark and Solomon are missing. We have to find them."

"Jamison said they lost him on the scanner. They think he went underground. That would be the only reason they would lose him. There has to be a tunnel or a cave around here. I had Jamison patch Mark's last known location to our GPS devices."

Kirk looked at his watch and saw the red dot blink on. "Let's go," Isis said. "Looks like it's a few hundred yards south of here. You up for a jog?"

"Always." Kirk couldn't shake the sinking feeling that they were not going to find Mark or Solomon. At least not alive.

They took the stairs that wound around the back of the house and ended up in the kitchen. The house was empty, but

Kirk still had a feeling that someone was watching them. It felt like the house was alive—it could see them as they walked through its chambers. The yellow Lamborghini still sat out back and mocked them with its presence. The owner was still out there somewhere…or maybe that's just what he wanted them to think. Stepping out into the knee-high grass, they started to jog toward the direction indicated on their GPS.

The hill came to a high point and then fell away into a small valley that was sheltered from the road and anything else that might be close by. Isis looked at her watch and pointed ahead. They spread out and combed the area, looking for anything unusual. Isis pawed through some brush and called out. "I think I found something."

Kirk rushed over and saw an old, wooden, cellar door half-buried in the dirt. He looked around, grabbed the rusted handle, and pulled. The door moaned, but opened with a loud creaking sound. Isis had her weapon out and soon Kirk did the same. Emily and Taras could be lurking in the shadows somewhere, and they would not hesitate to shoot them if they had the chance. The note said they were all dead, but they were not taking any chances.

Before they entered the dark tunnel, Kirk noticed something on the ground. Leaning down, he touched dirt that looked like it had some sort of shiny Jell-O splashed around it. Kirk lifted his finger to his nose and smelled the stench of iron and earth.

It was blood.

* * *

TARAS SAT IN A black, overstuffed chair and watched his sister's monitors as Kirk and a pretty, dark-skinned woman searched the house. They'd combed the house for him and now were outside. He had to smile at the detective who seemed to make it out alive from just about any situation. He recognized the woman from the airport and saw that he had been under surveillance for a while now. "Shelly, I still owe you dinner and a drink." He felt his heart race when he saw her and knew that he loved her.

He took another sip of wine and smelled the deep almond scent as it filled his pallet before he swallowed. He was right under their feet, and he thanked his sister for building the underground room with the walls and ceiling lined with lead and copper. *Not bad, sis. Too bad you're dead!*

The pair had found his note and soon left to search for their friends in the underground caves. He thought of the graves he had dug months before in preparation for this day. He had only dug two, one for Mark, and one for his sister, but sometimes you get lucky. The graves were in the middle of the first main cave, right off from where the main house was. Taras watched as Kirk led the young female into the dark and walked right over the top of where his friend was buried. It was sweet to see them scan the area and search. But they wouldn't find anything.

Getting up, he slipped through the kitchen and poured himself another glass of wine for the road. His Lamborghini waited for him, and he wanted to be relaxed for the show he was sure to see on TV tonight.

Taras walked onto the back porch that looked out over the ocean. It was beautiful, and with the day he'd had, it was the perfect end. He felt good, now that his urge had been fed. It was a sweet release that ran from his head down to his toes. Killing—there was nothing like it!

As he fired up the engine, he flipped open his cell phone and sent a text message. It read, "Go, Code: Dreamcatcher."

Looking at his watch, he waited for five minutes. As he crested the hill, he saw the city lights come into view, and a plume of smoke in the shape of a mushroom cloud rose from the earth with a red glow filling its underbelly.

The first school was a surprise even for him. He never thought that the American people would love their pocketbooks more than their children. But the calls into the hotline came back with 84% in favor of bombing a school. Their pride and arrogance was overwhelming. Maybe he would learn to love them after all. They thought like he did. *You can always make more kids, but oil is a scarce resource!*

* * *

A SINGLE, DARK HOODED man slipped onto the school grounds without much notice. The bomb he carried was the size of a cigarette lighter. He found the boiler room and strapped it to the main gas line that fed the entire school premises.

Harry S. Truman High School was bigger than he had thought at first. He had carried the keys on his Snoopy keychain and walked in like he owned the place. The chemical that he now carried would mix with the air, and a single drop would destroy anything within a hundred yards.

After setting everything up, he walked to the street where he grabbed a cab and headed away from the school. He knew The General could call at any moment, and he didn't want to be a victim of his own bomb. The city lights bounced off the side of the cab and back toward the neon city signs. It looked like a movie set with the roads wet from a short shower and the smell of fresh mountain air, even this far in the city. After ten minutes, he had the driver pull over and let him out.

He was a short man in his late twenties with a dark, braided goatee. Taras was not only his boss but also The Boss. His name was enough for the hooded man to cower in fear.

The bar had a soft glow from a half broken sign that used to say Gabe's, but only the *G* and the *a* remained lit. Pushing open the door, he found a place at the bar and sat down. He was known around this part of town, and the bartender slid a cold mug of moose drool in front of him.

"Thanks." He didn't feel like talking tonight. The city was on edge. The bombings that were soon to come was in the back of everyone's mind. Somehow, they just knew there was no way to avoid the chaos.

His cell rumbled in his pocket and his heart jumped at the same time. Looking at the number, he opened it up and read the text message. Reaching his hand into his coat pocket, he felt the cold metal of the remote detonator with his fingertips. *Time to pay for your sins.*

He mashed down on the device, sending an electronic signal through the air and over miles of buildings and radio waves. It found its target and ignited the small bomb. It sent a popping sound followed by a ripping shrill shriek through the night air. The world was about to change. The hooded man smiled and took a long drink of his beer. In five or six minutes, he could have all the beer he wanted. The bar would be cleared out as people ran from their homes and from the clubs to see what no one ever thought was possible.

Time to pay. The Red Dog had just released the hounds.

* * *

CARSON RAN FROM HIS office just in time to see the news come on the flat screen TVs that were placed everywhere throughout the FBI building. He knew what it was going to say when he saw the smoke rising from the New York skyline. Director Jacobson was coming from his office with three top agents in tow. Carson almost collided with them, and the director looked mad.

"Carson, what do you want? We've got an emergency on our hands!" He pushed up his thick glasses.

"I have new information. The WJA didn't do it. They aren't Chaos!"

"What are you talking about?" He pushed past Carson and headed for the elevator. "We've been called to an emergency meeting with the president. We don't have time for your theories!"

Carson slid past the closing elevator door and opened the file on the Karjanskis. "Sir, this is the person called Chaos. Her name is Emily Dobson. She is involved in the Russian Mafia."

"Mafia, what Mafia? The Russians can hardly blow their noses, let alone blow up a building. They were disbanded years ago."

"Just look at the file, please." Carson handed the thick file to Director Jacobson, and he thumbed through it. His eyes grew larger when he saw the photo of Taras Karjanski. "Oh, my goodness!"

"You know him, sir?" Carson didn't like the reaction from his boss. Not much got him worried, much less shocked.

"This is General Karjanski. He has been underground for years. We all believed he was killed in a bombing a few years back. He is ruthless and has the power to pull something like this off. Carson, where did you get this information?"

Carson pulled on his collar and turned to look away from Jacobson. "I can't say—it's an old friend of mine. I swore I wouldn't say, sir. But it's legit, I promise you."

Jacobson didn't like the answer but brushed it aside. "You're coming with us to meet the president. Tell him everything you know about this. You got that?"

"Yes, sir." Carson felt a lump the size of a potato fill his throat. He had never met the president, much less had a meeting with him. He adjusted his tie and tried to look like he wasn't scared out of his mind. *You had better be right, Kirk Weston, or my name will go down in history, and not for a good reason!*

CHAPTER TWENTY-SIX

KIRK MUTTERED UNDER HIS breath. He hated small, confined spaces, and right now, he was on his knees crawling through a tunnel that was getting smaller by the minute. They had been through two large rooms that led nowhere, and they'd been going through this tunnel for at least an hour. Isis called from somewhere up ahead. "I think I found the exit!"

The cave gave off a breath of fresh air as they emerged from underneath the ground. They had gone a few miles, and from the looks of it, they were farther inland and no closer to finding Mark or Solomon.

"See the bent grass. It looks like drag marks of some kind." Kirk said. The small trail of bent grass led them fifty yards west, where there were signs of a struggle. The second entrance had a few spent casings on the ground, and blood splattered on the dirt and rocks. Isis bent down and took a sample of the blood with her DNAX device, which would search the DNA against all government and WJA listings in a matter of seconds.

"It's Solomon!" Isis took a few more samples but couldn't find anything besides his blood, some fibers from his shirt, and some hair that turned out to be Solomon's, as well.

Kirk felt a sick feeling wash over him as he entered a cave that led downward to an old wooden door. He pulled on his glasses, scanned through the door, and saw that the room was empty. The door was half-open, and as he entered, he could smell the stench of dried blood and sweat.

The room was wrecked. One table was on its side, and sharp instruments were scattered all over the floor. A cold, metal table stood in the center of the room with blood-soaked straps for a victim's legs and arms. The table was red with blood. It looked like there had been a slaughter..

Isis took samples and found traces of Mark's DNA, as well as Solomon's. A third set was from Emily Dobson. *Taras must have killed her. Or maybe Mark put up a fight and wounded her*. No bodies or evidence of a body were anywhere to be found. After searching the room for over an hour, they called for a cleanup crew. The WJA would go over everything with a fine-toothed comb and clean the area, leaving no trace that anyone had ever been there.

Kirk sat in the tall grass and looked out over the rolling hills. He had lost the Red Dog once again. This game was beginning to get old. Isis sat down next to him and took his hand in hers. She looked up at him with her beautiful dark eyes and smiled. "We'll get him, we always do."

Kirk leaned down, kissed her on the forehead, then looked off in the distance. His cell phone vibrated, and seconds later Isis's phone was chirping as well. They looked at each other and checked the text message.

School bombed. Report back to base A.S.A.P.

* * *

WITH THE THREAT OF oil refineries going up in smoke, gas prices doubled over night. Security and private militia groups were hired and sent to scour each refinery to help protect them from a bomb or something worse. The military in each country that housed oil refineries sent out units armed with bomb sniffing dogs, and the massive hunt began.

OPEC put a lock on any oil being sent out, in case there was an emergency. They wanted to have enough in reserve to keep up with the demand. There were long lines at every gas station. Gas was now the most valuable substance on earth.

Taras landed in his G5 with a smile. He was having even more of an effect on the American economy then he could have imagined. He nodded to Abe and climbed into a waiting chopper. He took off to see the progress on his newly acquired refineries.

Equatorial Guinea was the same as he had left it, but it grew hotter with each passing week. After a dusty landing, and a wet rag placed over his face so he could breathe, he made his way to the main entrance. The brand new door looked nice, and the smell of fresh paint made Taras grin in satisfaction. He opened the door to meet the new supervisor, one of his own men from the old country.

"General, it is an honor to see you again." The tall blond man had a name, but Taras didn't remember it. He cared less for this man than he did for the choking dust that seemed to cover everything.

"Is everything in order?"

"Yes, sir."

"Good, I will inspect your work. You may wait for my report." Taras turned, followed Abe down the stairs, and sat in the waiting Jeep. The tour took over an hour. Nevertheless, it was worth it. The buildings and project were impressive by anyone's standards. He saw that everything was polished and painted, making the place shine. You could eat off the floor if you wanted to.

"What do you think, Abe?" Taras lit a fat cigar and took a long drag.

"Looks nice. You won't find a more beautiful operation on this planet."

"Well said. And true, my old friend."

The ride back to the top was quiet as Taras thought of the next stage in his master plan. He knew it would hurt him, but in the end, he would rise to the occasion and stomp the world under his feet.

The scared supervisor wiped sweat from his face and paced the room as he waited for the verdict. Taras enjoyed his torment, so he sat smoking his cigar without saying a word. Ten minutes went by, and then the Red Dog spoke in Russian,.

"Good, you may tell your family you did well." Taras blew a ring of smoke that drifted toward the scared Russian.

"Thank you, sir. Thank you!" The man bowed and watched as Taras walked out the door. The chopper took off and disappeared from view, making the supervisor sigh in relief.

Twenty minutes later, a single MQ1 Predator, armed with two laser-guided Hellfire antitank missiles with nuclear warheads, silently slipped through the air. The missiles engaged and dove toward the refinery with earth-shattering speed.

The Russian sat down in his high-backed chair and took a sip of his black coffee just in time to feel the reverberation of the molten fireball as it crashed through the refinery's office. The blast could be felt over one hundred miles away, and, to the tiny town nearby, it felt like a small earthquake. The next stage had begun. Operation Dreamcatcher was now underway.

* * *

THE GRAY, STREAKED HAIR of the president of the United States was disheveled, and he looked tired, with dark circles under his eyes. The news media and the country was in a panic, as, one after another, oil refineries and oil fields were blown off the face of the map.

The Joint Chief of Staff, Conner Wells, sat silently with the rest of the Cabinet and the FBI and CIA. The oval office was packed, yet the room was so quiet, you could hear the clock ticking on the wall. Tick, tick…it was a reminder of the precious time that was being wasted as they tried to gather information on The General, whose existence had just been revealed to the president.

"Gentlemen, ladies. I need something, anything! How do we stop this Dog—this, what does he call himself?"

"Red Dog, Sir." Carson was standing with his hands shoved in his pockets staring at the president. He was so nervous that he could feel his sweat running down his back and down his legs.

"Yes, Red Dog, whatever. I need more than who he is from an unknown source. Agent Carson, you know this source?"

"Yes, sir."

"So tell me, what do you suggest?" The president paced the floor between his desk and the rest of the group.

Carson wiped the sweat from his forehead with the back of his hand and looked at Captain Jacobson for some kind of support. His blank stare was confirmation that he was on his own with this one. The fate of America and maybe the rest of the world rested in what Carson had locked inside his head.

"Sir, have you ever heard of the World Justice Agency?"

Jacobson perked up and started to interject. Carson didn't give him the time to butt in. "It is an elite group of, shall we say, vigilantes, who are so well-funded and organized that we don't know who their leaders are or even where their headquarters are located. We have set up a special task force just for them, and in the last few years, even with all the information we have on them, we are no closer to finding them then when we first started."

"Go on."

After this little speech, he was sure he would be fired, if not sent to prison for revealing top-secret information to a room full of people who were not in the loop. The FBI had a way of taking their jobs a little too seriously.

"May I?" He walked over to the computer screen that hung on the wall, accessed the controls that slid from the control panel, and begun typing. He pulled up his personal computer remotely and opened up the file marked *Top Secret*.

"They are linked with hundreds, if not thousands, of hits. Murders of prominent villains. Al Capone, Hitler, Saddam Hussein, who, by the way was assassinated on the convoy that was transferring him to his trial. The rest was an elaborate hoax by the FBI to keep up appearances."

Whispers crossed the room as Carson ran through countless files and cases involving assassinations. "One thing is common through all of this. The symbol WJA is stamped or found at every site, connected with every case. If we won't punish the crime, then they will, down to the smallest cases like this one involving a small girl who was kidnapped and later killed. We never caught the killer, but a year later, a man turned up dead in a hotel room with a note pinned to his chest confessing to the crime. It was later confirmed that he was the killer."

Carson turned and suddenly was worried that he had said too much. They were sure to think he had lost his marbles.

"This is all very interesting, but what does this have to do with our current problem?" The president was now sitting in his high-back brown leather chair.

"We first believed that the WJA was involved in the Chaos notes, but I believe they're on our side. They're the ones who have given me this information on Taras Karjanski. They're the only ones who can stop him. We need to get them to help us."

Captain Jacobson jumped up and protested. "Now, hold on a minute! This is all circumstantial. We don't know whose side they are on, or that they didn't fabricate this whole thing to lead us on a wild goose chase!" The captain was red in the face, and Carson wondered where he'd be applying for his next job.

The room erupted with arguments and conjecture. Finally, the president held up his hand and called the meeting to order. "Okay, I can see that this is a touchy subject. I believe that, with the evidence before me, we don't have much of a choice here. We need to ask this WJA group for help. Through the papers or news media, I don't care how, just get it done. If they wanted to destroy America, they would have done it by now. Make it happen, people."

The meeting was dismissed, but Carson and Captain Jacobson were asked to stay behind. "Mr. President, I feel this is a mistake."

"Captain Jacobson, I hear your concerns, but I think this is the best course for the country. I need you on board with me on this, you understand?" The captain stood stiffly and nodded. He didn't like it when he felt pushed in a corner, but it was that or step down and do nothing.

"Agent Carson. You get to your contact and do whatever is necessary to get a meeting with this group. I want someone from the World Justice Agency in front of my desk by the end of business tomorrow. Got it?"

* * *

A MEETING OF EQUAL proportions was going on at the Merc Building down in the deepest parts of the WJA headquarters. Every agent and field operative was in attendance, and Big B was leading the charge. They had one case and one case alone.

Find and stop Taras Karjanski.

Isis couldn't help but feel a little guilty to have lost him at the Karjanski house. Not only was Solomon missing, but Mark was, too. It couldn't have happened at a worse time. *Mark, we need you! Where are you?*

The dark feeling on the minds of everyone around the World Justice Agency was that, in the biggest crisis of their existence, they had lost their leader. They didn't even know if he was alive. The jokes around the water cooler had stopped, and the energy that usually filled the halls of the Merc building had slipped away, leaving a hole in everyone's heart. Solomon, their leader, was feared to be dead, and the country they loved was being terrorized by a madman.

CHAPTER TWENTY-SEVEN

I SUCKED IN A breath of air and gasped for another. The dusty, stale air was thick with the smell of blood and body odor. I couldn't tell if my eyes were open or closed until I reached up and felt them. The dreams kept coming as I watched the world I loved go up in smoke, and a depression brought on by a bankrupt economy and the total cut-off of foreign oil ravaged my country. The bombs took out not only the oil across Africa, but ripped through Asia and Russia as well. The dead refineries in the Middle East couldn't be jumpstarted fast enough to keep up with the panic and fear that had set in. America was in an uncontrolled downward spiral.

The same dream plagued my mind as I lay in the dark, day after day. I tried everything to escape, but with each passing day, the air was getting harder and harder to breathe. My own stench soon was unnoticeable to me. My wounds didn't even hurt anymore. I was trained to block out any pain and keep my mind sharp and in control; however, some things are beyond training.

The time I spent asleep was the time I cherished. It was the only time I could see K and Sam. They came alive in my dreams. I could smell K's sweet perfume as it wafted across the room from her perfect shoulders. Sam would giggle and jump into my lap, demanding a story. She butchered the words, but nothing made me happier then seeing her.

Surely, I am dying. Why am I not already dead? Can I keep hoping for a miracle? Does anyone know where I am? My mind played tricks on me as I tried to avoid the thin line separating sanity and insanity. The only thing I could do was hide. Therefore, I created a safe place to go, deep within my subconscious. Sometimes, I feared it was the same place you go when you die. Each time I went there, I had to fight and struggle to make it out again. In this place, K, Sam, and I were in a small room, just talking. I talked with them about anything and everything. I would go to this place and for hours at a time shield my mind from the mental hopelessness that was pushing down on me. They kept me sane, alive.

When the mind is at the breaking point, it does weird things. I had no hope of getting out of this alive, and when you have no hope, you give up on everything. But, I had something to live for. If I was alive, then I could dream. I could see my wife and daughter.

Do I want to get back? Why not just give up and die? It would be over, and who knows, I might be able to see them forever. But then I shook off the thought, knowing there were only two places that the dead go. I didn't know which one I was going to—but I had a sneaking suspicion.

* * *

KIRK GRUMBLED AS HE looked at the text message from Agent Carson. He was now wondering if contacting him had been the right thing to do. He sent a text back and set up a meeting at a local coffee shop down the street from the Merc building.

The cleanup crew had combed the Karjanski house and found an underground command center with links to cameras hidden through the house. They found more DNA evidence from Mark, Solomon, and Emily Dobson. No sign of any bodies or anything to help trace to where they might have taken them. Taras was good. Far beyond anyone they had ever come up against before. Kirk had gone up against some killers and crazy people in his day, but Taras Karjanski took the cake.

Isis came into the now empty conference room and sat down across from Kirk. "So, what are you going to tell him?"

Kirk felt his throat tighten. "Tell who?"

"Come on, Detective Weston, you really think we would let you in here unsupervised and free to tell the world our secrets? Agent Carson, your old friend, at your meeting in half an hour."

"I can explain." Kirk said.

"No need. Just remember, we aren't the bad guys." Isis stood up and walked from the room.

Kirk breathed in deeply and closed his eyes. He should have known better. *Stupid!* Getting up, he walked down the long hallway and took the elevator to the parking garage. He was met by Isis at the top. She reached out and grabbed his hand. "Come on. I would like to meet your friend, Mr. Carson."

Kirk smiled and pulled her close and looked into her eyes. They seemed to sparkle as she looked up at him. "You are such a wonderful person, Isis Kanika." She beamed and kissed him on the cheek.

"You're not too bad yourself, detective!"

"Shall we walk?" Kirk said.

"Sounds good."

Kirk felt his heart skip a beat as Isis pulled him along. He didn't even want to think about what he was feeling for fear he would mess it up. *What am I, a teenager?* He felt as if he were floating on a cloud. All he wanted was to be by her side.

The day was bright and busy as people hurried from shop to shop, stocking up on flashlights, batteries, and food. The usual small talk gave way to frightened glances and lowered heads, as the general mood was that of fear. The sunshine and the birds that dodged through traffic didn't seem to mind, one way or the other. The birds sang and flew just as they did on any other day.

Kirk and Isis made good time, sat down by a window, and sipped their coffee. Isis liked the café lattes, and Kirk preferred his coffee black. They half expected Agent Carson to be followed by a team of FBI agents, but he came alone and sat down at their table. He looked tired and not quite himself, but everyone was pretty much in the same condition.

Kirk started things off with a handshake and a smile. "Hey, this is Isis Kanika. She is part of the WJA. She wanted to meet you and see if we could help."

Isis shook Carson's hand, and he looked at her in mild shock. "Wow, I never expected to meet someone in person like this. I'm honored. Thank you for coming."

"So, what's on your mind?" Kirk said.

Carson ordered a chai, and, opening his briefcase, pulled out a file. "As you know, we have next to nothing on Taras Karjanski. Most of what we now have, we got through you." He pointed at Isis and waved his hand in a circle in a frustrated motion. He was nervous, and it showed. "We need your help. I have a letter, signed by the president of the United States himself, requesting your aid in the capture of Taras Karjanski and his sister, Natasha Karjanski."

Isis took the letter and read it, then handed it to Kirk to look over. "We are doing everything we can," Kirk said. "But we will do it our way, whether the president wants it that way or not. I can't ensure that they will be captured alive."

"We understand. He would—that is, the president would—like to meet with you as soon as possible. In fact, he was adamant about that."

"Unfortunately, we can't do that. We have too much going on here and we cannot compromise our whole operation." Isis said. "Besides, he doesn't want or need to know who we are or what we do. It's better for him not to know."

"He will be very disappointed to hear that. I'll do my best to smooth it over. Do you have anything new on the case?" Carson took a sip of the hot chai and nodded to the waitress.

"Just that he has two of our own people," Isis said. "And from the blood we found, it would be a surprise if his sister is alive. She was the person who called herself Chaos. We believe he killed her, and now he has taken over, cutting her out of the picture all together."

Kirk leaned in and said, "You focus on sealing off the schools and the rest of the refineries. We will take care of Taras. I don't think he will blow up anything else until he has made contact with you again. He wants the public to fear him, so he'll drag this out as long as he can."

Carson nodded and informed them that the country was on Red Alert. Every school was shut down until further notice, including colleges. They had one week to find Taras or they believed the country would not be able to recover.

Kirk looked through the file Carson handed him and saw they didn't have anything new to report. They talked about their options, but they all knew there was only one option left. The whole meeting took only twenty minutes.

"Good luck, and nice meeting you, Isis." Carson shook her hand and then Kirk's. He was going to have a hard time explaining to the president that he wouldn't be meeting with anyone from the WJA any time soon.

* * *

THE SPICY, RICH, DARK Bartolo Mascarello 1989 Barolo ran down Taras's chin as he drank deeply from the bottle. Equal to its deep, ripe fruit flavor, it held a hidden hint of rose petals and tar. He would have sipped and savored the fine wine but he felt like indulging, and with his upcoming victory, who could blame him?

He watched the city from his balcony as it ran for cover in a wave of confusion. Their little world was being torn apart right before their eyes. And to make it even more brilliant, they chose their own fate! He thought of a very similar case in history where the raving mobs cried out for a rebel, Barabbas, instead of their true king. *His blood be on us and our children! So it shall, so it shall!*

He reclined and pulled his legs off the deck, lifting them to rest on the black, iron railing. He leaned back in his chair and took another drink. He thought about the last piece of his plan and how wonderful it was going to be to take down his most hated enemy. The mafia was his now, and the New York City mob was under his thumb. He could go anywhere, do whatever he wanted, and not fear anything.

The World Justice Agency was hard at work trying to find him and restore balance to the world once again. He looked at the Merc building and snickered. *Come and get me, boys. I'm right here, across the street!* His new apartment was on the top floor with a full view in all directions. The New York City skyline stood all around him, with Central Park to the west. He'd bought the whole floor and had it converted into a fortress. It had been under construction for a year now, and the end results were perfect. Nothing less would be accepted. He had a second apartment set up in a different part of the city to throw off anyone who might be trying to find him. So far, it had worked.

Hidden in the walls were surveillance cameras and automatic lasers that would cut just about anything in half within seconds. It could read his body-heat signature and allow him to walk through, unharmed, in the event the system was set off accidentally. The glass in his office was bullet proof, as well as bombproof. Nothing could get through if he locked it down.

The electronic room was the command center for all the sensors and monitors showing him who was coming toward his building. It also sensed any toxins, including lethal chemicals of any kind. He'd even built separate pillars that ran down the sides of the building to support his floor. The building could be blown right out from under him, and his loft would still stand. All of this wouldn't be necessary after he took care of the WJA once and for all, but he liked to have it anyway. He had created the perfect home in which to relax and be safe from anything the WJA could throw at him.

The note he had written was being read by *The Post* as well as the FBI as he drank the last of the 1989 Barolo. He ran over it again in his mind, and a smile crossed his face.

Dear World,

I want to introduce myself, as we have been drawn closer with each passing day. I am the great General they call the Red Dog. I am giving you one week to give me the justice I require, and, if you refuse, I will destroy every school and agency. After that, I will destroy your last defense: your military. You have one week.

With all my hate,
Chaos

A deadly virus was being shipped from Russia and would arrive in two days. It would be released into the Merc building and passed between each person without anyone knowing they were even infected. After three days, each and every person who came in contact with the virus would start showing signs of an outbreak. Boils would appear on the skin, and the internal organs would start shutting down. The process would be painful, taking another week to kill the host. They would die in wretched agony. Taras had a front row seat, and was waiting patiently to watch the show. Every one of his enemies would die.

He stood and walked back into his new home to look at his beautiful wife as she slept in their king size bed. She was exhausted after her flight from Rome, and after going over her week with him, they held each other until she fell asleep. He saw the slow rise and fall of her chest as she dreamed. He couldn't help daydreaming about killing her. His love could only be expressed in that powerful way. The ultimate sacrifice of giving her up, for their love!

Pulling a curved, thin-bladed knife from the dresser drawer, he stood over her peaceful body. The cold metal caught light from the open window, and he touched the tip on her smooth neck. She turned in her sleep, making a soft sigh as she rolled on her back, exposing her neck to her husband. The Red Dog's heart skipped a beat as he breathed heavier and raised the knife over his head, imagining the blade plunging deep into her neck and seeing the blood flood the pearl sheets in a magnificent display. In one quick movement, he swung the blade down and stopped a millimeter from her perfect skin.

Sweat poured from his face, and he was almost out of breath from the dramatic experience. He turned away from her, put the knife away, and looked at a picture on the dresser. His wife and their daughter swinging on a rope swing over a crisp blue lake. They looked so happy and so in love with each other. Taras could not have that, she was his—all his! The child was gone now, he comforted himself, and he pondered as he walked back out onto the balcony. One day they would have more children. He would only let a son live, to teach and carry on the wonderful right of being God!

Chapter Twenty-Eight

A DEEP, PULSING UNDERTONE vibrated the ground making small stones rattle like Mexican jumping beans. The sound was so low that it couldn't be heard—but it was felt. Thump, thump, thump!

I awoke with a start and instinctively tried to sit up but smacked my head on the top of the coffin. My head was throbbing with each heartbeat, and I could feel my body crying out in pain. The sound made my blood boil, thundering in a quiet, base tone deep within my chest.

I caught my breath and clutched my throat as the small bit of air left in my resting place exited my lungs. My lungs burned, and I could feel my whole body quiver as I gasped for air. None came.

I was out of air!

Thump, thump! I felt like knives were stabbing through my skull and deep into my brain. Each heartbeat made it worse as every cell and nerve ending exploded in a hot fire of signals. My dying mind struggled for life.

Thump.

The sound got louder with each gasp, and soon, I would be dead. My life didn't flash before my eyes like I'd always imagined it would. Just the sweet feel of K's lips and a giggle that filled my ears, as if Sam were here with me. I felt a strong wave of something wash over me, making the pain even hotter. I screamed out and cried as the invisible shock wave shot from my fingers and rushed from my chest.

What is happening to me? Just let me die. I can't take it anymore, please, God, please!

I didn't expect the answer to come, but it did, with my last heartbeat. Thump…thump…slower now... I felt it stop, like a train as it slowed on the tracks and rolled its large wheels one more time before coming to a complete stop. I could see something in the dark, a tiny, blue, glowing light hanging at my side. Moving my hand, I watched the flicker of the light as it fell from my fingers like mist or dry ice.

Thump.

I wasn't breathing, and even though I tried, no air would come. The vibrating was coming from my chest, and it made the light jump in the dark as if it were trying to get out of me. The next sound was not a sound at all, but a feeling. I was surprised I could still feel anything. White-hot pain blazed through my chest and shot through my arms and into my head as if I had just grabbed a live electrical wire in the rain.

K, all I could do was think about K. The pounding came faster, and my body convulsed with each shockwave. I could see the top of the coffin in the light that was now getting brighter and saw the wood start to splinter with the force. My brain could not comprehend what was going on, it just kept coming like a pounding barrage of fireworks shooting off for the grand finale. *This is it! My last stand, and I am going to die alone!*

Boom, boom. The force slammed my body around like a rag doll pushing me against the bottom of the casket. Then, in one last burst of force, an earth-shattering subsonic boom erupted, sending a bolt of light shooting from my body, crushing my chest.

Then, like the fading memory, I knew. I saw the darkness—I felt my death.

* * *

TRAVIS FOUST CRAWLED THROUGH the small cave entrance as he had many times before. He loved spelunking, and the old abandoned tunnels were a special delight. He grew up in the deep south with racial profiling and sneers at school every day, just because he happened to have different colored skin. He liked living in the city because of all the different people who found their home in New York. No judging, no sideways glances, just a melting pot of every race and color, and no one seemed to care one way or the other.

He'd found out about the underground caves a few years back and looked up their origins on the web. Once he discovered that they had been used to hide and transport slaves back in the Civil War era, he had to see them for himself. He was overjoyed to find the entrance and had made many visits in the last year.

Coming into the main room, he sat down to eat his lunch, a tuna and cheese sandwich. He set up a battery powered light and turned off his headlamp. The old, cracked brick on the south-facing wall still showed signs of its previous glory. Doors that went nowhere and dead-end exits could get the unsupervised high school kid lost, so Travis had closed them off, just in case.

Mid bite, he felt something shake under him like a mini earthquake, but dismissed it with a sip of Mountain Dew.

Thump.

This time he looked up and set down his drink as the sound vibrated through the very ground he was sitting on. It sounded, or rather felt, like a heartbeat, but it definitely wasn't.

"What the heck is that?" *Earthquake?* No, too small.

He looked at the ground and saw the fine, sandy ground move like a thousand tiny fire ants, the single grains of sand jumping with each throb from the earth. *It is an earthquake!*

Travis's first thought were the thousands of pounds of dirt that made up the roof of the cave, and, more specifically, the fact that he was right under those tons. Grabbing his backpack, he ran for the small opening that was the only exit. Just seconds before he reached it, a volley of dirt fell and collapsed the exit. He choked in the dust cloud. Looking around, he began to panic as the sound grew louder and he could feel the vibrations run up his legs. In the center of the large room, he could see a dip in the dirt as a hole started to open.

Boom, boom, boom.

Climbing into a doorway, with the plywood he had set up blocking the only place offering any semblance of safety, he cursed the fact that he had blocked it off just two months ago. Backing up as far as he could, he crouched under the archway and watched as the ground bounced and the falling rocks grew in size. It looked like a rock sifter on a gold mine, bringing the bigger ones to the top. Then, just as fast as it begun, it stopped. Looking around Travis wiped the sweat from his upper lip. He was breathing hard and laughed out loud at himself.

Boom!

Jolting him back under the archway, he just about lost his lunch as he clutched his heart with his hand. The sound came faster and faster as the ground split open and a burst of light and steam shot into the air. In one last thundering sound, the ground erupted like a volcano, spitting dirt and debris into the air, leaving an open hole the size of a Volvo.

Then silence.

* * *

DARKNESS SURROUNDED ISIS AS she climbed the outside wall of the building to the apartment where Taras was staying. Her thin, black suit looked like a wetsuit, but was made of a special material that looked like mesh up close. It held in 99.9 percent of her body heat and reflected light to allow her to blend in with her surroundings.

Kirk hugged the wall just ten feet below her and was in a much worse mood than when he had learned of the mission. He was ready to take Taras's head off, but he couldn't understand why they just couldn't use the elevator. He didn't trust the suction gloves that were supposed to react when you pressed them to a smooth surface. And now, two hundred feet from the street below, he was wishing he'd stayed in the car. *Man up, Kirk, aren't you supposed to be a hotshot detective?* Isis was making him look bad. She was in the zone and also had more experience in this crazy, jump-off-of-buildings stuff then Kirk did. *This is nuts! I am going to die in front of Isis. It's like high school all over again.*

The evening air had a bit of a chill to it, and the breeze felt cool on his face. Everything else was covered in the ridiculous suit. Kirk had grumbled as he put it on, but after looking up at Isis just about losing her in the reflection of the glass, he figured it was cooler than he'd first thought.

Taras was supposed to be home. With thermal imaging, they could see a heat signature in the apartment. The plan was to take him out and make it look like an accident. The whole team was involved, down to covering every possible escape route. Big B kept him in sight two buildings away with thermal and x-ray vision. He scanned the building for possible guards.

Kirk didn't expect any. Taras was far too arrogant to think he would ever be caught. He never had any protection, he didn't even try to hide from the law. He just seemed to be able to escape no matter what anyone did.

The team was split into four different groups: one was in the lobby sipping martinis at the bar, one covered the back, one was circling in a black helicopter just in case Taras decided to run, and Kirk and Isis were the fourth, going in to make the hit.

Kirk felt like Spiderman as they crawled up the side of the glass building. Isis signaled and pointed to a window to her right. Kirk pulled himself up and took the right side, and they looked in. The light in the kitchen was on, but no sign of The General. Kirk turned on his x-ray glasses and looked through the rooms leading into the bedroom.

A figure sat in a La-Z-Boy reading or watching television in the master bedroom. Isis whispered and started to set up the glass remover. After she secured the device in place, she hooked a small hydraulic arm and attached it to the side of the building with a suction plate. After Isis had locked in the arm, she attached the other end to the glass. Kirk was amazed how easily it cut the glass. Isis pulled it out, and then the arm lifted the window like a wing door on a Ferrari. Kirk quickly climbed in and Isis followed as he watched Taras, who still sat in the next room, apparently unaware of their presence.

Soft music was playing through surround sound, and a half empty bottle of wine sat on the dining room table. Isis pulled a canister from the hidden pocket on her arm and unscrewed the lid. It held a single ounce of Lithoyzone, bottled in a small glass vial. Once shattered, it would send out a burst of light that would instantly blind anyone whose eyes were exposed to it. They'd told Kirk that their glasses protected them from the harmful light.

Kirk pulled a dart gun from his hip holster, which held three rounds of a drug that would show up as narcotics. It would hit the target and slide under the skin, injecting a poison that would shut down the victim's blood flow within seconds. The microscopic dart would then inject the victim with enough narcotics to put down an elephant. The beauty of the drug was that, after death, it would dissipate through the pores, leaving no trace other than extreme stress on the heart and clotting in the blood. The coroner would test the body and find nothing. It would be assumed he'd died from a heart attack by the condition of the heart, and the blood clots would suggest the same thing. However, the fancy gun was not the only thing he packed—he had his .45 just in case. Isis had laughed at him for lugging "That heavy weapon!"

Kirk didn't care much for the whole kill-and-leave-no-trace thing. Considering what the madman had done, he would like to run the guy up for all to see. Isis had looked at him with a "that's not how we do it here" look. He had a hard time not doing it for revenge, but the WJA didn't want to draw unnecessary attention to themselves.

Kirk looked over at Isis as she slid to the left side of the doorway. Kirk didn't need to yell, "Police," or anything. He was an agent for the WJA now.

He reached for the door and swung it open as Isis tossed the Lithoyzone into the room. The man in the chair had his back to the door. A blinding light flashed then burned out as they burst into the room. Kirk put two rounds in his neck before he had a chance to react.

They swung around in a wide sweep of the room, and they came face to face with...Kirk dropped his weapon and rushed for the man strapped to the chair. He was beaten and bloody. But something wasn't right. Kirk's mind went numb, and his shoulders dropped as he realized that the man in the chair was the body of a man with a cardboard cutout strapped to his face.

The cutout was a picture of Solomon.

Isis ran for him but saw that he was already dead. He looked like he had been dead a few days. His face was blue, and his body was bloated and filled the room with a foul smell. Kirk froze as he swept the room with his eyes. They had walked into a trap.

"Abort, abort!" Kirk sounded into his headset.

"What's going on in there, man?" Big B could only see the heat signatures and x-ray, but nothing more.

"It's an unknown man with a picture of Solomon tied to his face. He's dead." Isis said.

"Can't be, he's showing a heat source!" Big B stuttered. "Get out, now. Isis, run!"

The impact of what was about to happen hit Kirk like a ton of bricks. He turned just in time to see the blood soaked writing on the wall behind them.

Game over, Detective.

"Isis!" Kirk grabbed her arm and nearly pulled her off her feet. He dove through the door leading to the living room, dragging Isis the whole way. She regained her footing, and, with a quick glance his direction, they ran for the open window.

A high-pitched whine filled the room as the explosive solution inserted into the dead man's body mixed and ignited.

Kirk had a million thoughts running through his mind as they headed for the window. *We're dead either way. Falling three hundred feet, or blown to bits.*

Isis was right in front of Kirk as they reached the window. Without slowing, she dove headfirst out the window and into thin air. Kirk followed a half second behind her, just as the apartment exploded into flames. The blast shattered the windows for five floors, and as Kirk fell, he could feel the heat and glass hitting his back with brutal force. He didn't even hear the explosion or see the half of the building that tore itself from its framework leaving a gaping hole, five floors deep. A rain of metal and glass showered down after the two as they fell.

Kirk regained his composure as the wind hit his face. He looked frantically for Isis. There! She was stiff and straight, as if she knew she was in control. He saw immediately what she was planning. The building just ten or twelve feet from them was made of glass, as well. She was diving straight for it. Kirk pulled his arms to his side and straightened. He saw Isis hit the side hard and flatten out, grabbing the side of the building as she tried desperately to get a grip on the glass.

Kirk fell into the building faster than he'd imagined. Hitting the glass wall, he grunted and bounced off like a rock skipping across a pond. The wind in his ears was so loud, he had trouble even thinking, and the fact that the ground was fast approaching did not help matters either. Reaching out for the window, he clawed and hit the glass with open palms, trying, hoping the suction devices in his gloves would activate.

Kirk had a brief thought. If he could punch through the window and try to hurl himself inside, at least he would land somewhere other than the concrete below. The ground was coming up fast and in one last effort, he slammed both hands on the glass in front of him. Wham! The gloves activated and Kirk slid down the side. Using the momentum from his fall, he swung his legs down in an arch and broke through the glass. Now the glass he'd been attached to broke into a thousand pieces as Kirk flew through the open space and tumbled head over heels into a storefront. The sound of falling glass rained down past him and hit the ground like a hailstorm. He opened his eyes and rolled off the pile of fur coats that had broken his fall.

Macy's storefront window was broken to pieces, and the path he'd taken was covered with glass and a dark red streak of blood on the tile floor. Gathering himself up, he felt a sharp pain in his shoulder. It was bleeding, but all he could think about was Isis. *Did she fall? Is she splattered on the pavement?* Walking to the open hole, he looked out to find that he was standing on the ground floor. The street was scattered with bits of metal and glass, paper floated in the air, and small fires were burning everywhere as fire trucks roared down the street. Looking around, he saw Isis walking toward him with her hood ripped off, leaving her jet-black hair hanging down over her shoulders.

"Isis, are you okay? Are you hurt?" Kirk ran to her and pulled her close. He kissed her all over her face, hugging her before he realized what he was doing. "Oh, I'm so sorry, I uh—"

"It's okay, I'm fine. Oh, you're bleeding!" She looked him over and saw that, outside of a few small gashes, they were fine. Isis took Kirk's hand and pulled him around the corner and into an alley. They had to get out of sight before the police started looking for witnesses.

"You guys okay?" Big B squawked in their ears.

"We're alive, come get us we are on the corner of—"

"Search the area in a five mile perimeter. He had to set that bomb off by remote. He has to be close by." Isis said.

"Roger that. You two hang tight. I'll send in the ground team to pick you up. Did we made it out with everyone?"

"Everyone but Solomon, but I think he's dead. He has to be." Isis looked down at the ground and a sob made it past her lips. Kirk wrapped her in his arms and they sank to the ground. For the first time in a long time, Kirk wept. He was falling in love with her, but everything was confused. He was torn between his training as a cop and this new way of looking at the world. Isis held onto him, buried her head in his chest, and cried. They sat there for a long time. Kirk Weston had a brand new chance at life. He was holding that chance in his arms, and he was going to make the best of it.

CHAPTER TWENTY-NINE

TRAVIS FOUST OPENED HIS eyes and looked through the dust-filled room in amazement. He choked and coughed as he staggered from his hiding place. A huge hole lay open in the center of the room and the dirt from it was piled all around, looking like a giant gopher had just dug a new entrance to his tunnel. Testing the ground, he made his way to the edge of the crater to investigate. He eyed the room and noticed the only exit was buried. He was trapped, and this hole in the ground didn't seem to be helping matters.

Great, just what I need. He thought about his girlfriend and the family dinner he would surely be missing tonight. He didn't like them much anyway. He was black and she was, well, not.

The pile of mounded dirt was well over his head, but he climbed it without much effort. At the top, he looked down to see a black hole that seemed to be empty. Dropping his backpack from his shoulder, he retrieved his flashlight and clicked it on. The small light flooded the darkness and shone on the face of a person.

Travis gasped and just about fell back head over heels, but he caught himself. "Hello! Are you okay? Hey, mister. Can you hear me?"

The man was covered with blood and wasn't moving. Noticing the shattered wood around him, he could tell that the man was in a simple pine casket. He sat down and sighed out loud and tried to think of an explanation for what he'd just seen. Maybe an earthquake had just occurred and jiggled the dirt loose around the grave. It was a stretch, but nothing else made any sense at the moment. He swung the light around the room to see if there was any other means of escape, when a grunt jolted his attention back to the hole. A groan came from the darkness. Swinging his flashlight around, he shined it into the gaping hole.

The man was moving.

He was still alive.

* * *

I OPENED MY EYES and saw a bright light. Just like I imagined—a bright light you follow into heaven or some afterlife. The pain was gone and everything felt like a dream. *I wonder if you dream in heaven.* The last thing I remembered was a blinding flash and a sonic boom, and then everything went black. Someone was yelling at me, maybe it was my spirit guide. I hoped I would have one. This whole death thing was new for me. "Hello, you okay? Hold on, I'll get you out, man!"

He sounded more like a human than an angel or a spooky, glowing ghost. A man! Then the light went away and my eyes adjusted to the soft glow coming from the open air above me. I turned my head to see the lid of the casket torn to pieces and jammed into the side of a crater. Wood pieces were everywhere.

As my memory came back, I realized I wasn't dead. To the contrary, I was alive, and not only that, something had happened to me. The pounding had come from deep inside my own body. My head had hurt so badly a few minutes ago, but now it felt fine. I looked at my fingers and saw they had black soot or ink on the tips. *Weird!* I bent my arm and struggled to my knees. The stench hit my nose as I stood up. I was covered in dried feces and urine. My body was caked with blood and sweat, but everything seemed to be working.

"Hey, man! What was that? I mean, I've never seen

anything like it. You like blew the ground right up off you."
The dark man went on and on about the miracle, but I didn't
hear much of what he said. I was alive! *How in the world am I
alive?*

"I don't know; I thought I was a goner. You got a rope or
something?" I rubbed my eyes and felt something warm. My
fingers were hot to the touch. Almost scorching hot. I looked at
them, but they looked fine. They didn't hurt.

"I'm Travis. I was doing some exploring when this, I mean,
that—whatever—happened!" Travis stammered and tossed
down a blue, woven climbing rope. "You strong enough to
climb up?"

"I think I can, just hold on to the other end." I grabbed the
rope and started to pull myself up. "I'm Mark, by the way. Sure
glad you were in the area, I might have been stuck down here
for who knows how long."

"You're one lucky dude, or very unlucky."

My muscles ached, and it took a few tries to make it to the
top. The week of not being used had turned them into Jell-O,
not to mention I was starving, and my mouth was dry from lack
of water. I was a mess.

"Thanks a lot, Travis." I reached out and hugged my new
friend. I was so overcome with joy to be alive that I just held
on like he was a superhero. He was, for me.

"No problem, man." He was nice enough not to comment
on my smell or the way I looked. After devouring the rest of his
lunch and the water in his canteen, we sat, and I filled him in
on the very vague details. I was kidnapped and had been buried
alive by a madman. He didn't need to know much more then
that.

Travis was a stout and strong man. He stood five-foot-eight
and looked like a cage fighter. His dark eyes flashed when he
talked, and I could tell that everything he did was with passion.
"One problem Mark, we're stuck." He pointed to the entrance,
which I remembered crawling through a few days earlier. It
was under hundreds of pounds of rock and dirt. So, we did the

only thing we could do.

Dig.

* * *

DARK BAGS COULD BE seen under the president's eyes as he looked at Agent Carson and Captain Jacobson. They were alone in the oval office, and the tension was thick as he thought about the country.

"This is unacceptable!" He hadn't taken the news of the WJA refusing a face-to-face meeting well. "I want this terrorist shut down, and I mean now!" He closed his eyes and sighed, rubbing his temples. "I'm sorry, this whole thing has got me angered beyond belief. I know you're doing the best you can, and I appreciate that. Really, I do. Carson, do you have any idea how long until we have confirmed reports on Taras Karjanski?"

"We know he's in the country, but what city is still up in the air. We believe he is in New York, but I can't say for sure. All the notes have been delivered to *The Post,* and he seems to like to be close to the WJA. We believe he's planning to dump the blame for all this on the WJA in order to draw them out into the open. Once the country finds out about this group, we will have a bigger mess on our hands. We have to protect them at all costs and sort through the rest later."

The president thought on this a few minutes, and then stood up. He was wearing a suit, but the knot was pulled to one side, and the top button was open on his shirt. He shook their hands, and with that, they were dismissed.

Carson hoped the president would take his advice. The WJA had a lot of power and influence, but if the world found out a group was doling out revenge or overstepping the law, it would spark an uprising and, possibly, a civil war.

Jacobson didn't say two words as they rode in the back of a black Escalade. He didn't share Carson's ideas about the WJA, and had on more than one occasion voiced his doubts to the president. The president shut him down much too quickly for Jacobson to take it well. Carson was the new pet, and with the president's ear, he was now in the crosshairs of his boss. The thought crossed his mind that Jacobson would think he was involved in the WJA, or even that the president himself was linked to them. He never said it aloud, but Carson could read it in Jacobson's face. Only time would tell, and with the country in a chaos, the threat of Martial Law was being seriously considered by the president and his cabinet. *Come on, Detective, we need a miracle!*

* * *

I BRUSHED THOUGHTS OF what had happened from my mind as Travis drove down the dirt road to the highway. I wasn't sure if it had all been a dream, or if I was going to die of a brain overload or tumor or something. Travis Foust didn't say much about it, which confirmed my suspicions that something weird had happened.

The sound of thundering deep inside my chest and vibrating through my skull was imprinted on my mind. And then there was the fact that I was out of my own grave, for no reason other than that something supernatural happened. I used to go to church when I was a kid, and I remember hearing stories about miracles and healings. But when something happens to you, it's really hard to bring yourself to even consider that something supernatural may have happened.

We had dug for hours before we finally saw light at the end of the tunnel. Once we made it topside, we got in his rig and headed back into the city. His truck was a late nineties Toyota, with more rust on the body than paint. I didn't care, I was just happy it ran. I could only afford to have one thing on my mind at a time, but it was a little hard to focus on the task at hand when I knew I should be dead. The pile of dirt and the empty grave stuck out like a hot pink dog would at a black tie ball. It didn't make sense, nothing did anymore.

The world was falling apart, and from the sounds of panic coming on the radio, Taras Karjanski had begun his plan to bring the world to its knees. He wanted to see them at his mercy, but I only hoped he had some—mercy, that is.

* * *

KIRK COULDN'T FIGURE OUT what he thought or felt about anything. He rubbed his shaved head and closed his eyes as if to shut off his brain for a few minutes. He was flooded with thoughts of Isis and how she made him feel. He wanted to make her happy. To wrap her in his arms and protect her from the danger that surrounded them. *Come on, man, she is an assassin! She can take care of herself.* He didn't care what it took. He would do whatever he could to win her love.

Kirk had been alone most of his life. Even when he was married, he was alone. He never did know how to communicate very well. He would get buried in his work, and after putting the bad guys in jail, he woke up one day, divorced and living in a dumpy apartment, eating pizza for breakfast.

Taras was long gone, or maybe just a few blocks away. For all they knew he could be in the WJA building at this very moment. Kirk walked down the dim hallway toward Solomon's office. The brickwork lining the walls was impressive; the lights imbedded in the walls and ceiling made the lobby and halls glow. No one was attending the front desk, and Solomon's office was open. Like a tomb, it had a cool edge to it as he entered. He looked around before beginning to go through the desk drawers looking for anything that might help them in their search for the new world terrorist.

Isis was going through files and computer hard drives throughout the complex. The satellites proved worthless. The one they used to track targets wasn't responding. Kirk knew that Taras was responsible, and it was just a matter of time before he took his revenge.

Solomon had kept everything in its place with towering dark bookcases holding thousands of books from ancient Rome to the most current political novel by Vince Flynn. Kirk ran his fingers over the backs of the books, hoping to feel something as he touched them. Some kind of answer. But all he felt was a wave of hopelessness and something else—fear. The feeling had come over him just in the last few days when he looked into the eyes of the people around him. His favorite coffee shop was closing tomorrow, and just about every other business was, too, as people went home to hide and watch the news coverage of the crisis. The country was being held hostage. The spirit had been sucked out of everyone as they watched and waited for the next attack.

Kirk stopped and looked at the one book that didn't seem to fit in with the others. The title was *Kreios*. It looked handmade, and the cover was thick leather. Kirk pulled it from the shelf and opened it to the first page. It had no author listed, and the pages were blank. Something was off about the large book. The pages seemed to shine and had a weird quality to them, as if they were hiding something that he just couldn't quite see. He turned each page and then turned the book over to stare at the back. Inside, nothing but white stared back at him.

What did it mean? Why make a book without anything in it? The back cover had an inscription in tiny print. Kirk walked over to the light on the desk and leaned in to read. *"B.C. 2700."* The words seemed to fade in and out as he read them. Kirk sank into the large, high-back chair and set the book down on the desk.

The sound of footsteps on the stone floor made him look up. Isis burst into the room breathing hard. "What's going on?" Kirk jumped up when he saw her.

"It's Mark. He's alive!"

CHAPTER THIRTY

TARAS LOOKED OUT OVER the city with a whole new sense of enlightenment, a feeling of raw power flowing through his body. He imagined going to the funeral services of the great Solomon. He would wear a disguise, and even go up to look at the casket. He knew no body lay inside; it was rotting next to his beloved sister. Just the thought of it made him smile.

He felt his wife's warm embrace as she slid her arms around his shoulders and let out a sigh. "Good morning, my love. I dreamed of you and me on the beach just enjoying each other's company, doing nothing at all."

"My sweet wife, you might find yourself closer to that dream than you think." She leaned over and kissed him on the cheek. The scent of her perfume reminded him of home. His mother used to wear one quite similar. It made him want to cry.

She moaned and hugged him. "Oh, don't tease me. You know I don't like it."

"I never tease. I will have you on a beach in the South Pacific by the end of the week. You do realize it is our anniversary next month!" He knew she never forgot an anniversary or a birthday. Taras kept a calendar of all the important events on his blackberry, so it reminded him a good two weeks in advance. He was a romantic at heart, though his idea of romance might be slightly different than anyone he knew.

She squealed with delight, ran around the bed, placed herself on his lap, and kissed his neck. He could see her smooth neckline and thought of how easy it would be to snap it—maybe two seconds, maybe less. He wanted to toss her off the balcony and watch her fall to her death.

"Baby, you spoil me, you remembered!"

"How could I forget?" *Kill her!*

His head ached, and the thing living in the back of his mind growled and stood up as if to step forward and take control. The passenger had left him alone for a day or so, but now it was back and demanding more then he thought he could give. *She will get in the way. You need to be free from this hag. Kill her now!*

Shaking his head, he took her head in his arms and looked deep into her sweet, brown eyes. She had a soul and he could see the spark of life swimming inside of her eyes just waiting to be set free. She looked back at him, lost in the dark secret of his black eyes. The spark was gone, and he knew it. The only way to make it stop was to obey.

Snap. He could hear his mind going. It was bending, and each fiber of his will and control was slipping and breaking like a twig.

"I love you so much. Please stay just the way you are right now, at this very second." Taras could feel his face flush red from the battle going on in his mind. A tear came to his wife's eyes as she thought that his embarrassment was because he was so in love with her.

Taras knew he was two, maybe three people in one. The Red Dog was a part of all of his entities, and their memories blended together, making one terrible life filled with all the evil of many killers. He wanted freedom from the nightmares and the lust to kill, but his desire to do otherwise was much stronger. "Oh, my love, my Taras. I will always love you. What would I do without you?" She closed her eyes and placed the softest, gentlest kiss on his lips he had ever felt. The spark for one brief moment passed to him and it rushed to his heart. Then he knew what he had to do.

He had to kill his wife just like he had killed his only daughter. No one got to the Red Dog. No one!

* * *

I KISSED K AND held onto her like it was the last time I would ever see her. I was sobbing as I kissed her lips, cheeks, and forehead. I couldn't hold it in any longer. She had to know what I did, who I was, and why, one day, I might not come home from work.

The time I'd spent in my own grave had brought a new light into my world. Life is a vapor. It flashes, then it's gone. It's like a wave as it comes in from the ocean. It rises into the air like a giant filled with power and wonder, then crashes to the shore only to disappear into nothingness. Each wave is another day. Some are great, with the birds singing, and the next brings a dark cloud with rain and thunder. They are gone all too soon, and if another one comes, you are blessed.

I had no guarantee of another day to see Samantha running down the stairs and sliding on the hardwood floor with a huge smile on her face. No guarantee of more soft touches or sideways glances at K, to see if she had noticed that I was hopelessly in love with her.

I'd been gone over a week, and K knew sometimes that's just the way it was. She knew by my reaction when I saw her that something was going on. Sam was at Grandma's house, and we had a few hours alone. My heart was bursting with love, fear, and hope that afterward she would still love me. "Mark, you know you can tell me anything." She could see the battle going on behind my eyes and scooted closer on the sofa and took my hand in hers. "One of those weeks, huh?"

"Yeah, you could say that." I'd cleaned up at one of our safe houses and put on a fresh shirt and clean blue jeans. Besides the few pounds I'd dropped, I supposed I looked normal enough. My ribs were sore and the other wounds were healing up fast enough, faster than they should have. "K, I've been trying to figure out a way to tell you something. Let me start from the beginning."

The next two hours we sat glued to the couch, talking and crying as I opened my world to K like I'd never done before. My fears of rejection and the disdain I thought she might feel towards me disappeared as she kissed me. I went back to when I was a baby, and Solomon took me in, and I began the program. I told her how my brain had been injected with dreams and thoughts, training me in everything from how to use weapons, to hand-to-hand combat. The machine he created was used as I slept from the age of one year to four years old. The things that were implanted in my subconscious would be forgotten, and at the age of twelve, I was adopted by my parents.

I told her about the mission of the WJA and how they were on a path to bring the country back to a place of peace by righting the wrongs that we have let go unpunished for far too long. I told her about my glimpses, and how I could get brief looks into the future, but was still trying to learn how to control it. She took it all in and smiled, as it explained some weird behaviors that had bothered her in the past.

Then I brought her along with me on my last mission, and when I got to the part where I escaped, we both could not believe it. I was beginning to wonder if it was my imagination or the fact that I was just about out of my mind and about to die. However, no matter what we thought, I was here sitting in my own living room with my wife, and the casket lay open and empty.

* * *

A PICTURE OF TARAS Karjanski from two years prior was broadcast on every television across the country. A massive manhunt was underway, but only Taras knew that the picture was of his dead brother. He'd had a few reconstructive surgeries to alter his face and even had his femur shortened to make him a few inches shorter.

The president was days away from declaring Martial Law

and locking down the ports, and the whole country for that matter. His advisors screamed for something more than a slim hope in a group that didn't seem to even exist. He was beginning to have his own doubts, but he had promised them more time, and he was a man of his word, no matter what evil may come of it. He sent out the report on Taras Karjanski to the news media and hoped they would do what they did best: blow it up and make it so the murderer couldn't leave his house without fear of being turned in or shot.

"Mr. President?" James Centerfield walked in, and from the look on his face, he didn't have good news.

"What is it, James?"

James was the Secretary of Defense and a close personal friend. His balding head and slanted eyes made him look like a cat. "We intercepted a transmission from Russia to China. They look to be joining forces and planning an attack on the US."

"I was afraid this might happen."The president ran his hand through his salt-and-pepper hair and sighed."It was only a matter of time before the world started to think we're behind the bombings in an effort to take over the world's oil reserves."

"I have one more thing that might be worth looking into." He was silent for a moment.

"Spit it out, James."

"According to our satellites, there is movement in the Middle East. They're mobilizing, sir!"

The president stood and turned to look out the large window that opened up to the beautiful green White House lawn. "They've been fighting for thousands of years, and now they come together. Who would have believed this day would come? I hope you went to church on Sunday. We're going to need all the help we can get!" He let out a sigh. "God help us!"

* * *

A MEDIUM-SIZED SCROLL WITH a wax seal made its way to the desk of Yang Hu Chin. It was a cool morning in the People's Republic of China. The president took a sip of black tea with a drop of honey before he excused the servant.

The roll opened with ease and the president read the contents over a few times to make sure he was reading it right. He had dreamed of this day. The simple note held weight that made the dark-haired president pick up the phone and call for an emergency meeting.

Taking the note in his hands again, he smiled and took off his glasses. He knew that in his lifetime something wonderful could be accomplished, but this would leave his name on the lips of the people for many years to come!

Time to wake the sleeping Bear!

* * *

THE SAME NOTE, BUT written on plain white paper and stuffed into an envelope, made its way to the desk of the president of Russia. Before he had time to finish reading it, he got a buzzer in his ear from his secretary.

"Yang Hu Chin is on the line for you, sir."

"Put him through."

* * *

I COULD STILL FEEL K's sweet kiss as I drove to the Merc building. Isis called and could hardly contain her happiness to hear my voice. She filled me in as I drove, and from the looks of the city, I could see a difference right away.

Most of the businesses were closed, and only a few cars drove lazily along the streets. The feeling of dread and grief could be cut with a knife as Taras Karjanski held the city and the country hostage. I stopped to fill up at the only gas station I saw open, and after handing over four hundred-dollar bills, I could see why not many people were driving around. A few kids with ball caps on backward and big coats that looked like pieced-together life jackets were throwing rocks at a store window. They bolted when a bike cop hassled them and yelled after them to go home.

I had a good idea how to find Taras, but I needed to sleep, and with all the excitement, I didn't know if I could.

I put Isis off about where I was or how I got out by just telling her that I escaped. She didn't press me further and told me about the apartment where Taras had had a body and a bomb waiting. I told her about Solomon and Emily Dobson. I tried to control my anger, but this time I was not going to kill for justice. This time, it was personal!

CHAPTER THIRTY-ONE

AFTER A FEW SLEEPING pills and a bed in a quiet room down deep within the Merc building, I fell asleep. My mind was running in a thousand different directions like a computer downloading a large file. I knew Taras Karjanski was up to more than we could even guess, and at the same time, I could not help thinking that it was my fault somehow. I could feel a dark, sinister blackness fill my mind as the mind of the Red Dog opened up to me. It wasn't like I could just see what might happen, but I could feel the thoughts of the person. In most of my glimpses, I was me, but this time I wanted to get into Taras's head. The pit of my stomach hurt as the conflicting thoughts and one very strong voice took over. The hate and the power I felt rushed over my body like electricity hitting a pool of water. I saw nothing but darkness and heard a faint sound of heavy breathing. In deep, then out, then a long sigh.

He was sleeping.

I tried to move but was trapped like dead weight inside of the killer. "Wake up, you murdering sadistic monster!" I yelled as loud as I could. "Guess who?"

My eyes opened, and I bolted straight up out of bed. A woman was sleeping next to me, and the room was dark except for a flickering candle on the dresser. I could feel the thoughts rolling around in his head, looking to see what had woke him. I was drenched in sweat, or rather, Taras was.

To this day I can't get out of my mind the thoughts and memories that filled my head. It's like a bad song that gets stuck and just plays over and over again in your mind, tormenting you. He was a twisted monster that only wanted to kill. He loved the act of killing more than anything else in the world.

Rubbing my eyes, I got up and pulled myself toward the window. He looked toward the bathroom, but I turned to the window, and soon after, his legs followed. It was a weird feeling, his thoughts and mine mixed up, all of them screaming to be obeyed. I put all my focus to the task at hand. One thing I didn't want was for him to see the other way. I wasn't sure how it all worked, but I was almost positive that if I stayed in too long, he would know it was me. I needed to see where I was, to give me some idea where to start looking. A street sign or an address of some kind would be the best, but I was not prepared to see what I saw next.

The night air and lights made a shimmering fog lift from the city streets, making the streets glow. Walking to the window, I looked down to the street where a single cab waited for a passenger. The next thing I saw woke me up in a cold sweat. Right across the street from where I, Taras Karjanski, was standing, I saw the entrance to the Merc building!

* * *

ALIVE! MARK HAD CALLED in and talked to Isis and she'd updated him on everything that was going on. Kirk caught part of the conversation, and from the sounds of it, Mark had been kidnapped by Taras and left for dead. *He has more lives than a cat!* Mark had come in a few hours later and they rushed him into a small room with a comfortable couch with soft music running through the sound system. He was going to try to find out where Taras was, but Kirk had his doubts. The whole dream thing seemed a little too farfetched, but Isis seemed to be on board with it, so he brushed his doubts aside.

Kirk held onto the leather-bound book and sat in Isis's

office thumbing through the blank pages. It was a bit confusing to have a book with nothing written in it. The pages had a slight yellow tint to them and the cover was bound with old, rough cords intertwined through the pages on one side. It looked to be well over a hundred years old, maybe even older.

Isis came in and sat across from him in a love seat that was in the corner of her office. "He's asleep. I hope he finds out something. Anything at this point would help." She wore a dark blue sleeveless blouse that was smooth like silk, and a pair of black slacks with tiny white pinstripes. She leaned back and closed her eyes. It had been a long night, and they had been up for fifteen hours now with no sleep. Kirk was still wearing an old beat up t-shirt with "AC/DC," stamped on the front, and a pair of stained blue jeans.

"So you believe this dream stuff?" Kirk thought it sounded like a much more reasonable question in his mind, but coming out, he sounded like a grumpy, old cop.

"Yeah. I didn't at first, but he's saved my life before with information from a dream, and he knows things he couldn't have known otherwise. Why? Do you think he's making it up?" She looked at him with a sideways smirk.

"No, I've just never seen anything like it outside of the county fair and an old hag with a crystal ball."

"Well, we'll just have to wait and see. You find out anything in that book?"

"The pages are blank. It just seems weird. You ever seen it before?"

"No. And Solomon never mentioned it." Isis sat up and ran her hand through her hair.

Kirk looked at the cover again, then placed it on her desk and stood up to walk around to where Isis sat. "Come on, you look like you could use some coffee. The cafeteria should still be open."

Grabbing her hands, he pulled her up, and for a moment, they stood face-to-face, just inches from each other. She looked up and stared at him with her big, dark eyes, unflinching—just content to look at him. Kirk could smell her faint perfume and felt the heat rising in his face.

"The world is going to hell all around us, and all I can think about is you!" The words came out without Kirk even thinking, but there they were.

Isis smiled, pulled him close, and hugged him, burying her face in his shoulder. The soft movement was simple and filled Kirk with warm sensation that flowed from his head down to his toes. Kissing the top of her head, he closed his eyes, and they stood there for a while. It didn't matter; he had found someone that made him feel alive again. This tiny woman and the mystery that surrounded her made him love her even more. The timing stunk though. They had a terrorist on the loose, Mark came back from the dead without a reasonable explanation, and the president and FBI were hungry for his hide unless he found Taras quick, real quick! And now he was falling in love with a woman he had no business even being with. She was way out of his league and yet she gave him the time of day.

I love you, Isis. I swear, I will love you forever!

That was the first step toward recovery—admitting you have a problem.

* * *

DEEP INSIDE THE TWISTED mind of Red Dog, something was hiding. Something that shouldn't be there, and yet it watched in the shadows like the grim reaper. Taras looked out the window at the Merc building and listened to the voices in his head as they battled. Control was no longer his, but someone had to be in control. Soon he would be alone again, which was the way he liked it. Granted, he loved his wife, or at least liked being with her. But something was always off when she was around. He thought about confiding in her and letting her see his other side, but something stopped him every time he got the urge to spill his guts. *She wouldn't understand! Just tell her what she wants to hear. Women don't want the truth no matter how they whine that all men are liars!* They wanted to be noticed and loved, it didn't matter if their men mean it or not. *If she knew the truth, she would leave you—or worse, turn you in.*

He grunted and folded his arms across his chest like a soldier looking out over a battlefield. What did he care if she loved him or not? All she cared about was what she perceived him to be and what she thought he felt toward her. She didn't want the truth. She would be happy to live a lie and believe in her own perfect, little world than hear the ugly truth.

Truth?

There is no truth!

Taras turned his head and watched the form of his wife. She was his wife now.

Taras was bigger than one person. He was not only Taras, but also the Red Dog, and The General. The dark passenger liked to keep him in the dark, and would only let him have a few memories of the others. He wondered how many in total made up who he was now.

What was he supposed to do, tell her he was not Taras but, he was…then it hit him: he didn't remember who he was anymore. *You are what I make you!* The thing ground its teeth and tugged at the controls. Yes, this was his destiny, his dream, his desire. He was the Red Dog, and in time, he would be so much more then that.

The alarm clock would go off in an hour, waking his sleeping wife. Her flight would take her to Spain, leaving him to get on with his plans for a few days more without her to distract him. Sliding back into bed, he made sure he didn't make too much noise. She needed her sleep.

The shadows made black shapes all through the room as the moon shone bright through the open window. Taras didn't fall back asleep, and when the buzzer went off, he closed his eyes and breathed in deep, holding it for a moment, then let it out like a rush of wind. The sounds of a man far gone in another world lost in his dreams.

But then that, too, was a lie—wasn't it?

* * *

NAYDA KARJANSKI ROLLED OVER, hit the alarm, and sat up placing her feet on the floor. She looked over at her husband and noticed his breathing. He always was a deep sleeper.

Her flight would only leave her a half hour to get ready, so she ran the hot water in the shower and pulled her luggage out from under the bed. She liked flying, and even though they didn't need the money, she needed the human interaction. Clicking on the TV that hung from the wall in the large bathroom, she brushed her teeth and gave only half of her attention to the news. The same dribble over gas prices and the mad bomber who called himself the Red Dog or something dumb like that. Her airline had expected to lose customers, but the opposite had happened. People were buying one-way tickets to Spain, England, and other quieter countries. They were scared, but somehow, it didn't seem to bother her. Things were always better than the news media wanted you to think. They got off on getting people all worked up.

The steam from the shower fogged up the mirror and she turned away from the television to get in as a picture of her husband came up on the screen. Shutting the door, she let the warm water wash through her hair, and a shiver crept its way up her body. The television was on mute so she wouldn't wake her beloved husband. The fact that she knew what he looked like before his surgery would pass by unnoticed. He'd had a bad auto accident that scarred his face, and with the plastic surgery, he looked totally different then the two-year-old picture. But she still loved him. He would always be her Taras, no matter what he looked like.

In a matter of seconds, the story changed to the local weather. It looked like it might rain. Cats and dogs.

* * *

THE NEWS CONFERENCE CALLED by the president of the United States of America made it across the airways into Africa and to the coasts of Japan. The stock market was hanging on by a thread, and the oil industry wouldn't recover any time soon.

A bombing in Baton Rouge took out the highest-producing refinery in America. Just about five hundred barrels went up in a cloud of thick, black smoke each day. The fire would burn for weeks, if not longer, as emergency crews tried to contain the blaze.

The president called a news conference as soon as the story hit. The people of America would be in mass panic if they didn't see some sort of hope of an end to this madness. He felt frustrated with the FBI and their response to the attacks. Taras Karjanski was behind it and they had one day left to figure out what Taras wanted, or he feared it was going to get a lot worse.

"You're on, sir." The intern with a clipboard pushed his thick glasses up on his nose and waved at him from the edge of the deep blue curtain. He smiled and adjusted his tie, which was fine to begin with, but he had to do something to calm his nerves. Cameras flashed like exploding cannons in the dark as he walked up to the podium with the presidential seal stamped on front.

"Ladies and gentlemen, I come to you tonight as a fellow American, and a father. We are under attack by a terrorist group living here in the United States. The cowardice and violent nature of the attacks are proof that we are dealing with a weak and scared adversary." The last few words came out like a pounding gavel on a hardwood desk. The president stood tall and looked at the cameras, stern and in charge. He felt just the opposite inside. As he spoke, he thought about the decision to challenge Taras Karjanski. It could go over horribly and enrage him, but they needed to get him to make a mistake. Something to draw him out. The military was mobilizing, and all airports, schools, and utilities were on lockdown. He was going to break the news that the country was going under Martial Law. He hated to do it, but he didn't have a choice.

CHAPTER THIRTY-TWO

I WAS COVERED WITH sweat and my mouth felt like i just stuffed a handful of cotton balls down my throat. i ran to the window and looked out over the street, following the building all the way up to the top. A new penthouse was just being finished that overlooked the park and the Merc building.

He was across the street the whole time! The FBI and CIA were looking all over the country for the terrorist, and he was sipping on some expensive wine right across the street. I could feel his presence like a fog rolling in low over the carpet, grabbing anything unlucky enough to be caught in its path. For the first time ever, I felt like my purpose in life was clear. I knew what I had to do, and I was the only one who could do it. I had put so many lives in danger, and this time it had gone way past personal. I was a killer, a vigilante, or whatever name you wanted to brand me with. Maybe I was doing the world a favor by cleansing it of the filth that plagued its streets, or maybe I was a little loose in the head. Whatever the outcome, I knew one thing: Taras Karjanski had to die.

The thought made me shudder as I slipped from my room and silently stole down the hall to the elevator. I was going to kill for a different reason this time. I was ticked that this creep had messed with my friends, with my family, and my country. This was not justice, even though it would be seen as justice by the world. This was revenge.

I had to think this through. Was it wrong? Was I now just as bad as he was? Then, I came to what I thought might be the answer. I was past thinking and knew that, in life, sometimes, you've just got to do what you've got to do. Sometimes, you have to get your hands dirty and get it done. This was one of those times. Besides, this is what I was trained to do.

I was an assassin.

* * *

A LITTLE OLD LADY with silver hair pulled back in a simple bun served Isis a steaming cup of coffee and smiled. The media was going over the president's address for the tenth time on the TV in the background while Kirk stared at the woman he was in love with.

"What's with the book?" Isis looked up from her coffee with a curious look in her eyes. " Kind of hard to know what it says if there is nothing written down." Kirk thumbed through each page and looked at the blank, white pages hoping to find something or see some words magically appear. "I don't know. I just have this feeling that it means something. Why have a book this old with blank pages? It doesn't make any sense." Kirk swore and shut the cover with a thud.

"I'll have the lab look at it when we get back. It might have some encoded message or something. Solomon had his way of doing things. Sometimes, he lived on the edge of the edge, if you know what I mean. I have a hard time believing he would keep it if it was worthless."

That made Kirk feel better, and with everything going on, he needed to focus on the case at hand. Taras was out there, and if the bombings kept up, the country would spin out of control and never pull out of it. "When is Mark supposed to be done with his—whatever he's doing?"

Isis just about choked on her hot drink when she saw a dark figure run across the street. "Guess he's done!" She pointed to a man in a dark hood as he turned and disappeared into the alley behind the new condos across the street.

"Was that…?" Kirk stood up so fast he knocked over his coffee, spilling it all over the floor.

"That was Mark!" Isis slid from her seat and bolted out the door with Kirk right behind her. The leather book with blank pages sat on the table, forgotten. But something was happening to it as some of Kirk's coffee droplets fell on the surface and soaked into the leather cover. A ripple moved over the face of the book, and for a split second, it seemed to move.

The little silver-haired lady came from behind the counter to watch the two young people run across the street in an awful hurry. "Kids, you forgot your book!" The two didn't seem to hear her so she picked up the leather bound book and put it under the counter in case they came back for it. She muttered something about the city and how everyone seemed to be in a hurry.

* * *

THE BASEMENT WAS ALL but abandoned, which was fine by me. I didn't want to be seen, and if I died, I didn't want anyone to have reason to blame themselves. The weapons room held everything I could dream of, from high tech armor to bio-weapons under lock and key. I needed the lightest armor with the strongest defense against whatever Taras would throw at me. I found what I was looking for hanging in a liquid-cooled container. The suit molded to your form and adjusted to your body temperature. We called it, "second skin." It would take a bullet at point-blank range, and was fireproof, water proof, and breathed like a cotton t-shirt.

I had a good idea that Taras would know I was coming for him. If I felt him, then he would be able to feel me. The dream was too close to the inside of the madman, and I had no illusions that I could go that deep into his head without being discovered. I felt a tinge of fear. I didn't consider myself a brave man or even very out of the ordinary. I just did what had to be done. Nevertheless, something about this mission had me a bit scared…okay, very scared.

Zipping up the last of many zippers and strapping a knife

to my calf, I stole from the weapons room and down the hall toward the elevator. I had to get out of the building without drawing too much attention. Isis, and even Kirk, would insist on going along to help. I needed to know that they were safe.

The elevator was empty, and the parking garage had only a few cars left in the many parking spots. I ran along, staying in the shadows, ducking between cars and the thick, round, cement pillars that held up the building. A car was pulling into the parking garage. I could hear the squeal of tires as it made its way up the circular ramp. I hurled myself over the rail, grabbed the edge of the railing, and looked down. The three flights offered a soft landing in a flowerbed below. I took it. I hit with a thud, rolled, and came up on my feet, looking around to see if anyone had seen me.

So far, so good. The street had light traffic compared to a normal day. Jogging around the building, I came to the back alleyway and scanned the tall building in front of me. It took sunlight in and threw it back at a thousand different angles. The newly remodeled building had huge, stone-covered columns rising up the side and stopping at the penthouse on the roof. It was like a spider sitting on a wall with its legs dangling down. The high-rise could crumble beneath it, and the lavish penthouse would still stand unharmed. *Not bad, Taras, way to think ahead.*

A yellow cab passed, and I ran out into the street. In seconds, I was in the cover of a dark alley. The alley stunk of wet boxes and rotting food that filled the dumpsters all along the side of the building. Evidently, the Sanitation Department had shut down, too. I ran down to the end of the alley and found a door marked "Fire Riser Room," and picked the lock. The fire sprinkler room was humid, and with the boilers and other pumps running, it was loud. The noise calmed my nerves just enough to take the edge off. I knew my instincts would kick in, but that usually didn't happen until just before I needed them.

The fire riser had a pump on it and four different risers

all tied into the main sprinkler system. I pulled off the covers to the flow switches and blocked them with a pencil that I'd broken into four pieces. The flow switch would notify the fire department if a fire broke out in the building or a sprinkler head discharged. By blocking them, it would bypass the alarm, and no one would get a signal. Confusion would be on my side for an escape. If I did escape.

At the back of the riser room was a door that led to the service elevator. It wouldn't go all the way up to the penthouse but it would save me some stair-climbing, nonetheless. The door opened with a ding, and a short, round woman with a cart full of dishes glanced up at me. A look of fear crossed her face. I grabbed her, placed my hand over her nose and mouth, and waited for the poison embedded in the fabric of my gloves to put her to sleep. Her heavy body slumped to the ground, and I dragged her into the pump room and laid her on the floor. She would wake up in an hour or so with a bad headache and no memory of how she'd ended up in the pump room.

"Sleep well, my plump maid. You don't want to remember me, anyway."

Taking the elevator up took a minute and a half. When the door opened at the top, I looked down the hall to find a service hallway. The lights flickered and gave off a slight green tint, making it look like an old hospital.

Empty.

The stairs were around the corner, and I took them two at a time, making my way up to where a murderer was waiting for me. I knew he was there, and I was sure he knew I was coming for him!

* * *

THE DARK ALLEY WAS empty when Kirk caught up to Isis. "He's gone!" She huffed and looked around. "What's he doing?"

Looking up at the side of the building, Kirk walked around to the back and tried every door on the way around. They were all locked. "Let's go inside and see if we can find him. He must have seen something in his dream-thing." Kirk and Isis walked around to the front entrance and through the glass doors that opened into a huge lobby.

Light from the sun filtered in through etched glass, making the marble floors swim like water. Men in tuxedos were milling around a tall, rounded front desk, helping the occasional tenant with their groceries or the elevator. The high-priced condos ranged from seventy-five million to hundreds of millions of dollars for the larger, furnished ones.

Isis walked to the register on the wall and looked through the names of the tenants to see if any looked suspicious.

"May I help you, Madam?" A tall, well-groomed doorman looked down at them with an arrogant air.

"Yeah, NYPD." Kirk flashed his badge fast enough for the man not to notice that it was a Detroit badge. "We need to see a complete list of the people residing in this here, what do you call this place?"

"The Grove, sir. I'm afraid you will need to speak to a manager. This way please." He never cracked a smile or even changed his expression as he led them to the elevator. Isis eyed him, but Kirk didn't look at her. He didn't know what he was doing, but the badge had sounded like a good idea at the time.

The third floor housed a restaurant, the management offices for The Grove, and a day spa exclusively for the residents. The administration office was just as nice as the front lobby, and a slender, good-looking redhead sat behind a desk using an earpiece to talk on the phone. It gave her more time to do her nails while not missing a call.

"Miss Devrioe, will assist you further. Is there anything else I can get you?"

"No, this will do." Kirk brought back his gruff demeanor and looked at the man as he left.

"What are you doing?" Isis leaned in and whispered so only he could hear.

"Just play along."

The redhead sat up, put down her ruby red nail polish, and

smiled up at them. "May I help you?" Her tone was sweet but had a hidden disdain for the lower class being in her office.

"Yeah, you can start by getting the manager out here!" Kirk flashed his badge again and stood up straight with his chest out. He was getting impatient. "You hard of hearing?"

"No need to be curt. I can help you in any way…"

"Let me be frank, I am having a bad day, and you are hindering an investigation." Her voice made Kirk want to scream. It was high and snotty-sounding, just like his ex-wife's voice.

Her face turned as red as her hair, and she huffed as she pushed the intercom on the phone. "Mr. Bushi, there are two detectives here to see you."

A brief pause, then a voice sounded. "Send them in."

She turned and looked toward a door to her left, and Kirk led the way with Isis in tow. The large office was decorated with décor from Asia, right down to a small, golden Buddha sitting on the oak desk. A thin man stood and looked at them through a pair of thick glasses. "Do come in."

"Detective Hatcher, and my partner, Detective Rush. We're conducting an investigation that has led to a tenant in your building." Kirk took out a note pad and pretended to look through it for effect.

"Oh my. We screen all our guests and only allow the best class of society to even darken the doors, I assure you." He pushed up his glasses with his index finger and looked around as if he'd lost something in the pile of papers on his desk.

"I'm sure you do. But we need to take a look at your register of all residents and recent visitors. If you could please make it quick, we're in a bit of a hurry."

"Well, our records are confidential, and I don't know…"

Kirk moved forward and leaned over the desk staring the fumbling man right in the face. His breath stunk of old coffee and he let a little spit fly as he poured on the intimidation. "Are you hindering an investigation? If you want a search warrant and a team of my biggest, meanest goons tearing this place apart, just continue to be uncooperative. I'll even bring my favorite reporter from *The Times* to do a piece on your crummy establishment. I swear to you, when I'm done, you won't be able to get the bums on Fifth Avenue to stay here!"

Mr. Bushi turned pale, and sweat ran down his forehead as he stuttered and climbed from his chair muttering. He tripped his way to a large file cabinet. "No need to get rash. I will cooperate…I…Please don't tell anyone. I could lose some very good clients!"

Isis spoke in a soothing voice and walked toward him as if to calm him down. "Don't worry Mr. Bushi, we will handle this information with the highest amount of sensitivity possible. I can assure you, this is very important to our case. You understand."

He nodded, pulled out a CD, handed it to Kirk, and stepped back, wiping the sweat on his sleeve. Kirk walked behind the desk and slid the CD into the drive.

Moments later, a list of popped up on the screen. Ricky Martin, Sylvester Stallone, and many others. *Come on, give me something!*

Isis was looking over his shoulder as he rolled the mouse and scrolled down the page. "Wait, back up. There on the guest register from last week."

Kirk backed up and followed Isis's finger to the name of a woman. A Russian woman.

Chapter Thirty-Three

A DARK SHADOW STOOD over the man who called himself the red dog. A dark green mist fell from its nostrils and trailed down to the floor, surrounding Taras as he lay, passed out on the floor. It was midday, but even with the windows open, the room was pitch black. The figure had yellow eyes that were almost invisible to the naked eye. It reached down with long, sharp claws and dug them deep into Taras's skull. Taras twitched and thrashed as the beast slithered into his body. With each twist and pull, Taras writhed in pain. His eyes shot open, and blood ran from his nose as he screamed.

Then, just as fast as it happened, there was calm. A breeze blew the dark mist away, and the sun flooded the apartment with warmth. Taras blinked and sat up. He felt lightheaded and in dire need of a stiff drink.

He's coming for you!

I know, don't patronize me. The bottle of Vodka hit the spot as he tipped it back and then wiped his face with a warm wash rag. He felt stronger than ever. His reflection in the mirror above the sink showed his rippling muscles. His jeans were torn, and he didn't even remember where his shirt went. The blackouts came every now and then, but this last one was, by far, the worst.

Throwing himself on the overstuffed couch, he held the

bottle of Vodka to his head. He needed to think. Placing the bottle down, he reached for his 9-milimeter that lay on the coffee table waiting for him to take it out to play.

He didn't need to look at the surveillance footage that showed Mark making his way up the back stairwell. He knew. After a quick check to make sure he had a full clip, he closed his eyes and waited in silence.

* * *

I FELT MY HEART jump into overdrive as I reached the thirtieth floor. I didn't know what floor he was on by anything other than the dark feeling inside of me that was trying to tear my chest apart. The closer I got to the top, the stronger it was, like a demon pulling me into its lair.

Looking at the doorknob that led from the stairway to the main hall, I stopped and just stared at it like I'd never seen a doorknob before. It was brushed copper and round with a dead bolt above it. I turned it and saw that it was happening again. My fingers were glowing at the tips, even through my gloves. I could see the light fighting to escape. What was happening to me? I had put the last few days out of my mind on purpose. I had no way of explaining what had happened to me, and I didn't have time to sit and think it through. Solomon, what did you do to me? With Solomon dead, I feared that I might never know.

The door opened, and I stepped out into the hall. I walked toward two, large, wooden doors. They led into a lobby. On one side was a private elevator for the Red Dog only, and on the other side was a metal door without a handle. A soft song floated over the speakers in the lobby area, the words like a prophecy. "Near, far wherever you are…"

"I'm coming for you, Taras. Wherever you are, I'm coming for you."

The cold, silver, metal door faced me like a monster's mouth, daring me to enter. I knew what was on the other side. A cold-blooded killer, and maybe my death. I thought of K and Sam as I took a plastic explosive from a small pouch on my sleeve.

Thump...thump.

I could feel my chest tighten and my head start to throb as the familiar hard *thud* feeling thundered in my ears. *Not again. I don't need this now. I have a job to do!* Placing the device on the door, I ran back to the stairway, and a few seconds later, an explosion sent a cloud of dust under the door.

Then, just as I'd come to expect, my heart slowed, and a wave of energy and power flooded over my entire body as I bolted from the stairway toward the open hole where Taras Karjanski's door used to be.

Thump...Thump...thump...

* * *

THE FIRE AND SMOKE from the explosion didn't even budge the Red Dog as he lay on the couch. He felt the cold steel of his 9-milimeter and listened to the sinister voice that rang in his ears. He was a hundred feet from the front door, and with the building armed with invisible lazars crisscrossing the pathway between him and his attacker, he wasn't worried.

His only regret was that he wouldn't be able to squeeze the life out of Mark himself. Taras even thought about turning off all of his security devices just to make it interesting, but he couldn't move. Taras was dead, and the beast called the Red Dog was in control. And he had a plan. No matter what, today, Mark Appleton was going to die!

* * *

I FLEW THROUGH THE door and rolled to the floor, taking refuge behind a huge vase filled with bamboo.

Thump...thump...

I looked around and couldn't see anyone, but I didn't trust my eyes. He was here waiting for me. Standing up, I took out my Glock and dropped it to the floor with a clang. Then, I unstrapped my boot knife and my other weapons.

I could feel something filling my arms and legs like cold metal. A lone figure stood up from a leather couch and walked out into the open. He had no shirt on, and his skin seemed to be an unnatural grey color. He smiled, and with hands palm up, he raised his arms out to his side like a man without fear. We stood looking at each other like a showdown in the old west.

Thump…thump…thump!

I walked forward and felt something hot hitting me all over. I looked down to see red dots burning holes into my suit. Like an engine being cold started, I jumped into action, running forward as Taras pulled a 9-milimeter and squeezed the trigger.

My head felt like it was going to explode as the pounding filled my ears. I couldn't even hear the discharge of his gun, I only saw the flash from the barrel. The bullet caught me in the chest and threw me back, just about knocking me off my feet.

He looked shocked when I didn't fall, and in two steps, I was face-to-face with the Red Dog.

Thump…thump…*thump!*

Faster than I thought possible, he stepped back and pointed the gun between my eyes and fired. I closed my eyes as a pulse of light compressed and shot from my body, hitting Taras in the midsection, throwing him back into a glass table, shattering it into a thousand pieces. The bullet flew back and crashed into the wall behind where Taras landed.

I couldn't believe what was happening, but at this point, I wasn't going to question it. My hands were glowing, and my chest looked like the sun itself. Lifting my hands in front of me, I sent a pulse of light toward Taras like a ball of energy. It hit him and threw him another ten feet, slamming him hard into the wall. My body was glowing white, and it was like everything was happening in slow motion. My hands were weapons, and this strange light was acting like a sonar pulse gun. I didn't know what to do or how to control it, but it seemed to know what to do on its own.

Before I knew it, Taras was on his feet, blood running from his ears and nose. He smiled and yelled something in Russian. A thick glass came up from the floor and down from the ceiling, making a cage all around us. I was trapped with the Red Dog, and I had no way out.

* * *

TARAS LAUGHED AS HE yelled another command and a mist of deadly gas poured into the sealed room from vents in the floor. "You think you can make it out of this alive? You fool! You have no idea who you're messing with. I am the Red Dog! I am not afraid to die, I am already dead. And soon you will share my fate!" He spit and foamed as the gas hit his eyes and started to burn them. "The great Mark Appleton had a few tricks up his sleeve, but you forget, I am God! And, today, you die!"

Taras started laughing as blood squirted from his mouth. He pulled a second 9-milimeter that had been stuffed in the back of his pants and unloaded it at Mark ,who stood twenty feet in front of him. *Die! Why won't you die?*

* * *

CHOKING AND COUGHING ON the gas, I could feel my eyes burning. Then I heard the distinct sound…Pop, pop, pop. He was shooting again.

Thump!

Thump!

Thump! I could feel a cold metal flow from my toes up to the top of my head. It hurt more than anything I'd ever felt before. I leaped into the air and came down with my fist crushing into the floor. Light shot out of my chest and hands, and the floor cracked as a force of raw energy and light hit it, sending out a flood of light with a bomb-like force. All around me, glass shattered, and the thick bomb-proof cage blew apart as if it had been made out of paper.

The force hit Taras right in the face and ripped through his body, crushing every bone and melting the skin! He screamed as his heart exploded, and within seconds, he slumped to the floor in a bloody heap.

I could feel hot pain shoot through every nerve ending, and my world started spinning. I tried to hold on, but whatever had just happened drained me of everything I had. I looked up just in time to see the glass in every window explode outward and rain down on the street far below. The gas was sucked out the window, and I fell over and crumpled to the floor. This was it. My last act was killing the worst terrorist the world had ever seen.

Then everything went black.

* * *

THE ROOM WERE THE Red Dog had built a fortress was ripped apart. Mark now laid beside a gaping hole in the floor, unconscious. All the furniture and everything else in the room had been shredded and pushed up against the outside walls. The thick glass from the protective cage lay in chunks on the floor, and seconds later, the fire sprinklers went off, raining down black, rusty water on the apartment. Hot steam rose from the floor as Mark lay dreaming.

The Red Dog is dead!

* * *

HITTING THE BUTTON A few more times on the elevator didn't make it come any faster. Kirk muttered and looked around as his eyes darted back and forth. He knew now why Mark was in the building, and worse yet, he had a bad feeling that the Red Dog was home.

Isis had a cool look on her face that told Kirk that she was in the zone. All business, and she was good at her job. A ding sounded as the stainless steel doors opened. Looking Isis in the eyes, he almost forgot how she made him feel. She was like a lion tamer, and with one look she could melt his heart. They nodded and he punched the top floor. As the doors closed, Kirk pulled out his trusty .45 with a brand new laser site he'd put on himself. He could remember using this gun for many a shootout with a drug runner, and one time a hooker who was hell bent on killing off the male species.

4...5...6...7...

Isis didn't say anything as she put her sleek, black gloves on. No matter what she wore, she was always prepared. Throwing knives tipped with poison. Even all their sunglasses were equipped with thermal and x-ray vision. She had small vials filled with gas to wipe the room of any hostiles, and some that would put any poor soul in range to sleep. Side effect? One bad headache in the morning.

15...16...17...18...

"I called it in. We should have a team here in five minutes." Isis was looking down at her watch. It was glowing red, which was the emergency signal. With this, they could track all the team members as long as they were wearing their watches.

"Hope we're right. Hate to get everybody running down here for nothing!"

Just as the words came out of his mouth, the elevator shook and the lights blinked out. Kirk swore and the elevator came to a jerking stop. The emergency lights came on, and then a second sound that hit like a sonic boom shook the now stationary elevator.

"That's him! We've got to move!" Kirk tried to pull open the doors but they wouldn't budge. "The hatch. There should be a hatch in the ceiling for repairs, I'll boost you up." Kirk got on one knee and Isis stepped into his cupped hands. She pushed up on the tile that made the roof of the elevator.

"Got it...can you lift me higher, just a little?" Pushing with her forearm and shoulder, Isis managed to push the trap door up, and it folded back on its hinges, making a two-by-two opening.

"Good job, Isis, now, up you go." Kirk pushed her through, then jumped and grabbed the edge of the roof opening and pulled himself up.

"Just like old times in your little prison. Guess something good came from it." Isis blushed. "Sorry about that, I..."

"Never mind, we've got to climb up that cable and try to find a way out of here. I have a feeling Mark has no idea what he's gotten himself into."

Kirk grabbed a hold of the elevator cable and started to climb, hand over hand, up the cable. Isis followed.

One floor at a time, they slowly made their way up to the thirtieth floor. The elevator doors were bent and half torn off their hinges. Kirk looked down at Isis, who had a bead of sweat forming on her forehead. "We've got to swing this thing. It's too far to reach the door!"

Kirk and Isis started to swing the cable back and forth, and as it swung toward the wall, Kirk took a leap and grabbed the edge of the mangled door. He grunted as his body hit the concrete wall and he started to slip. His fingers wiggled and he pawed at the floor for something to grab hold of.

Isis was still swinging, and as she came around, she leaped for the opening and dove right over Kirk's head, landing in a tuck and rolling to her feet. She turned and grasped Kirk's hand just as he was about to lose his grip altogether. Pulling him up, she fell backward. He landed next to her, huffing and spitting as he tried to catch his breath. Kirk looked over at Isis, who was brushing herself off, and grumbled as he got up. "What was that?"

Isis laughed. "I was a long jumper and a champion pole-vaulter in high school."

Kirk shook his head and pulled out his .45 from his shoulder holster. He motioned toward two, huge, wooden doors that were hanging from their hinges. The small lobby was littered with debris and broken furniture. Water was running down the hall from the condo in front of them. Kirk walked through the twenty-foot hole in the wall and into the Red Dog's lair. The room was stripped, and the fire sprinklers were raining down on the gutted apartment.

Then he saw Mark lying in a heap in what looked like the living room. He lay by a hole about twenty feet around with hardwood splintered up around him like teeth. "Mark!" Kirk and Isis reached him at the same time. From the looks of the bloody mess next to the far wall, the Red Dog wouldn't be terrorizing anyone again.

"Mark, can you hear me?" Isis turned him over and felt for a pulse. "He's alive. Mark, come on, hang in there!"

Kirk took his hand and noticed Mark's shredded gloves and the tips of his fingers. They looked weird, not normal. They almost looked transparent, like clear plastic, but he couldn't see through to the bone. They seemed to glow!

Chapter Thirty-Four

THE PRESIDENT OF THE united states of america held his head in his hands as the Joint Chief of Staff and his top military leaders sat waiting for a response. There was no way out of this and he had to make the most important decision of his career. For that matter, his life!

Martial Law and a war that would be fought on American soil. He didn't know if the people could take another war. They had just gotten out of the Middle East, and now it seemed they were coming to the US. Reports were coming in from China, Russia, and Iran, to name a few. It looked like they were banding together to put an end to the self-declared police of the world.

"When I took that sacred vow to serve the American people, I knew that, one day, we would stop policing the world and just take care of our own. I'd hoped to do it in stages and teach the nations we aided how to live without their hands out, and how to turn their countries around. But it seems the countries we have helped and fought for have grown tired of our presence. Hospitality is a fickle thing, ladies and gentlemen. I knew this day would come, I just hoped it would be in some other lifetime."

The president was exasperated, and his tie was torn off and balled up on his desk.

"Look, we can argue all day about what we should have done, the problem is, what do we do now? We can't fight three countries at the same time. We all agree on that?" The room muttered with approval and a few nods. "Okay then. We have a few options. One is to fortify and defend. I know it's not in our nature, but why not let them come to us for a change. Let them kill their economy and pick them off one at a time. Or we can pull out the "N" word, hit hard and fast, and settle the problem in a week."

"Sir?"

"Go ahead, Jim."

"Thank you. The people are too soft to bear the responsibility of another nuclear strike. The media would have our heads, and the spirit of the people would be destroyed."

"Noted. But sometimes, Jim, a traitor and a murderer in time is seen as a hero. What do you think will happen to the morale if we have to fight a war on our own soil?"

A tall blonde in her twenties stepped into the room and handed the president a folded piece of paper. He opened it up and his eyes widened. Picking up the phone, he said. "You sure? Thank you very much. We are in your debt."

Placing the phone back in its cradle, he looked up and a smile crossed his face. "That was our friend from the FBI. Taras Karjanski is dead!"

* * *

TWO HUNDRED MILES OUTSIDE of Incirlik, a covert team of fifty-five Iranians drove through the mountains in armored Humvees. The mountains of Turkey proved to be not only treacherous, but, literally, a wasteland.

Hours later, they crested the ridge that overlooked the Incirlik Air Base. From here, the United States housed thousands of military families and deployed servicemen. The base was its own little city. It had a movie theater, supermarkets, and a medical park. Soldiers flew in from Iran, Iraq, and other Middle Eastern countries on their way to the

United States, using the base as a stopping point.

A short, stocky, tanned man spoke into a headset in Arabic. "We are in place. We will paint the target, send in the fighters! Allah be with you!"

The base had a very high level of security. Fighter jets within the base perimeter wouldn't go unanswered, but the F15 Eagle that carried a special passenger was still a thousand miles off. A fat man drooled on his black beard as he squawked into his mouthpiece once again. "Paint the target!"

The fifty men had moved up and down the mountainside, taking refuge in the rocks and behind large, spine-covered cacti. They each held a brand new Russian "Electronic Target Enabler," or E.T.E., that sent an invisible beam of infrared light over the base. Each soldier had a specific target. Hospital, airplane hangars, and the command center. Forty-five different targets, and in less than five minutes, they would all be a pile of rubble.

The headset sounded. "Package is away!"

The "Ghost" dropped from the F15, and two tiny wings shot out from its side as a burst of fire ignited and rocketed the device forward. It housed a nuclear tip on fifty separate missiles. Each rocket had an onboard computer that would read the exact signal from the locked in corresponding E.T.E.

As Ghost came within two hundred miles of the base, it split apart and the fifty missiles shot forward as they dove for the ground. Just before impact, they turned like fingers and raced toward the air base only twenty feet above the ground. The base wouldn't even see them coming!

* * *

HEIDI MILLER HAD NO time for the now very upset five year old in the back seat of her minivan. "Joey, I said no! We'll go to McDonald's another day." The yelling for a happy meal continued without even the slightest recognition of his mother's authority. Heidi sighed and decided to ignore her son. It was hot and the air base was not her home.

This was a far cry from Texas. Heidi had blonde, straight

hair, and her five-year-old had his daddy's dark eyes and brown hair. She was a beauty queen back home, and now all she seemed to be was eye candy for all the soldiers, except her husband.

"Military life." She muttered. If she'd known what was in store for her life, she would have never married Bill. But, too late now. He was a good man, but all the moving and the long tours were killing her. She couldn't take much more, but what could she do?

The sound of a jet engine was not an odd noise on the base, but this particular sound made her look up. Just as she pulled onto Fifth Avenue, she saw a rocket blazing a trail right for her minivan. She let out a scream as the impact tore through the van and hit the gas station behind her. The building rolled with a huge fireball that consumed everything in its path. Heidi Miller was dead before she felt the pain of being cut in half.

* * *

I COULD HEAR THE faint sounds of a familiar voice. It was like being underwater, and everything is muffled and only the base sounds come through. I opened my eyes to see K leaning over me with tears in her eyes. I gave her a weak smile and hugged her.

I could feel her body shaking as she sobbed in my shoulder. I hurt all over, and memories flooded back from the time I'd spent in the hospital after the explosion that had killed K and Sam. Then again, that turned out to be a dream, but I still could feel the glass and metal as it cut into my skin.

I opened my mouth to tell K that it was okay, but all that came out was a deep mumbling sound. She looked up at me with her big, beautiful eyes, and spoke in a slow precise manner. I only heard base rumblings, but I read her lips.

"Mark, you lost your hearing!" She held her hands up to her ears then touched mine. I couldn't even hear the soft sound her hand made when she touched my ear. "Don't worry, they think it will come back. I love you, baby!" K kissed me with her sweet lips, and I tasted the salt from her tears. I pulled her close and kissed her neck.

K sat up as Isis and Kirk walked into the room. I suddenly recognized the room I was in. It was in the infirmary at the Merc building. Isis smiled and waved at me. Kirk walked up, looked me over with a stern expression, and then shook my hand. A grin crossed his face, and he put his arm around Isis.

The television monitor hanging on the wall showed a white screen, and Isis handed me a wireless keyboard. She had one too, and as she typed, I saw it up on the screen. "Welcome back! And don't ever do that again! We filled K in, and may I say, she is lovely."

I pulled myself up on my elbow and got into a comfortable sitting position. My head throbbed, and the room spun for a few seconds, but then it all went back to normal. I typed. "Thanks for coming after me; I had to do it alone, I hope you understand. K, I love you so much, and I will be fine, so don't worry. I'm taking some time off so you can have me all to yourself."

K took the keyboard from Isis and said. "I love you too, baby. They want to watch you tonight, and then in the morning, you can come home. I'm just glad you're alive. They told me who you were with. I'm just glad it's over!"

I tried to hide my fear behind a big smile. But deep down inside, I had a funny feeling that it was just getting started!

* * *

MAC HAD A GOOD job with UPS, and with the changing times he felt as secure as he could in a job. He figured that, if the federal government went south, then his job would, too, but everyone would be in the same mess, and his job would be the least of his worries.

He pulled on his brown socks and muttered. They would always slip down, and he liked them up high to complete the uniform. Brown hat, brown shorts, and a brown shirt. He never told anyone, but he even had brown underwear. He was a big man with a thick head of black hair that he liked to wear to show off his African roots.

"Mama always said to be proud of who you were if you had something to be proud of." He chuckled to himself and looked one last time in the mirror before he left the driver's seat and hit the elevator button. He was a track star in college, and after getting his degree, he opted for the call of "Brown." His mama never asked why, but he knew that she suspected the truth. He went to college so he could prove he could, and graduated with honors.

The doors to the elevator opened, and he smiled at the tall blonde he saw just about every time he went to the Merc building. "Hello, Stacie, I see you are in your stunning splendor once again this fine morning." Mac let the words spill from his mouth like sweet oil as Stacie blushed and hit him on the arm.

"Mac, you flirt. You know I'm a sucker for the tall, dark, and might I add, handsome!" Mac let his polished white teeth show his delight, and he pretended to be shy.

"You may, and will I be enjoying your company this evening at, shall we say, eight?" Mac had tried to get a date with Stacie for a year now. One day, he would get her to say yes.

"My, my, Mac. You are not one for mincing words, are you? Let me see…" She looked up at the ceiling like she was deep in thought about what she would do. "Ask me next week, and I may just go out with you." With that, the doors opened to the fifth floor where Stacie got off with a flip of her hair. Mac stood staring after her and shook his head. *One day, one day.*

Heading back down to the first floor, Mac entered the lobby of the environmental magazine and smiled as he approached the front desk. "Miss Molly!"

The gray-haired woman at the front counter smiled and signed the electronic pad Mac handed to her. "Mac, are you messing with my girls again? I thought I heard some sort of goings-on in that there elevator?"

Mac put on a serious look and said, "Well no ma'am." The older lady eyed him and huffed in disbelief. They played the grandma and grandson bit all the time, and she rather enjoyed it. Mac could brighten her day by just walking by her desk.

"Thank you, Miss Molly. Have a good day now!" With that, he turned and strolled toward the elevator. The brown package was the size of a shoebox and was addressed to the Global Advisor. Miss Molly placed it with the rest of the mail on the mail cart, not knowing that inside, something was already working.

The tiny, unnoticeable holes let a clear, unscented killer out and into the air. The little grey-haired lady sitting at the front counter breathed in the invisible virus, not realizing that she would be dead in fewer than two weeks. It filled the main lobby and was sucked up and into the main air-conditioning ducts. They carried it throughout the building, and after it was exposed to every living thing, it melted away, settling on the plants scattered through the building.

In a matter of hours, all the plants in the Merc building were dead. Their leaves curled up and turned brown just before they crumbled to dust and fell to the floor. The package sat on the mail cart waiting to be delivered. Inside, as a last gift to the World Justice Agency, was a small, dead dog.

A Red Dog!

The End

Check out more titles by Aaron Patterson at:
www.StoneHouseInk.net

About the Author

Aaron Patterson is the author of the best-selling WJA series, as well as two Digital Shorts: 19 and The Craigslist Killer. He was home-schooled and grew up in the west. Aaron loved to read as a small child and would often be found behind a book, reading one to three a day on average. This love drove him to want to write, but he never thought he had the talent. His wife Karissa prodded him to try it, and with this encouragement, he wrote Sweet Dreams, the first book in the WJA series, in 2008. Airel is his first teen series, and plans for more to come are already in the works. He lives in Boise, Idaho with his family,

Soleil, Kale and Klayton.

PREVIEW

In Your Dreams
Book Three In The WJA Series

CHAPTER ONE

B.C. 2012 Havilah, Arabia

KREIOS RAN THROUGH THE dense forest. His long robe fluttered behind him like a frightened bird. He could hear the things behind him cursing and spitting in fury as they searched for him in the darkness.

Kreios was a big man with strong arms, chest, and legs. He did not hesitate as he leaped over a dead log in his path. In spite of his size, he was fast, and moved through the forest without a sound.

The warm night sky loomed overhead, and a fat, low-hanging moon looked on with indifference. Kreios clutched a book in his left arm and ducked under a branch to avoid a head wound. The two beings behind him crashed through the underbrush like unskilled hunters. Kreios ran without looking back. He knew that he must keep the book safe at all costs, even if it meant his life.

A howl erupted from his flank, and Kreios dove for cover under a huge willow tree root. He calmed his breathing, tucked the leather-bound book tighter under his robe, pulled the hood up over his blond hair, and curled up in a ball. He waited.

A snort and the footsteps of the two attackers came close to his hiding spot; nevertheless, he was not discovered. Two hours passed, and the two beasts gave up their hunt and moved out, heading west, back to their camp. The Seer would be very angry with them and might even take their lives because of their failure. Kreios did not mind. In fact, he hoped they would die and leave him with one less of their kind to kill.

Working his hand free, he removed the book and looked at it with awe and wonder. Words glimmered as he wrote in it every night, but he was surprised to find that, each morning, the words disappeared. However, by just a thought, they would reappear and shimmer like diamonds.

The book had his name on the cover and contained the complete history of his kind and their fall. In the wrong hands, it would mean death and enslavement. Climbing to his feet, he ran into the small creek and ran north. He had escaped this time, but he had many more battles to fight before the book would be safe.

* * *

ALONE, LYING IN A hospital bed, a man breathed through a tube and thought of how he came to be here. He was smart, in fact, he was a genius by the world's standards. Here he was, alone, with no visitors. Not even his mother had come by to see him.

He could still see the flash of the gun barrel as two shots rang out and the fire he felt as they hit him in the chest. He was a lucky guy, or so his doctor told him, but he didn't feel lucky. He felt abandoned, betrayed, and his anger boiled over like a pot on a hot burner.

Mooch hated the feel of the feeding tube, and the hoses and wires made him feel like he was in a sci-fi movie, or like he had been abducted by aliens and was about to be experimented on. How could they leave him to die, a friend who had and helped them. *See what you received in return?*

His thoughts brought Kirk Weston to the front. He could see Kirk's stupid face looking down at him. He was the reason he was in this mess, he was the one who held control over him, and just look at what he did! Here I am, shot up, left for dead, and alone! *You are not alone, not anymore. Invite me in and you will have your revenge.*

"Who are you?" Mooch could feel something tickle the back of his mind, and the feeling was nice. It was like an old friend, a chum that you thought you would never see again. When you needed someone to confide in, here he was.

I am whatever you want me to be, I am fear, I am desire, I am need, and I am the power of the most high. Trust me, and you will not die!

Mooch opened his mind and soul for the second time in his life and felt a warm, wonderful wave of beauty fill him. He felt stronger and his chest didn't hurt anymore. "Thank you, thank you for staying with me."

Mooch was talking to himself in an empty room on the third floor of a second-rate hospital in Manhattan. The ambulance had received the call, and when they had gotten on scene, they had found Mooch alone in the basement, bleeding from two gunshot wounds to the chest. They tried to revive him, but could not get a pulse. On the way to the hospital, he jerked and somehow regained a heartbeat.

Sometimes weird things happened, and for some, it just wasn't their time to die.

Made in United States
Orlando, FL
12 June 2022

18739743R00189